The Shadow of Woodmyst

THE WOODMYST CHRONICLES BOOK VI

Robert E Kreig

WHITEKEEP BOOKS

THE SHADOW OF WOODMYST

For Barry and Cheryl.

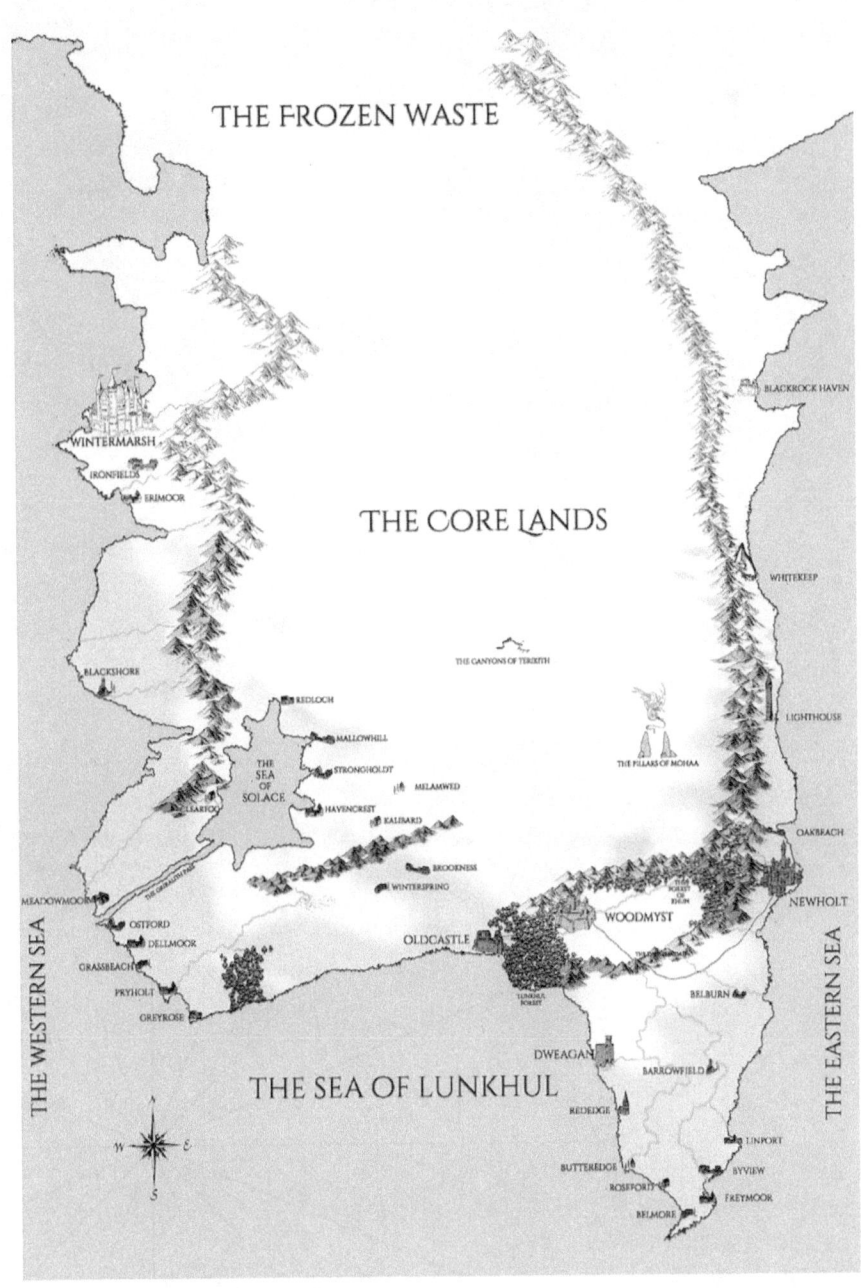

THE FROZEN WASTE

THE CORE LANDS

BLACKROCK HAVEN

WINTERMARSH

IRONFIELDS

ERIMOOR

WHITEKEEP

THE CANYONS OF TERIXITH

BLACKSHORE

REDLOCH

MALLOWHILL

LIGHTHOUSE

THE
SEA
OF
SOLACE

STRONGHOLDT

MELAMWED

THE PILLARS OF MOHAA

HAVENCREST

KALIBARD

CLEARFOO

OAKBEACH

BROOKNESS

WINTERSPRING

WOODMYST

NEWHOLT

MEADOWMOOR

OSTFORD

DELLMOOR

OLDCASTLE

BELBURN

THE WESTERN SEA

GRASSBEACH

PRYHOLT

GREYROSE

LUNKHUL
FOREST

DWEAGAN

BARROWFIELD

THE EASTERN SEA

THE SEA OF LUNKHUL

REDEDGE

LINPORT

W   E

BUTTEREDGE

BYVIEW

ROSEPORT

FREYMOOR

S

BELMORE

Prologue

Embers rose into the chilly night air, lifted high upon the heat emitting from the large fire in the middle of the tiny settlement. A thin dusting of snow covered the thatched rooftops and ground, frosting the tall pine trees lightly as a chill breeze from the north drifted listlessly over the mountains.

"One more story, Opa," the little girl begged, sitting on her grandfather's knee and resting her head against his chest. Her legs dangled high above the ground as she hugged her arms against her body and shivered slightly.

"You're getting cold, Danica," the old man replied, looking across the fire at a young woman feeding an infant, and a young man seated by her side. "And it's very late."

"Please," she whined, almost singing.

"Your Opa is right," the young man interjected, rising to his feet to move around the blazing hearth. "It is time for all good children to go to bed."

"But Papa," she protested. "I don't want to go to bed. I want to stay up with you."

"Look around you," he said, lifting the tiny toddler from the old man's lap. "All other children have gone to sleep. Most other mothers and fathers have gone to bed too. Your Opa, your mama and I are awake, waiting for you to fall to sleep too."

"But Edan is still awake," she argued, looking at the infant attached to his mother's breast.

"Edan will be fast asleep before you and me," the young man replied as he carried the girl to a small hut a few yards away from the fire. Some goats, penned to the side of the dwelling, snorted and bleated as the man passed by.

"The goats are awake," Danica pointed out, looking for any reason to stay up.

"You are persistent, aren't you?"

"What's that mean?"

"It means you really want to stay awake," the man answered. "Don't you?"

"I don't like my bed," she told him.

"Why not?" he asked, entering the dwelling. The old man followed close behind with a lit lantern to help them both find their way into the dark hut.

"Goodnight Gunar, Marcille, Opa Hadlee," called a tall man walking to his own small house. "Sweet dreams, Danika."

"Say goodnight," the young man told the little girl in his arms.

"Goodnight, Dieter," she waved with one hand as she wiped her eyes with the other.

The baby cried as his mother bade the neighbour a good night, rising to her feet to follow the others inside.

"Shhh," she tried to soothe the infant as the young man carried the little girl to her bed.

"There you are," her father said, pulling the covers over her. "Nice and warm."

She suddenly became quiet and withdrawn.

"What is it?" the old man asked her, listening to the soft cries of the baby as his mother brought him through the door of the hut.

"The shadow men will come again," she whimpered. "I don't like them."

"There are no shadow men, Danika," Gunar, her father, told her. "We've talked about this before. The shadows are just from the light of the moon shining through the trees. Nothing more.

"Your Mama and I are in the next room with Edan," he continued. "Your Opa is in the other room next to ours. There are no shadow men in our rooms. Just moonlight dancing on the walls."

Opa Hadlee turned his head towards the front door. The breeze was still coming through.

"Marcille," he called softly. "You left the door open."

There was no reply.

The crying of the baby had ceased as well.

"There will be no more talk of shadow men," Gunar instructed his daughter. "Do you understand?"

"Yes, Papa." She frowned.

"Marcille," Opa Hadlee called again, leaving the girl's bedroom to investigate.

"Can I have a candle?" Danika asked. "Please?"

"Papa?" Gunar turned to see where the old man was going with the lantern.

His gaze followed Opa Hadlee. The old man held the lantern high as he moved back towards the front door. It swung open, creaking softly as the wind pushed it in.

Tiny white flakes of frost floated through the air and landed softly on a dark puddle that had formed on the floor.

"By the gods!" the old man gasped, as he followed a trail with his eyes, leading from the puddle and across the ground outside the cottage.

"What is it?" Gunar asked, rising to his feet and rushing to his father's side.

There was no sign of Marcille or little Edan.

Only a deep, dark layer of blood trailed into the night.

"Where are they?" The young man bolted into the cold air, looking this way and that.

He could see more dark streams coming from the open doors of the cottages near to him.

"Arm yourself, Papa," he said, staring at his neighbour, Dieter's, door. The blood appeared black and glistened in the moonlight.

There was no reply.

"Papa?" He turned to see the lantern sitting on the floor just inside the door. "Papa?"

Gunar raced back inside, stepping over the lantern before moving back to his daughter's room.

"Papa? Danika?" he called, making his way through the dwelling. His heart raced in his chest so fast he thought it might explode. His stomach bunched into a tight ball and the taste of bile had reached the back of his throat.

"Danika?" he called again as he stared at his daughter's bed.

Empty.

They had pulled the covers back, and a dark smear of blood stained the bedding.

His legs weakened, causing him to drop to his knees.

His mouth fell open as the urge to scream filled him.

But no sound came.

It stared at him from a dark corner of the room.

A shadow.

Stepping forward, into the moonlight coming in through the window, Gunar saw the smooth, black skin of the creature.

Its rapier-like fingers stretched towards him.

Its mouth expanded wider and wider to reveal needle-like teeth.

When it sank its sharp fingertips deep into his shoulders, closing its lips around his crown, he felt excruciating pain for only a fleeting moment.

Just a mere moment.

After that, he experienced elation, bliss, ecstasy.

His eyelids felt heavy.

His mind swam as if in a dream.

There was no time to scream.

There was no time to run.

There was no way to wake from this nightmare.

But why would he want to?

A loud crunching filled his head as the creature closed its jaws.

Darkness flowed over him like a wave, filling his senses.

Elation.

Bliss.

Ecstasy.

Nothing.

One

The beast snorted, blowing from its nostrils dust that had been irritating it since the party had left the grasslands. Dust was constantly being blown around as the icy winds swept from the mountains, across the plains, and into the core lands. Some found its way into the rukyul's nose and were proving difficult to dislodge.

Alice reached over from her chestnut stallion and rubbed the predator's shoulder, moving her fingers through a thick clump of fur.

"Haigok." Nola'ee pointed to large rock formations in the distance that resembled spires stretching into the sky. Her leathery hand lowered back to the reins of her steed as she peered at the girl beside her.

Alice turned her attention to the team, keeping the three hundred horses in a tight herd as they moved across the wasteland. She pointed to the rock formation.

"We can see our destination," she called to them.

"It'll be dark by the time we reach it," David shouted, shielding his eyes as he looked up to the mid-afternoon sun.

"I don't think that will make a difference to the Night Demons," his son replied. "We could camp here, but I believe they will come to investigate. Surely, they have spotted us by now."

"No camping." Alice shook her head. "We get this done and leave for home as soon as we can."

Plodding along, continuing to direct the steeds into the harsh lands, they gradually drew nearer and nearer to the spires. Even at such a distance away, the pillars appeared quite impressive. Their massive form towered high above the ground, twisting into sharp tips that reminded the girl of teeth.

Alice swivelled slightly in her saddle to check the two pack horses led by the Agrodien female and herself. Their leads tethered to the horns of their saddles.

The rukyul growled menacingly, setting its hackles on edge as it glared towards the stone pillars.

"Kayl'sro," Bein hissed. He gestured to the air just above the nearest spire.

A black dot spiralled higher and higher into the air.

Alice didn't need to observe it for too long before she realized it was a dragon.

There was no doubt in her mind that they had been spotted.

The Agrodien warriors reached for their weapons.

"No," Alice commanded them, shaking her head and holding up her hand. "No blades."

"Wouldn't be of any bloody use anyway," David said. "Richard is the only man that I know that has ever killed one of those buggers."

"Kayl'sro?" Nola'ee objected. "Dragon come for us. Agrodien fight. Protect Kayl'sro and husband and father of husband."

"We didn't come to kill dragons," Alice told her. "We didn't come to kill Haigok. We came to make peace. No blades."

"Yes, Kayl'sro." She bowed her head before relaying the instruction to the other Agrodien in the party.

Alice moved her attention to the speck in the sky, sweeping around far and high to their right. It moved swiftly against the wind before banking sharply towards them.

The figure grew in her vision, changing from a small, dark object into something more perceivable. She noticed the wings and tail first as it drew nearer.

"Wave to it," she commanded the others, lifting her hand in a friendly gesture.

"You've got to be kidding?" David grunted, unable to look away from the approaching menace.

"Do it," she barked. "Or you may end up cooked."

Reluctantly, he lifted his arm and followed her lead.

The dragon fell slowly towards the earth, keeping its body level as it sped towards them at an incredible speed.

The six travellers continued to hold their arms high, trying to convey that they approached with peaceful intent.

Dust lifted from the ground as the great winged beast skimmed over the surface. Its broad, membranous wings stretched out far to its sides. Its jaws clamped shut, a few of its giant yellow incisors protruding over its lips.

Alice tore her attention from the dragon to the rider upon its back. Cloaked in black, his tattered cloth trailing behind, he held the reins steady as he swept his eyes over the herd and the riders.

She held her other arm up, palm exposed for him to see that she concealed no weapon.

Still, the dragon glided closer.

All it would need to do was keep on its bearing and it would wipe her out as its form impacted with hers. She pictured herself, Nola'ee and a few horses and a rukyul toppling through the air before settling in a mess some yards away.

With a thrust of its wings, the creature swooped back into the air and over their heads. Dust exploded from the ground, enveloping them in a dry, brown cloud as the dragon and its rider climbed higher into the sky, turning back towards the stone spires.

As the dust settled, Alice turned to the others, squinting to keep the sand out of her eyes.

"Is everyone all right?"

"I think I swallowed half of the desert," Arthur replied, coughing intermittently.

"Nice way to welcome people," David quipped, brushing the dust from his face.

"Kayl'sro, they no attack?" Nakra asked.

"I think we would be dead if they intended to attack," Alice answered.

He grunted, frowning and nodding as he peered at the shrinking object in the air.

The rukyul shook himself, flinging dust into the air and all over Alice and the stallion. Snorting in protest, the steed stomped his feet and moved his head towards the beast beside him, seeming to give the other a look of contempt.

Nola'ee stared at the ground, wide-eyed and bemused.

"What's wrong?" Alice asked her quietly.

She lowered her head. "I afraid, Kayl'sro."

Alice tried to bring some comfort to the other by reaching over to her and placing her hand on that of the Agrodien's.

"Me too," she confessed before calling to the others. "Let's keep going. They know we're here and will be expecting us. Might as well try to pick up the pace a little."

Driving the horses onward, the troop made ground as the sun slowly drifted towards the western horizon. The rock spires grew into looming towers that seemed both beautiful and terrifying. The windswept around them, blowing a deep sound that filled the riders' ears.

Several hooded figures awaited the approaching herd, armed with curved blades and bows. As the travellers drew close, one of them stepped forward.

Alice noted a horn attached to the Haigok's belt. It was fashioned from a ram and decorated with markings that she didn't recognize.

"Stop there," the cloaked figure hollered over the sound of the wind. "State your business."

It surprised Alice to hear him speak in her tongue.

"We have come to treat with you," she replied.

"You are a child," the Haigok replied. "Why does your man not speak?"

"I am in charge," she informed the other, a lump growing in her throat. She felt her heart racing, but maintained an unflinching demeanour. She hid her fears far beneath the surface. "I will speak for my people."

"Who are you?"

"My name is Alice Gyfford," she announced. "I am Kayl'sro of the Agrodien and a daughter of Woodmyst."

"Woodmyst?" He stepped towards her slowly. His bulbous, yellow eyes held her gaze for a long time before moving to the three reptilians travelling with her. "These ones stole our horses."

"I know," she replied as he stepped within a few yards of her. The rukyul growled. She held her hand out to the beast, signalling it to be still.

"Those creatures cannot be tamed," the Haigok stated, turning to look at the angry rukyul. It had closed its mouth and stopped snarling, but it still glared at the hooded figure.

"It is not tame," Alice informed him. "My people took your horses under the leadership of the previous Kayl'sro. I have assumed his role and have come to remedy any offences committed."

"How did you?" he asked sceptically.

She looked at him confusedly, unsure of what his question meant.

"How did you assume the role of Kayl'sro?"

"I killed him," she answered. "I tore his head off with my bare hands."

"Why?"

"It was him or me."

He seemed to accept the answer.

"My people," he began. "They gave chase to the Agrodien thieves. Only the dragons returned. Do you know what happened?"

"I killed them too," she replied. "They attacked me on my land."

He stared at her. She couldn't tell if he was angry or inquisitive.

"Did they suffer?"

From the corner of her eye, she saw David shift uncomfortably in his saddle. Nola'ee turned her head to the girl, preparing for the order to strike.

Instead, Alice searched for the correct words, the ones she thought he wanted to hear.

"They each died a good death," she assured him. "They died as warriors."

He dropped his gaze, his head nodding slightly as he considered what she had said.

"We should not have come so close to your homelands," he replied. "My father promised one of yours that we would not return."

"I hope that by returning what is yours," Alice gestured to the herd of steeds, "we may have peace between our people."

"There are more animals here than were taken from us," the Haigok replied, looking over the chargers.

"Then accept the additional horses as gifts," she offered.

He moved his attention to the sun, sinking slowly towards the earth.

"It will be dark soon," he said. "You must join us tonight. Make camp near our village and sup with us. Please."

She was hesitant to reply, looking at her husband, who seemed to share her sentiments.

"It will give us a chance to talk terms," the cloaked figure offered. "A peaceful relationship must be built upon trust; don't you think?"

"You're right." She jumped down from the stallion and reached her hand out to his. "We accept."

"Good." He smiled, shaking her hand. "My name is Gruloch, Lord of the Haigok."

***

A long fire pit had been lit, and many animal carcasses positioned over the flames, roasting slowly and filling the village centre with a wonderful aroma. They ushered Alice and her party to a position by the fire, near the raised seat set aside for the Lord of the Haigok.

Gruloch rested, cross-legged, with his back against fat cushions covered with a variety of animal hides. Rugs made of goat skins covered a small platform where he was situated, overlooking the area where his people gathered for the night's meal.

"We are having goat tonight," he told Alice. She was rubbing the ear of the rukyul, resting beside her and eyeing the meat hungrily. "Are you sure your animal would not be more comfortable in our stables?"

"It would devour your horses by morning if he were to be locked in with them," she assured the other. "Everyone, including your livestock, will be safer with him by my side."

The Haigok inclined his head, accepting her words.

"Your knowledge of our tongue is excellent," Arthur commented. "How is it you came to learn it so well?"

"Believe it or not," Gruloch said, "we encounter other men from time to time. Nomads who traverse the Core Lands. Some of them we even trade with. My father thought it would be wise for me to learn the language of men, so he offered livestock and iron in exchange for men to teach me."

"May I ask what happened to your father?" Alice turned to the Haigok as others started carving the meat, placing portions upon steel trays.

"The Mirikin killed him," Gruloch answered. "They marched their army across the sand from the west. We destroyed them, but not before one witch broke his body with her sorcery."

"I am sorry." She peered into the flames. "My father was killed by one of them as well."

"But he still managed to inflict a fatal wound to the bitch before it was all over," David said proudly.

"What colour did she wear?" Gruloch asked.

"White," Arthur replied as one of the Haigok females held a tray out towards him. There was a stack of unleavened bread at one end, with shavings of steaming meat next to it, some thin portions of goats' cheese and some leafy greens at the other side. He looked to Gruloch for help.

"Take the bread," the other instructed. "Put a little meat in the middle of it. Sprinkle a small amount of cheese over it and then some leaves over the top. Fold the bread over it and try not to lose any out of the ends as you eat."

Arthur followed the other's directions. Biting down on the end and getting a good portion of the mix, Arthur spilt a little upon himself. The Haigok chuckled quietly.

"I've gone and made a mess already," the lad muttered.

"It takes a very skilled individual to not spill any, my new friend," Gruloch told him as the iron tray containing the ingredients moved to Alice. They offered another platter to the Agrodien and David.

The rukyul looked along the line, salivating slightly as he observed the others eating. Gruloch placed the mixture onto the bread when he noticed the beast looking at him.

"Don't worry, big one," he said, pointing along the side of the hearth. "Your share is coming now."

Alice turned to see two Haigok males carrying a fresh goat carcass, skinned and cleaned. They placed it before the creature. The rukyul didn't hesitate. It sank its teeth into the rump and tore a large piece of flesh away.

"The white was their leader, if I heard correctly," Gruloch said.

"She was." Alice nodded, trying not to spill her food.

"And all of her followers were defeated?"

"All but one," the girl answered. "The Queen of Newholt allied herself with Woodmyst and fought against the White Witch."

"And now the colours have appeared again." Gruloch looked to the travellers. "The Black Witch rules from Woodmyst."

Alice felt her stomach tighten.

"How do you know this?" she asked.

"The words on the wind speak frequently to one another," he told her. "I listen to their tales. I listened to how a young girl with strange abilities was shunned by her own and sent into exile. I listened to how that young girl became a leader of a nation and willingly opened her homeland to others seeking refuge. I listened to how she defeated my warriors and frightened my dragons with sorcery.

"I so wanted to meet this girl. I needed to see this one the shadows talked about. I must admit that I knew far more about you than I originally led you to believe, Alice."

"What do you intend to do with us?" David asked, seeing the Agrodien beside him tense with anticipation.

"Treat with you," Gruloch assured them. "Make peace. As I said before, my people should not have ventured so close to your home. But in their defence, we do require payment for those things taken from us.

"You have paid for the crimes of one that no longer lives," he continued. "This act reveals more about the kind of person you are, Alice. You are a person I wish to treat with. I think our peoples are going to need one another before long.

"If the colours have returned, days of doom will surely follow. We must be allies and we must find others to ally ourselves with."

Alice reached over to her husband and took his hand.

"You had me a little concerned," she admitted.

"I apologise," Gruloch replied.

"If all goes well," she said, "the Queen of Newholt will receive my envoy and treat with us also. But you must know the Black Witch is my mother's sister. The others, the women of colours, have been friends to my family since long before I was born."

"You are hesitant to fight them," Gruloch said. "I understand your concerns. But listen, Alice. A small piece of advice. Sometimes close friends make the worst enemies. They will use your love for them against you. Take care when you're with them."

She peered to the ground, considering the Haigok's words. Her mind raced back to the last time that she saw her Aunt Joanne. To Alice, the witch in black appeared different to the woman she knew as her mother's sister. Even though Joanne professed her love for the girl, it was clear at that moment that she had planned to take over Woodmyst for a very long time.

"So!" Gruloch clapped his hands suddenly, looking at the girl with a smile. "I have something for you to see."

She responded with a quizzical stare.

"One of my dragons has not come out of her cave since she encountered you," he informed her. "She lets her keepers feed her and clean her den, but will allow no one to get close enough to even touch her. This is proving to be a little vexing as I need to assign a new rider to her."

"And if you can't get her to accept a new rider?" Arthur asked.

"She will only be good for breeding," he replied. "But to do that, the dragons need to keep their strength up. This means that they need to be flying and breathing fire. She can't do that inside a cave."

"I don't know what you expect me to do," Alice said, furrowing her brow.

"Truthfully," Gruloch said, frowning, "neither do I. But I can see you have a bond with this creature beside you. Perhaps your influence can be imparted to a dragon also. I would be grateful if you would at least come and look at her with me."

Alice nodded.

It wasn't very often one got a chance to see a dragon. The last time she had the opportunity was one when she was engaged in battle. Perhaps, with no one attacking her, she could admire the beast rather than try to think of ways to defeat it.

"Of course I will," she replied. "But my people must be allowed to join us."

"I had already assumed they would," Gruloch replied.

Two

They sat upon their horses, resting at the top of a hill that overlooked the city by the sea. A magnificent palace with high walls surrounding it, constructed atop a rocky mound in the centre of the community.

Just to the east of the palace, near the docklands, stood a tall clock tower with four faces that reminded them of the one on top of the assembly hall in Woodmyst. Reflected light beamed upon the timekeeper from all sides so they could clearly see it during the night.

Street lanterns had been lit and from many windows flickered the orange candescent glow of candlelight and fireplaces. A few people moved about on the paved roads between the buildings, but most had retired to the warmth of their dwellings.

"We should find a tavern," Akasati suggested. "We have enough coin for a room and a good meal."

"Let's not go too close to the docks and try for one closer to the middle of the township instead," Gustav offered. "I don't particularly feel like listening to old sea songs or the sounds of whores making money. Perhaps an inn would be a wiser option?"

"We could just camp out here," Sharek put in.

"I really want a warm meal that we didn't have to kill beforehand," Akasati said.

"Agreed." Rhydra nodded. "Besides, if there is enough leftover, we could all use a bath before seeking an audience with the queen."

Gustav urged his steed forwards, ambling down the hillside. The three Erilian women followed closely, their steeds plodding towards the city of Newholt.

The clip-clop of their hoofbeats echoed through the near-empty streets as they made their way through the town. Those they saw roaming about welcomed the travellers with a wave and a smile.

The city seemed relaxed and at ease.

As they drew nearer to the palace, Gustav noticed a pair of soldiers patrolling along the road on foot.

"Excuse me," he called to them.

"Can we be of service, sir?" asked one man. He turned his attention to the three women and touched the brim of his helmet. "Ladies."

"I certainly hope so," Gustav replied. "We are looking for an inn for the night. Would you be able to point us in the right direction?"

"You could try the *Wolf and Maiden* a little further along the road here," the soldier said, pointing towards the castle. "It's a quiet establishment, if that's what you're seeking."

"What's your business in Newholt?" the other asked, eyeing them suspiciously.

"Sorry." Gustav placed a hand on his chest. "How impolite of me. My name is Gustav. These are Akasati, Rhydra and Sharek. We come from Woodmyst in hope to seek an audience with the queen."

"Woodmyst?" The second soldier inclined his head. "I thought you ladies looked familiar."

The Erilian women glanced at one another, shaking their heads.

"Apologies, sir," Sharek said to him. "But we don't recognise you."

"Of course you wouldn't," he replied cheerfully. "I was just a soldier amongst many others. But I recognise you. I saw you fight on the battlefield when the white witch fell. It would be inconsiderate if I allowed you to stay at the *Wolf and Maiden*. Sure, it's a fine establishment, but you deserve better than that. I would offer you my home immediately, but the queen would reprimand me if I didn't inform her of your arrival.

"If she cannot see you tonight," he continued, "then my door is open to you. Please, let us accompany you at least as far as the guardhouse?"

"We're a might bit ripe after travelling," Akasati put in.

"I know the queen would not concern herself with that," the first soldier told her.

"Thank you, gentlemen," Gustav said, lowering himself from his horse. "Please, lead on."

***

The guardhouse was a large structure just inside the gates of the palace grounds. The interior split into two sections; sleeping quarters at the rear and a mess hall to the front. Several long tables with bench seats stretched from one end of the room to the other. Gustav and the Erilian warriors sat here, amongst a few of the Newholt men who had visited to Woodmyst during the attack of the Mirikin.

"I was expecting larger quarters for your soldiers," Rhydra commented as she peered about the room.

"Most of the men dwell in the city," a man seated across from her, dressed in chain-mail, replied.

"Are you expecting a battle?" Sharek gestured to the apparel.

"I hope not," he answered. "I am due to go on gate duty soon. We all wear the mail beneath our armour. You just never know when you may need it.

"I see you don't bother with such formalities," he said, eyeing her clothing. "How do you defend against attackers without proper protection?"

"I move out of the way of their heavy swords and cut their throats open with my blade," she smiled.

Gustav chuckled quietly and shook his head.

"Besides," continued Sharek. "All that iron slows you down. It inhibits your movement. I don't know how you could fight in it."

"With a great deal of training and practice," said a man's voice from the door.

The soldiers sitting along the tables instantly rose to their feet and stood rigid.

Gustav turned to see a tall man, dressed in formal attire, standing at the edge of the room. He wore a red jacket with gold buttons and trimmings. His dark trousers were decorated with a long gold stripe along the hem, leading down to a shiny pair of black leather boots. Upon his head, he wore a large, black tricorn.

"Sit, gentlemen." He gestured for the soldiers to resume their seats as he approached the visitors. "My name is Jonathon Brondt."

"Ay." Gustav stood to shake the other's hand. "I remember you. I'm Gustav. These lovely ladies are Rhydra, Akasati and Sharek."

"The Erilian warriors," Brondt bowed slightly. "I've come to escort you to the queen. She is helping in the kitchen, preparing something for you at the moment."

"She needn't bother," Akasati replied. "It's not necessary."

"Amicia always looks after her friends, my lady," he replied with a grin. "And she considers any from Woodmyst to be her closest."

"A meal prepared by royalty," Sharek uttered. "I can't say that has happened to me before."

"She has arranged rooms for you and hot water for your baths," Brondt continued. "Your horses are stabled and are being fed as we speak. I've asked my men to groom them for you as well. You might not recognise them afterwards.

"Come…" he tilted his head towards the door. "Let's get you inside to freshen up and then you can join us for a fine meal of whatever it is that Amicia is working on."

***

Refreshed and dressed in fine clothing, the visitors were seated around a long table in the dining quarters of the palace. The room was light, with whitewashed walls, adorned with tapestries and iron torch holders jutting from timber fortifications, small flames illuminating the area with orange and yellow.

Upon the table, a silver plate of bread had been placed beside a large candle stand containing six large white sticks of wax. The wicks were lit, spreading a bright glow across the faces of those seated about.

Five young women from the kitchen staff, dressed in dark dresses and white aprons and with their hair covered in bonnets, served large bowls of steaming stew to the visitors. The four of them dug straight into the broth, slurping portions of the casserole from their spoons.

"Good," Gustav muttered between mouthfuls.

"My lord," one woman said, gesturing to Amicia seated at the head of the table. "You forget protocol."

Gustav and the three Erilians peered at the queen sheepishly. She and Brondt, seated to her right, were still waiting for their bowl of stew.

Amicia was smiling happily.

"No need for formalities," she told the kitchen girls. "These guests have come a long way and appear to be in dire need of good food tonight."

"We're sorry nonetheless," Akasati told her. "We've been enjoying most of our meals around a fire of late."

"Please continue." The queen gestured to the stew as a girl placed bowls before her and Brondt.

"Meals around a fire?" he questioned. "You are not talking about your journey to Newholt, are you?"

"No," Gustav replied, wiping his mouth on a napkin. "Some of us have moved to a glade not too far from Woodmyst. I'm not certain if you were told about the caverns."

"Not that I recall," Brondt said as he lowered his spoon into the stew.

"Many years ago," the other began, "Woodmyst was attacked. The children were kidnapped and taken to the caverns a small ride away. Tomas Warde was one of them. They were kept there while the invaders destroyed everyone and everything inside the village."

"This part of the story I know," Brondt interjected. "Dragons tore the walls down and destroyed the town. Richard was the only man to survive."

"Ay," Gustav agreed. "The children were later returned and left to rebuild their community. The caverns look upon a wide and long glade and, by unwritten agreement, belonged to Tomas. All who knew him well would tell you it should be his children who have claim to it. And the family would tell you that Alice, his youngest to Emily, had more right to it than any other.

"She is more at home out there than she ever was in the city. She can out-hunt, outfight, and outlast any man I know. Additional to that, she has displayed the traits and gifts of a sorceress."

"A sorceress?" Amicia looked up.

"Ay," Gustav said. "She can communicate with animals on an elemental level. She told us she could make fire dance when a dragon attacked her. She is still learning her abilities.

"Because of that, some feared her, and she was exiled from Woodmyst. Some of us left the city to be with her. As amazing as she is, we consider ourselves loyal to her because we were, and still are, loyal to her father."

"Of course." The queen looked down at the table. "And the Seven? What of them? Where do their loyalties lie?"

"Now that," he said, raising his eyebrows, "is a whole extra complication in itself. The Seven, it would appear, have not been the women we thought them to be. They left the council and accompanied us to the caverns. Then, there were some murders, including two council members, one of who was married with two children. His family suffered the same fate as he."

"Was magic involved?" Amicia moved her gaze to the candles flickering in the middle of the table.

"Yes," he answered. "The Seven were responsible."

"And now they sit in a place of power."

Gustav nodded.

Amicia Elynbrigge, Queen of Newholt, the once Fuchsia Mistress, sighed a deep breath and frowned.

"It's the prophecy." She shook her head. "The Maji will rise."

"That child?" Brondt furrowed his brow.

"He won't be a child forever," she replied.

"Wait," Akasati blurted. "You're talking about Takmel. He took his father's name and married Catherine Warde. He's harmless."

"Joanne and the other six were able to blind you," Amicia said slowly. "The boy may have only realised recently who he really is. Perhaps the union with the young lady sparked the furnace. She possesses power too, does she not?"

"If she does, she hasn't made it known," Rhydra answered.

"She *is* the daughter of Emily Warde," the queen reminded. "The niece of Joanne Warde. You can almost guarantee that both of the girls possess power."

"But I don't understand." Sharek looked to the others questionably. "How are the actions of the Seven, and Takmel's and Catherine's marriage, in any way linked to this prophecy about the Maji?"

"He's surrounded by magic," Amicia told her. "It feeds him and strengthens him. Until now, we have only ever heard of witches or sorceresses with such abilities. The Maji will be a first of his kind."

"A man-witch," Gustav grunted.

"A warlock." She clarified. "The coven has the duty of ushering and guiding such an individual into a position of authority. With the Mirikin gone, the burden fell upon the Seven. It would appear they understood this for a long time. Perhaps even before the battle of Woodmyst. Or somehow, he is able to influence them.

"In any case," she continued. "It's clear to me that the Seven have taken the place of the Mirikin and have situated themselves into a place of authority to guide Takmel into power. Be assured, we are about to see the rise of the Maji."

Three

Gruloch led the troop along a well-worn path, past several large caves with torchlight emitting from deep within. They could hear growls and deep snorts reverberating from inside the caverns.

"Are there dragons in all these?" David asked, peering along the path ahead of them and seeing light flickering in the mouths of many more openings into the rock wall.

"Yes," the Haigok answered. "We have twelve adult females, three males and five new pups. There are seventeen unhatched eggs. It can take several months for the pups to emerge. Would you like to see them?"

"The eggs?" Arthur asked excitedly.

"Yes," Gruloch replied, pausing in front of a cave. "They're just in here."

"Absolutely!" The young man looked enthusiastic.

Alice grinned, squeezing his arm tightly.

"You're just like a little boy going for his first hunt," she told him.

"Only taller," his father quipped.

"Come see." The Lord of the Haigok entered the hollow.

As they walked along a wide passage lined with torchlight, they listened to the guttural rumblings of a gigantic beast deep inside. Shadows danced upon the rock as they ventured deeper and deeper.

The cave opened into a large chamber where two Haigok males were tending to an enormous creature. One used a large scrubbing broom to rub the beast's thick, scaly skin. It responded by closing its eyes as it rumbled a deep resonating sound from its chest.

The other was filling a hand wagon with faecal matter, discarded by the dragon. He scooped heap upon heap of the sloppy substance into the cart, clearly not enjoying his task as much as his comrade.

"I thought you said we were going to see the eggs," Arthur said disappointedly.

"We are," Gruloch informed him. "This is Meera. She acts as egg mother. In nature, a dragon will stay with her eggs until they hatch. Only then will she leave to hunt.

"My father was convinced that the young inside the eggs hear the sounds of the world through the shell, so we have always kept a female by the eggs so the young can hear her breathing and moving. Once they hatch, we take the young to the nursery cave where they are cared for by Haigok only."

"You don't wait until they no longer need to suck?" Arthur queried.

"Dragons do not give milk," the Haigok replied. "They require meat from the moment they hatch."

"Fascinating," the boy murmured.

"Come." Gruloch gestured for them to follow him. "Meera is harmless. She won't fight like the others, which is why we assigned her to this duty."

To prove his point, the Haigok moved to the large creature and raised his hand to her snout. She responded by tilting her massive head so he could rub the spiny ridge that ran above her eye.

"Come," he said to Arthur. "She won't bite."

"Go on." Alice pushed him gently, feeling her heart race with excitement.

Arthur stepped tentatively as he moved towards the beast. She watched him as he approached, never taking her eyes from him.

"By the gods," David whispered as he observed his son reaching his hand towards the dragon.

Meera, the egg mother, stretched her neck and pressed her snout against his palm. The rough scales rubbed against his skin.

"Oh my," he gasped. A lump formed in his throat as a wide smile stretched across his face. The dragon rumbled a deep rattle from her chest as he moved his hand over her top lip, touching the protruding incisors as he passed his fingers over her. "She feels warm to the touch," he observed.

"Dragons are fire," Gruloch told him. "Quite beautiful when you get to know them. Dangerous if left to their own devices."

"That's why you keep them?" David asked. "To control their will?"

"My people have always been the keepers of dragons," the other replied, moving away from the beast and towards a group of objects resembling large, black stones. "The Haigok never intended to use them to attack. Rather, we protected them from the men who almost wiped them from the world."

"Yet..." David lowered his brow. "They were used to destroy my home once."

"And others." Gruloch crouched by the objects, placing a hand gently upon one. "My father's act of vengeance was not one that I agreed with. You must understand, David. I am not my father."

"What are those?" Alice asked, gesturing to the objects, attempting to soothe the air between David and the Haigok leader.

"These are dragon eggs," he replied.

Arthur turned from Meera to look at the objects.

"How long before they hatch?" the boy asked.

"The little ones inside won't see the light of day until well after winter," Gruloch replied as he lifted himself upright. He then said something to the other two Haigok males, to which they replied with a wave and a nod. "Come. We should see Liana."

"Liana?" Alice frowned.

"The dragon I was telling you about," he replied, moving by the troop and back to the wide passage. "Her den is a little farther along the path."

Moments later, the party had entered another cavern and stood in a chamber with a massive beast. This one cowered against the wall as the visitors drew within sight of it.

Upon seeing Alice, it roared before trying to back away, pressing itself against the cavern wall. The sound was deafening, causing the troop to cover their ears with their hands.

"As you can see," Gruloch said, "she has become timid. This one cannot be ridden again until she moves past this state of being. I'd like to know what happened out there for her to be like this."

Alice stared at the beast. It bunched into a ball, curling its long tail around itself to hide its face, keeping its eyes fixed upon the girl.

"I remember her." Alice stepped forward.

"Kayl'sro?" Nola'ee muttered, reaching out to the other. She was too late. Alice had already moved out of reach.

"What are you doing?" Arthur asked her.

The dragon roared again, opening its jaws wide to expose its long teeth.

Alice continued forwards, slowly stepping within striking distance of the giant creature. She scrutinised the beast as it slid its nose behind its tail again and tensed its muscles.

"Liana," Alice said soothingly.

The dragon seemed to relax.

Slowly, it lifted its face into view.

"Liana," the girl whispered, reaching her hand out to the creature.

It stretched its neck towards her, lowering its head towards the girl's hand.

"I won't hurt you," Alice assured the dragon as she swept her hand over its snout.

It emitted a deep rumbling rattle as it pressed its nose against the girl's hands.

"By the gods," David gasped, shaking his head.

Alice lifted her other hand and embraced the dragon, placing her arms as far as she could around its snout.

It closed its eyes and rumbled a pleased sound again.

"I have never seen such a thing," Gruloch admitted, turning to the others, only to see that they were just as astounded as he.

Alice turned to face the others, moving to re-join them. The sound of rustling as the dragon attempted to follow her caused her to stop.

"No," she said, holding her hand up to the beast. "You must stay here."

She turned to walk away, only to hear the creature calling after her with soft chirping.

"Well, well!" Gruloch shook his head. "It appears I cannot use this dragon after all."

"Why is that?" Arthur asked as Alice came to his side.

"That sound you hear is the call all dragons make to their keepers," he explained. "It's the sound of belonging. Liana has decided she belongs to your wife."

"What?" Alice felt the colour drain from her face and a knot form in her stomach.

"She is of no use to me," Gruloch told her. "She will fret without you. She will starve herself and die. She will need to be with you from now on."

"First a rukyul..." Arthur smiled. "And now this. What will your mother think?"

"Not funny," Alice told him, slapping him on the arm.

"Yes, it is," he replied.

The dragon chirped again, calling after Alice.

"Liana is yours whether you like it or not," Gruloch informed her. "She has chosen you and that is the way it is with dragons."

"David, what do I do?" the girl asked.

"The diplomatic thing would be to accept the gift as part of the peace agreement," he shrugged.

"It would be a gesture of good relations between our peoples," Gruloch offered.

"Go on," Arthur said, giving her a little shove.

Alice breathed a deep sigh as she looked upon her gift. The dragon inched towards her, lowering its head submissively as it chirped.

She placed her hands upon its snout again and rubbed the scales above its nostrils. A soothing rattle resonated from its chest as it fell into a deep sleep.

"I have a dragon," Alice said to herself.

Four

He rested in a high-backed chair by the fire, slumping down into the cushions as he stretched his old legs towards the heat of the flames. His woollen socks felt warm against his icy skin, and the multi-coloured blanket wrapped about him was a welcome addition.

The flickering light and the balminess emanating from the stone fireplace would usually cause him to drift off into sleep. But not tonight. Instead, his mind raced with concerns about the city; concerns that made him wonder if his thoughts were overreactions or reasonable.

"What's the matter?" Courtney asked from beside him. She was knitting another pair of socks, peering over to him worriedly.

"I don't know," he admitted. "Something hasn't been sitting right since Alice Warde was exiled. Don't you get the sense that something is wrong?"

"Since when is it right for a little girl to be exiled?" she replied. Her expression was sad.

Ruttger looked over at her and wondered why she had stayed with him. She was still young and beautiful and could easily win the heart of any man. But she had remained with the old soldier, professing to love him many times in a day.

"I feel as though I'm back on the western plains." He looked back at the flames.

The young woman stopped knitting and lowered her needles and wool, placing them in her lap. She then reached over to him, taking his hand in hers.

"What do you want to do?" she asked. "I'll stand beside you no matter what."

He shook his head.

"I don't know." He looked into her eyes and tried to smile before lifting her hand to his lips. "What do you think we should do?"

She frowned as tears welled in her eyes.

"We should pack up and leave for the caverns," she told him.

He felt a strange knot form in his stomach. It wasn't the answer he was expecting.

"I'm afraid," she confessed. "I feel like I'm cupbearer for the Lilac Mistress again and I don't know why."

He pictured the Seven seated upon the chairs in the assembly hall. Only, instead of wearing the faces of the women he was accustomed to seeing in Woodmyst, he saw nothing. Blank faces like the surface of eggshells.

"It's the Mirikin all over again," he muttered. "Isn't it?"

"I'll stay here for you, Ruttger." A tear streaked down her cheek. "But I would prefer it if we were to leave."

He got up and moved to stand before her, leaning over to kiss her forehead.

"Pack what we need," he told her. "I'll fetch a wagon and our horses."

"It's late," she told him. "You'll arouse suspicion."

"I don't care," the old soldier replied. "My wife is afraid and I don't feel safe in the city. The sooner we leave, the better I will feel about it."

***

Fire rolled across the land from the north like a giant wave, engulfing everything in its path.

Joanne watched as it scoured the mountains, bleeding through the dales and sweeping over the peaks before swooping towards the city.

A terrible roar filled the air as the giant flames appeared to stretch outwards, spreading wings of light and heat across the sky.

Screams and cries filled the streets. Men, women and children fled towards the southern end of the town, many coming to a standstill as they packed onto the bridges to cross the steaming river.

Frost-covered rooftops melted and caught light as the immense heat radiated from the wave of fire.

The smell of burning flesh poured from the buildings as flames enveloped those still trapped inside.

Giant ribbons of heat lashed over the forest to the west and caused the canopy of dry leaves to erupt into orange balls of fire.

She could hear birds and deer calling in agony as they cooked alive.

The oak, standing in the ruins of the Great Hall, burst into light. The flames reached high into the air.

She watched with disbelief as a form emerged from the blazing tree, stepping onto the path that encircled it.

A girl.

Unburnt.

Undamaged by the fire.

Alice.

Only, she was different.

Streaks of her hair, extending from her temples, were as white as snow.

Her eyes were a piercing blue.

Joanne's heart skipped a beat as the girl's appearance reminded her of the White Witch, Sumaiyya Tarkin.

Alice stepped towards her, holding her swords in each hand. She lifted one, pointing the blade directly towards Joanne's chest.

The girl opened her mouth and spoke.

Her voice seemed dark, distant as she plunged the sword into her aunt's breast.

"Sovereign."

Joanne sat up with a start, clutching at her chest.

She was soaked in sweat and breathing rapidly. Her vision focused, gradually seeing objects about her in the dark. A chest of drawers beside her. The light of the moon crept through the drawn curtains. The wardrobe against the far wall.

She was safe and alone in her bedroom.

Her hands were shaking and her body quivered as she pulled her knees up to her chest. Without warning, she burst into tears.

Slowly, Joanne lowered herself back on her pillow and closed her eyes.

The flames were still there. The image of Alice thrusting her sword was etched in her mind.

She wasn't sure whether it was simply a dream or something more profound. Perhaps a vision of something yet to come.

Her tears dribbled onto the pillow. Using the sheets, she padded moisture from her cheeks and continued to cry.

***

Nursing yet another mug of tea, she stared blankly into the flames of the hearth. A few had stayed awake with her, keeping vigil through the night.

"She'll be fine." Karlena leant over and touched Emily on the knee. "They're probably on their way back to us now."

"I won't have a proper sleep until she's here," the other replied, moving her gaze to the mountain peaks, barely visible against the night sky. "I miss her so much." Emily sobbed. "I miss Catherine and Joanne. I miss them all."

"Hey!" Jeremy lifted himself from his seat and strode past his wife to crouch beside the auburn woman. He wrapped his arms around her shoulders. "I know everything must look like a mess right now, and I know this is of little comfort, but you have us. We're not going to leave you.

"Besides, maybe Catherine will come to her senses and return to you. I'm not saying it will all go back to normal, but maybe something good will come of this."

Emily shook her head.

"My sister is responsible for the deaths of five people as far as we know." She frowned, wiping her face on her sleeves. "One of my daughters has chosen to live with her rather than with me. How can any good come from that?"

"There is still Kayl'sro Alice," Yuri put forward with his gravelly voice.

The others by the fire looked to the Agrodien as he leaned forward and poked at the cinders with a stick. Galonia, his wife, muttered something to him in words that the others didn't understand.

Yuri nodded as she spoke. "Kayl'sro Alice is strong," he told them. "She fight Haigok and frighten dragon. She made fire turn. She more stronger than sister. She more stronger than Seven. She killed Kayl'sro Greil. She rip his head open with her hands. She more stronger than Q'sharh."

"Yuri!" Galonia gasped, surprised by her husband's blasphemy.

Emily smiled as he tried to explain himself to his wife, using their own words.

His words were simple, but kind. Still, the pain she felt persisted in clinging to her like a weight in her chest.

"She'll be fine," Karlena said again. "Yuri is right. She is the strongest of all of us."

"Stronger than all of us," Jeremy corrected. "She could take down an army."

"Not yet." Emily was still wiping tears away as she peered into the flames. "She is still discovering what she is and what she is capable of. But I know Joanne fears her. I could sense it."

***

Alice felt Arthur's body pressing against her back. She was on her side, facing the dragon inside the den.

Gruloch had granted the party permission to stay the night inside the cave with the beast. The girl's presence appeared to soothe the dragon, so they had laid bedding, lit a small campfire, and the troop settled in for the night.

Arthur had pulled the covers over them before slumping his arm over his wife's waist and drifting off almost immediately. The others with her had a little trouble falling asleep in the presence of the magnificent creature, but soon enough, their exhaustion won out and they were all slumbering.

All except Alice, who fought her tiredness to watch the dragon resting.

Its breaths were deep and long. The rumbling, rattling sound continued to resonate from its chest as it slept. She assumed the noise was one of contentment, like a cat purring.

The rukyul, lying on its stomach, shifted its paws as it dreamed. A soft trumpet fart emitted from beneath its tail to echo gently around the cavern. Alice stifled her laughter so as not to wake her companions.

"You all right?" Arthur mumbled drowsily. Her movement as she giggled quietly must have woken him.

"I'm fine," she whispered. "Go back to sleep."

She needn't have worried about telling him to do so. She heard the change in his breathing pattern that signalled he was already out.

Alice watched the dragon for a while longer, observing the nostrils expanding with each inhale and exhale. She noticed tiny twitches in its face as it dreamed.

Wondering what dragons envisaged in their sleep, Alice felt her eyelids growing heavy.

"Goodnight, Liana," Alice whispered as her eyes closed and she started drifting away.

***

Concealed within the shadows of the trees, its black form writhed unnaturally along the ground as it crept along the ridge. Pausing at the crest, glaring at the tiny hamlet nestled in the clearing below, it sniffed the air and hissed a long breath.

Baring long, white, needle-like teeth as it pulled almost translucent lips over its gums, it discharged clear strings of saliva from the corners of its mouth. Pulling itself along the surface with thin, muscular arms and sharp claws, the creature crawled down the slope towards the village.

The scent of flesh was irresistible.

The aroma of blood, enticing.

Silently, purposefully, it moved closer, closer to the source of the odour.

Placing a hand upon a wooden fence post, it eyed the swine that had moved away to the far side of the pen, flicking its tongue past its teeth to taste the air.

Turning its head, it hissed and made a soft clicking sound with its throat.

A reply from beyond the ridge resounded as another heeded the call.

Then another.

And another.

Soon enough, many black forms were creeping into the village, keeping to the shadows and hiding from the firelight that flickered through the windows.

The creatures spread themselves around the hamlet, taking up positions near cottages, stables and pens.

A dog growled but was quickly silenced by a moving shadow as a fine spray of blood stained the ground by its kennel.

The other hounds suddenly met a similar fate before a few of the dark forms fed.

The beasts in the pens and the barns were next.

No noise was heard.

No struggle was made.

Quick.

Soundless.

One by one, the doors of the huts slowly opened.

Silently, the creatures moved into the dwellings.

Positioning themselves near their prey, they stood upright like men and prepared to strike.

Men, women, and children slumbered, oblivious to the dangers standing beside their beds.

There were no calls or signals.

There were no cries of pain.

There was just blood.

Copious amounts of blood.

Five

A deep crimson glow breached the horizon far to the east. A gentle breeze swept in from offshore, over the city and onwards towards the mountains.

Gustav leant against the stone banister of one of the palace's many balconies, peering towards the ocean as the birth of the new day began, dressed in nothing more than his breeches.

The smell of salt in the air and the sounds of waves crashing on the beach carried over the rooftops to the castle perched above the community, still sleeping below. Sea birds called as they glided across the sky, searching for scraps left in alleys before they resorted to scanning the tide for schools of small fish hidden beneath the waves.

He missed this and rose early to savour as much of it as he could. All would have been complete if only the balcony would rock gently with the ebbing sea.

With a deep sigh, he watched as crimson turned to pink and the morning stars blinked out one by one.

The sun would not be too far behind.

Gradually, more and more of the eastern sea became visible.

How easy it would be, he thought, *to board a vessel moored at the docks, to sail away and never return.*

"Gustav," a soft voice called from behind him. He turned to see Sharek pulling a robe around her naked flesh as she walked from the bed towards the door that opened onto the balcony. "How long have you been standing there?"

"A while," he replied, smiling as she wrapped her arms around him. He slid his hands over her waist and pulled her close, kissing her lips softly. "I didn't wake you, did I?"

"I got worried when I woke and found that you weren't beside me." She placed her head upon his shoulder as he turned to look over the roofs of the city to the ocean again. "You miss it, don't you?"

"You don't?"

"Sometimes," she admitted, running her fingers over his back.

"We could do it," he told her, his attention fixed upon the flat horizon. "You and me. We could find a ship and just go."

"No." Sharek shook her head. "We don't belong out there anymore. Our home is west of here. Not out there."

Her words saddened him. He still longed for the sea, but he knew she spoke truthfully. Their time at sea had past. The only ship that made him feel at home out there was now sitting beneath the waves of the Sea of Lunkhul.

"My home will always be with you, my sweet." He kissed her forehead.

She saw the grief in his expression and perceived his love for the sea. Gently, she ran her hands over his chest and around his neck.

"We still have time before the others wake," she said. "Take me back to bed."

"Well..." he frowned, lifting her off her feet and carrying her back inside. "Seeing as you twisted my arm, and all."

She giggled as he dropped her onto the mattress, proceeding to laugh out loud when he took the robe away from her roughly.

***

"Sleep well?" Akasati asked, grinning cheekily as she bit into a slice of toast.

Sharek and Gustav sat across from her with sheepish expressions. Both reached to the centre of the table, taking toast and tea from the spread placed there by the kitchen staff.

"I would have thought you two would have exercised some restraint considering you are guests in another's house," Rhydra commented as she leant back in her chair, nursing a warm mug in both hands. Her face remained expressionless as she stared at the two. "I was all the way along the hall from you and I could still hear everything. Imagine what the queen will say."

"Is she awake?" Gustav asked.

"Everyone in Newholt is awake after that episode." Akasati chuckled. "All women in the city are jealous, for certain. I'm wondering what you have hidden down there, Gustav, after hearing the cries of joy she put out."

"Oh, no." Sharek lowered her eyes in shame.

Gustav placed his elbows on the table and lowered his face into his hands.

Rhydra couldn't contain herself any longer. She burst into laughter after watching the two try to sink away in their seats. This set Akasati, who was already giggling, off.

"Rather jovial at this time of the morning?" Amicia Elynbrigge said as she and Brondt entered the dining room.

The four guests immediately rose.

"Please!" the queen gestured with her hands. "Sit down and enjoy your breakfast. Such formalities belong in public. Not here behind closed doors."

"We need to discuss a few issues with you," Brondt announced, as they all were seated. "We've thought about the situation you have brought to our attention. We need to say we will always consider Woodmyst an ally of Newholt. But the ascension of the Seven has us somewhat concerned.

"We will make a treaty with Alice Warde," he continued. "We will also keep our agreement with Woodmyst. This will mean that we won't get directly involved in any conflict that may occur between those of the city and those of the caverns."

"But you just admitted that you had concerns about the Seven," Akasati said as she reached for the pot of tea sitting in the middle of the table.

"We do." Amicia agreed. "And we may yet face another threat, just like that of the Mirikin. But there are innocent people in Woodmyst too. We just don't know enough of the details to understand what the Seven are up to.

"What I can be certain of is that it can't be good. Five people, you say, are dead. Maybe more for all we know.

"My concern is for the family," she continued. "Two sets of sisters have been separated. Emily from Joanne. Catherine from Alice. You may not have realised this, but the younger are the more powerful. Joanne and Alice.

"Joanne relies upon the strength of her coven. Sumaiyya Tarkin was the same, as was Yasmeen Svoboda."

"The Sovereign," Sharek hissed.

"The Sovereign." Amicia acknowledged as she poured a cup of tea for herself. "Yes. Both of them were the younger siblings of their families, and both drew upon the power of their followers. Joanne has that ability as well.

"Alice, however, seems to be a mystery. Until now, according to what I know, a sorceress would need to commune with others of her own kind. But it would appear something has changed.

"Let me ask you..." the queen leant forward. "Did she ever make it a habit to tarry near the Seven?"

"Not even in her younger years," Akasati answered, placing her mug on the table. "She always preferred the company of animals and often wandered off on her own."

"Then her power comes from within," Amicia stated. "This is truly unheard of."

"But we've seen other witches use their abilities without others being present," Gustav put in. "The White Witch made straw men attack us. She made the weather turn."

"She drew upon the Sovereign and me to do so," the queen informed him. "Alice is a standalone sorceress, and there is much power in her."

"The point is," Brondt added, "we will not stand against Woodmyst directly, but we will oppose the Seven if they prove to be a threat."

"Do you perceive them to be a threat?" Gustav questioned.

"It's hard to say," Amicia admitted. "I don't have the ability to see what others are thinking or even gauge their mood from such a distance. I can sense two forces rising in the west. They both give me a feeling similar to when a powerful storm is about to strike.

"It appears calm, but you can almost touch and taste the energy in the air. For now, they neither align nor oppose one another. But they are two separate entities."

"Good or evil?" Rhydra asked.

"Good and evil are only a matter of perspective," Amicia replied. "The ones you may consider evil could see their own actions working for the benefit of others. They wouldn't see you in the same light or darkness as you see them.

"However," the queen added with a grimace, "as you have told me, they have slaughtered children using magic, and I don't see how any good can come from such actions."

"We have some other matters to discuss with you." Brondt lifted a steaming cup from the table. "I dispatched a regiment this morning to investigate the lands to the north. We've not heard from several settlements for some time."

"You're about to ask us to join your men on the journey," Gustav perceived.

"Not at all," the other replied before sipping from the cup. "We simply feel that there is a possible threat out there and would urge you to take precautions on your return home."

"In fact," Amicia interjected. "I would prefer it if you stayed with us until we heard from our men."

Gustav eyed the two seated at the end of the table carefully. He could see a deep concern on their faces.

"What is it?" he asked. "You're afraid. Why?"

"It may be nothing," Brondt replied. "They could all simply be set-tling in for the winter. It is getting colder by the day. The snow will fall soon. Perhaps they're using their time to build their supplies."

"But?"

"But," and here the commander locked eyes with the other man, "they are long overdue for resupply of certain goods. Our dockyards have stock waiting for the settlers farther to the north to gather.

"We sent some perishables to the farthest outpost along the coast, but the word back was that there has been no contact with the north-erners for weeks."

"How far north is your outpost?" Rhydra asked.

"Blackrock Haven," Amicia replied.

"By the gods," Gustav grunted.

"Others have gone farther to the north?" Akasati questioned.

"There are many settlements along the coast and in the mountains from here all the way to the frozen waste," Amicia replied. "There is iron, gold and bronze in the higher grounds, and more has been discovered in greater quantities to the north.

"Settlements along the coast have opened the road to the north. We have built a road and reclaimed land that once belonged to Yasmeen Svoboda and Sumaiyya Tarkin."

"So, what's north of Blackrock Haven?" Sharek asked.

"Nothing that we know of," Brondt answered. "There used to be farmhouses long ago, but they were either raided by the White Mistress when she fled to the west or abandoned not long after you were last there. Why do you ask?"

"I was just thinking that perhaps the settlers encroached onto the grounds of someone, or something, that doesn't take kindly to intruders."

"We considered that also," the other replied. "Which is why I've dispatched men to investigate."

"Seems a long way off to be concerned with our safety, though," Gustav put in. "I mean; Blackrock Haven is more than a few days' ride."

"You're right," Brondt said. "But one settlement due to gather supplies is situated not too far from the fallen lighthouse, north of Oakbeach."

"I remember the lighthouse," Gustav told him. "I watched that monstrosity tumble down."

"Then you remember it is not all that far away," the commander said.

"Whatever is happening out there," Amicia said, leaning forward, "whatever is keeping those people in the mountains is moving towards us. I don't know what it is, but I sense a shadow moving along the range."

"Alice!" Sharek blurted suddenly.

"What?" Gustav turned to her.

"Alice went north to treat with the Night Demons," she reminded him.

"She'll be fine." He placed a comforting hand on her shoulder. "She's nowhere near the mountains."

"No," Akasati acknowledged. "But she needs to climb them on her return home."

"What do you speak of?" Amicia asked, looking at her guests with a perplexed expression.

"Alice has become the leader of a race called the Agrodien," Gustav replied.

"The lizard warriors that attacked Woodmyst?" Brondt queried.

"The same," the other answered. "It's a long tale, but as they moved to the south, they stole horses from the Night Demons. Alice has gone to return their property with hopes to treat with them."

"She would have gone to the Pillars of Mohaa," the queen surmised. "Even though she is well into the Core Lands and some distance away from the mountains, the Pillars of Mohaa are as far north as the fallen lighthouse.

"If she returns by using a direct route to the east, she may venture into danger. Would she do such a thing, or would she move south first?"

"I'm uncertain," Gustav told her. "I'm unfamiliar with the land. But she would take the terrain that is the easiest for her companions. She travels with David, three Agrodien warriors and her husband."

"Our hands are tied here," Amicia admitted. "We cannot get a message to her in time. For all we know, she could be in the mountains as we speak."

"She defeated the Night Demons," Akasati said proudly. "She defeated the Agrodien. She may defeat this shadow you speak of also. Others have underestimated her before and she has shown them what she can do. I believe she will make it home safely."

"She will," Gustav agreed. "But I'm still concerned for her. She has a husband who is only a boy and his father in her care. She will feel the need to protect them before she defends herself. You know it. It's who she is. She always thinks of those she loves before herself. That's her weakness."

"It's not a weakness," Rhydra snapped. "It's her strength. She will be fine."

Sharek reached over and took Gustav's hand in her own. He turned to her, seeing moisture glistening in her eyes.

"She will be fine," she told him. He knew she directed her words more to herself than to him. But he nodded before she repeated them again. "She will be fine."

Six

"How often should I feed her?" Alice asked Gruloch as she tied down her bedroll onto the back of her saddle. "And how much of what should I feed her?"

"Dragons don't eat as often as you would think," he replied, helping her with her belongings. "If you can spare a goat every few days, or half a cow, that should suffice. She will be slower in winter, preferring to sleep more, so she won't need to eat as frequently. If she's active, flying and moving about, she will need meat."

"So, she'll need to eat when we reach home, then?" Arthur asked as he lifted himself onto his steed.

"She has eaten little since her first encounter with you," the Haigok said to Alice. "So yes, she will need to eat. She may fret at first, being in a strange place, but it won't take her long to adjust."

"We'll start with one heifer," the girl replied, peering up into the sky to watch the creature circling high above them.

"It would be easier if you just rode her," Gruloch told her.

"I wouldn't know where to begin with such a task," she replied.

"It's easier than you think. You simply lean into the direction you wish to go and she will take care of the rest."

"What of the reins?" Alice asked, looking over at the large bundle enveloped in canvas that sat upon the back of their packhorse.

"If you pull back on them, she will stop in the air," he replied. "Apart from that, they really have no use."

"So, to make her climb?"

"Lean back," Gruloch answered. "To dive, lean forward. It's all very simple."

"What if she falls out of the seat?" David asked.

"Impossible," the Haigok replied. "You must strap yourself in. You will see when you unwrap the package. It will all make sense."

He looked at the sky and smiled.

"Thank you, Gruloch." Alice held her hand out to the other. "Lord of the Haigok."

He took her hand in his. Tears slid from his yellow orbs.

"I am so happy," he said. "Liana has not been out of her den for days. Now she flies with joy. You did that, Alice. Kayl'sro of the Agrodien. Ally of the Haigok, and my friend. You and your people are welcome here any time."

"As are you in my home." She lifted herself up on her chestnut stallion.

"Safe travels," Gruloch called to all of them as he lifted a hand. Many Haigok had gathered to see them off, all waving goodbye as the troop set off along the path that would take them out of the valley.

***

Eventually, the six riders and one rukyul were back upon the desert sand, moving towards the east. The morning sun was well above the horizon, and a gentle breeze caressed their faces as they plodded along.

Above them, Liana stretched her muscles by circling around, barrel rolling and looping through the air. The Agrodien watched the beast in awe, commenting to each other and gasping loudly as the dragon performed feats of amazement.

From time to time, she swooped down low and swept over their heads before climbing back into the sky. Nola'ee, the female reptilian, let out uncontrollable soft squeals of joy as she grinned like a small child at a fair.

The dragon spiralled high into the air before falling back towards the ground, tucking its membranous wings tightly against its body. The troop watched as it drew closer and closer to the ground, holding their breaths as it plummeted faster and faster.

Alice appeared unmoved as the beast suddenly spread its wings at the last moment, swooping just in time to avoid contacting the surface. Liana manoeuvred her body just above the earth, leaving a cloud of dust in her wake before climbing back into the sky again.

"She's trying to impress you," Arthur said to his wife.

"She doesn't need to try," Alice replied with a wide grin on her face.

***

The troop travelled for most of the day, reaching the edge of the heathland by late afternoon. As the sun sank towards the ground to the west, the travellers set up camp in a shallow dell.

There was little shrubbery around to consider making a fire. Even the tufts of grass were sparse and considerably dry. The hobbled steeds munched on what they could, but there was little for them to enjoy.

Alice peered to the east, sighting the mountain peaks far in the distance. She estimated another day's journey before they would reach the foothills.

The rukyul stood by her side, seeking attention after the long day of walking. She rubbed its shoulder before moving her hands underneath its chin. It lifted its head, welcoming her touch. It groaned with pleasure as Alice moved her fingers along its thick neck, scratching deep into the thickening fur.

"I guess that I'll need to get a brush for you," she told it. "I'm not having your hair all over me when you shed your coat after winter passes."

The creature let out a soft growl as the dragon slowly drew lower to the ground. Liana extended her talons and flapped her large wings, sending small whirlwinds of dust into a flurry around her.

Gently, she touched the earth and gave herself a great shake to remove the dirt from her thick, leathery skin. Lowering her giant head, the dragon crawled towards the girl, using her folded wings as forelimbs as she chirped quietly, calling to her new keeper.

"Quiet," Alice said to the rukyul, who was still growling and setting his hackles on edge. "Be nice."

The girl turned to the dragon and reached a hand out to her snout. The beast chirped again as she pressed her nose against Alice's hand.

"You must be tired after all that flying," the girl said. She turned towards the camp. Tents were erected in a small circular formation and the others gathered on canvas rolls that they were using as make-shift seats.

"I've broken out the dried food for us tonight," Arthur told them. "I think we should give the rabbits from Gruloch to the rukyul."

"Might as well," David agreed. "We can't cook them without a fire, anyway."

"What dried goods do we have?" Alice asked, sitting down beside him.

He opened a satchel and looked inside, pulling out bits and pieces and handing them around to the others.

"Some smoked fish from home," he said, giving a bundled package to his father. "Dried beef strips from our new friends, the Haigok. We've no vegetables or fruit."

"It will have to do," Alice said, taking the beef and removing a strip before passing the rest on to the Agrodien. "We should be closer to the forests by this time tomorrow. With luck, we will be able to hunt something and make a fire to cook it."

She bit into the beef. The meat was tough and needed a firm jaw to tear a bite-sized portion off.

Arthur retrieved two dead rabbits from the satchel and tossed them to the rukyul, who was watching intently as they passed the dried meat around. It practically inhaled the two carcases, pelt and all.

Turning to Liana, Alice could see the great dragon curled up behind the tents and already asleep. It wasn't long afterwards when the rukyul lowered his head upon his forelimbs and closed his eyes as well.

The sun was setting, turning the sky into a deep red glow.

"I don't think I will be awake for much longer," Alice admitted.

"It's been a long day." David turned to observe the two beasts sleeping nearby. "For all of us, I see."

"I stand guard, Kayl'sro," Nola'ee offered.

Alice shook her head. "No guarding tonight," she replied. "We all deserve some rest. This one will alarm us if any intruders approach." She gestured to the rukyul sleeping beside her.

The light in the sky dissipated, and stars twinkled to life.

One by one, as their eyelids grew heavy, the travellers retired to their tents. The last to remain was Bein, who scrutinised the rukyul with fascination as it slept.

He cocked his head as he observed the rising and falling of the dark creature's ribs as it inhaled and exhaled slowly. He admired the sleek form of the beast and the enormity of its shape.

One of its eyelids flickered open suddenly, and it stared directly at the Agrodien.

The reptilian felt his heart stop as he quickly rose to his feet.

"I go sleep now," he blurted, pointing to his tent, assuring the creature that he meant no harm.

The rukyul followed the Agrodien with his eye as the reptilian slunk away, disappearing beneath the tent flap with a friendly wave goodnight. Only then did the creature close his eye and return to his slumber.

Seven

She knelt on the grass before the great oak, staring up into its branches as the boughs swayed gently in the breeze. The many-coloured leaves fluttered and rustled softly as she watched them move, a dark silhouette against the night sky.

She pulled her black hood over her head and her hands rested listlessly in her lap as she looked at the tree, waiting for an answer or a sign.

It offered nothing to her.

Not a whisper.

"What does it mean?" she asked in a soft breath, hoping that by voicing her thoughts, a response would be given. "I don't understand."

A tear streaked over her cheek and down to her chin.

It dropped upon her chest and soaked into her cloak.

"Please." She placed her palm against the rough skin of the trunk. "Please, Tomas."

"Joanne?" A voice drew her back to reality. She turned to see a figure standing by the gate of the enclosed grounds. Tricia Bell was peering at her, a quizzical expression upon her face. "What's the matter?"

Joanne wiped her tears. "Nothing."

"Don't lie to me," the other said, moving closer as Joanne lifted herself to her feet. "You are my prime, and I can sense when there is something wrong with you. We all can."

"It's Alice," the woman in black answered. "I had a dream about her."

"And it worries you?"

"She set the city aflame." Joanne frowned. "Then she pushed a sword through my breast and called me *Sovereign*."

Tricia placed her hand on the other's shoulder.

"It was just a silly dream," she assured Joanne. "It means nothing."

"What if it does?" Joanne asked, shaking her head, tears streaming down her face. "Every time I close my eyes, I see her. I can almost feel the heat of the fire. What if it is something yet to come?"

"She's your family," Tricia comforted, pulling the other woman into her arms. "She's not going to set the city on fire and stab you."

"What if what we did was wrong?"

"Don't say such things," the scarlet woman warned. "If the others heard you, they would doubt that you deserve your place amongst us. You are our prime. Together, we will set the way for the Maji. We can't do this without you."

"But what if the Sovereign's prophecy is true?" Joanne pressed. "What if the Maji is evil?"

"Do you think the Maji is evil?" Tricia asked, looking Joanne in the eyes. "Besides, the prophecy doesn't say that the Maji is evil. It says that the Maji is the Heir of Darkness. The ruler of all. Nothing more. There's no word of the Maji being evil or good for that matter."

"We did the right thing?" Joanne questioned. "Tell me we did the right thing."

"We did the right thing, Joanne," she replied. "I have no doubts about it."

"Then why do my sister and my niece remain at the caverns and not here with me?"

"I don't know," replied Tricia. "Perhaps they simply can't see what we can. Give them time. They'll come around."

"I'm not so sure," the woman in black said, starting along the path to the gate. "I wonder what Tomas would think of all this."

"You should go home, Joanne," the other said, trying to direct her friend's mind away from painful thoughts. "Little Antony needs you."

"And why are you out so late?" Joanne asked as they stepped onto the street.

"I came looking for you," the scarlet woman answered. "I sensed something wasn't right. So, I came right away."

The woman in black pulled her robe tightly around her.

"I think you're right," Joanne admitted. "I should go home. These things will either work themselves out or they won't."

"I'll see you tomorrow, then." Tricia embraced the other.

"Tomorrow," she replied.

**

Entering the house, she found Lucy sitting in a chair by the fire, nursing a steaming mug. Takmel and Catherine were in the kitchen cleaning up after a late supper.

"The children?" Joanne asked.

"They've been in bed for some time now," Lucy answered, a hint of anger in her voice. "Where have you been?"

A knot tightened in Joanne's stomach. She sensed hostility from the three of them. Lucy kept her gaze on the embers as Catherine and Takmel continued tidying without looking in her direction.

"I was at the oak," she said, moving into the sitting room. "I didn't realise how late it was. I'm sorry."

"He asked after you," Lucy told her. "I told him you would be back to put him to bed."

Joanne looked towards the passage that led to the bedrooms. The corners of her mouth drooped.

"Don't bother," the other woman said. "He's finally asleep."

"I'm so sorry," Joanne said to her. "I'm sorry that you had to..."

"I didn't," Lucy interjected.

Joanne stared at the other, bewildered.

"I did," Catherine announced, turning to face her aunt. "Sit down. We need to talk."

The woman in black shifted her gaze over the three of them. Only Catherine and Takmel were looking at her. Lucy continued to peer into the flames, unable to bring herself to face the other.

"What is it?" Joanne asked, sitting in a chair beneath the window.

"This has gone on too long," Catherine told her, lowering herself into a seat across from her aunt. "You have been out at that tree every day. You sulk and weep on the grass while your son cries for you here."

Joanne felt a lump grow in her throat as tears streamed down her face. "I didn't know," she admitted.

"We know you didn't," her niece informed her. "But now you do. The question is, what are you going to do now that you know? Will you be a mother to your son, or will you continue to go to that tree and cry to a husband who is long dead and unable to help you?"

Joanne glared at the girl. "That's your father you speak of," she muttered.

"That's your son that I rocked to sleep." Catherine pointed toward the bedrooms. "I did the same last night and the night before because you were brooding by a tree. It's time to come back to reality.

"Your sister has turned away from you," she continued. "How sad. *My* sister and *my* mother have turned from me and you don't see me being so upset about it. There is far more at stake than having our family by our side.

"The time approaches. The Seven are needed. You, as their prime, need to remain on task. We cannot afford any mistakes. Not now.

"What lies in the past will remain there. A new beginning is imminent. We need you to get us there.

"In the meantime..." Catherine leant forward. "You will not visit the oak on your own any longer. You will act as the prime of the Seven, as you are meant to be. And you *will* be a mother to Antony. Understood?"

Joanne wiped her eyes, keeping her attention fixed upon her niece. She bit her lip and nodded slowly.

Catherine stood up and crossed the room to her aunt. She bent over and placed her hands gently on either side of Joanne's face, and kissed her softly on the forehead.

"I love you, Aunt Joanne," she said. "Please don't put me in such a position that requires me to bring correction again."

"I won't," the woman in black replied. Her heart thumped rapidly in her chest. The lump in her throat throbbed. The knot in her stomach tightened. The fear she felt caused her muscles to tighten. "I promise."

***

"How are you keeping?" Emily asked as she sat in a seat by Courtney and Ruttger, handing the woman a warm mug of tea.

The fire was fading. Yuri placed another chunk of wood onto the hearth and poked at the embers with a long stick. The flames quickly bit into timber and sparked to life.

"I'm fine," the young woman replied with a grateful expression. "It feels safe here."

Emily looked around at the faces gathered nearby. It was quite astounding to see such a gathering. Old friends and new sat around, sharing each other's company as if they had been doing so since forever.

Glaun and Lilen no longer only sat with the other northerners. Now, they were mingling with those who had turned from Woodmyst as if they had always done so. The Agrodien shared the heat of the fire with the humans, along with stories, laughter and moments of sorrow as they glanced to the north, waiting for the return of their Kayl'sro.

It felt safe here.

They were a people. A society. A family.

"We're glad to have you here." Jeremy looked to Courtney before turning to Ruttger, sitting to her side. "An extra set of hands will go a long way as we continue building our new huts."

"I don't see too many of those," the old soldier observed with a wry grin.

"Construction is slow," the captain admitted. "We've hit a few problems recently."

"What construction?" Emily questioned. "Everyone seems preoccupied with hunting and gathering supplies. I haven't even seen ground broken for foundations yet."

"And that would be one of the many problems," Jeremy admitted.

Karlena shook her head as she snuggled against her husband.

"We need our stores filled," Baldwyn put in. "The frost on the grass lingered longer this morning. The snow will come soon. We need to be ready."

"We need shelter too," Ewan Cunningham informed them. "The canvas on the wagons will only protect us from the weather for so long. We need houses and stoves. We won't be able to gather around this fire forever."

"Make groups," Gharnef grunted. He was leaning forward, towards the flames with his scaly palms stretched towards the warmth.

The others looked at him questionably.

"Groups," he repeated before turning to his wife, Evalad, and holding a quick conversation with her. "Hunters. Builders. Fishers. Groups."

"Agrodien hunters," Yuri was swift to say. "We hunt."

Gharnef nodded in agreement. "We good hunters," he said.

Baldwyn chuckled. "I like that," he snickered. "You lads come up with a grand idea and quickly place your mark on what part of it you want to do."

"Sounds fair to me," Emily told him. "If the Agrodien want to hunt for us, then they should be allowed to hunt. I, in the meantime, will fish and tend to the flocks. I will need help with that."

"I'll help you," Courtney offered.

"I help," Corandra, Yuri's daughter, said. Her father reached over to her and rubbed her head affectionately.

"I guess that leaves us men to build," Glaun suggested.

"Not all of us." Baldwyn tightened his arm around Elka. "Some of us need to work the quarry. We made a deal with Woodmyst. The snow will hinder our progress with cutting stone. We should get as much done as we can before the weather turns for the worse."

"We'll make do," Emily said. "We will keep our word to Woodmyst. What men remain will need to start construction here."

"The next question is," Ruttger put in, "where do we build our little community?"

Everyone looked to Emily, who felt suddenly exposed. She glanced around at each of them, who were eagerly waiting for an answer from her.

"I..." She looked past the flames to the western edge of the glade. It was pitch black and obscured by the shadow of night. "I guess we should start in that direction. We have livestock to the other end of the clearing. And this side is a little higher."

"The stream runs close by, also," Karlena added. "And the close mountains offer a little more shelter from the winds here. I think that may be why Alice built here in the first place."

"Alice built here because of her father." Emily frowned. "He came out here often and knew these caverns almost as well as she does. This is home to her more than Woodmyst ever was. And now it is our home too.

"Why she built her hut within that cavern over all the others here, I could not say. I would only be guessing.

"We should look into using the other caves at this end of the glade as possible shelters before committing to building upon open ground. By building in the cavern, Alice was able to save on wood."

"No roof and sidewalls," Jeremy said, peering back to the cabin. "The cave offers those. She just sealed the gaps with some kind of residue."

"Wax and mud," Ewan informed them. "Beeswax from the hives near Woodmyst and mud from the edge of the stream. She told me so."

"Clever girl." Jeremy smiled.

Eight

Bein continued to glance over his shoulder at the massive black creature seated next to Alice and her chestnut stallion. It was watching the girl intently as she whispered to her steed. But now and then, he felt a shiver run up his spine, forcing him to turn and peer into the staring eyes of the rukyul.

Hastily, each time this happened, the Agrodien would turn his face back to his horse and continue strapping an item down. He had no intention of angering the large beast.

The travellers were packing their horses for another day of riding. The silhouette of distant mountains stretched across the eastern horizon as a faint glow of morning pre-dawn light reached across the sky.

"Another clear day." Alice smiled, turning to the others.

"Good," David said as he and Nakra lifted one of the rolled tents onto the packhorse's back. "We should make the foothills by dusk."

"I'd like to get as close to the forest as we can," the girl told him. "A fire would be nice. It was a little chilly last night."

"Even with my warm arms around you?" Arthur raised his brows.

"I could feel you shivering against my back," she replied. "It kept me awake most of the night."

"A fire would be nice," Arthur said sheepishly.

Liana, the dragon, chirped softly as Alice tightened the straps holding her bedroll in place. She turned to see the giant creature looking at her eagerly.

"You're a needy one, aren't you?" the girl said, leaving her stallion to see to the winged beast. Liana chirped again as Alice raised her hands to pet the creature's snout.

The dragon nuzzled the girl's chest, almost knocking her off her feet. Alice laughed and rubbed Liana's nose. The beast made a deep rattling noise, purring at the girl's touch.

A deep rumble emitted from the dragon's belly.

"What was that?" David asked, perplexed.

The Agrodien warriors gazed at the creature.

"I think she's hungry," Arthur presumed.

"Hungry?" David frowned. "You keep her under control, Alice. If she eats my horse or me, I'm going to be rather upset."

"You be dead," Nakra informed him.

"It's a joke, you scaly bastard." The other shook his head.

"Joke not funny," the reptilian replied.

Alice turned from the dragon and mounted her steed.

"Are we set?"

"Ready," Arthur said, settling into his saddle.

Nola'ee pulled her horse to Alice's side as the others climbed onto their chargers.

"Liana," the girl called. The dragon immediately looked at her. Alice gestured by sweeping her arm towards the sky. "Fly."

The beast spread its giant, membranous wings and beat them up and down, sending dust and silt into a flurry. The creature bounded once, twice on its legs before leaving the ground.

Alice peered after the dragon as it turned to its right, beginning a circle around the travellers as it climbed higher and higher into the air.

The dust settled back to the earth as the troop brushed dirt away from their faces and clothing. The rukyul gave a great shake, creating small puffs of dirty powder around him.

"You'll need to rethink that through for next time," Arthur told his wife.

"Sorry," she told them.

The dragon gave a loud, shrieking cry as it glided through the air.

Alice urged her stallion forward, directing him towards the mountains.

***

"We must return home," Gustav told the queen.

The table was being cleared by the young girls dressed in white after the company had enjoyed a hearty breakfast.

Amicia held a hot cup of tea in front of her lips, blowing on it gently before taking a sip. It was still hot, causing her to wince slightly.

"We've only just sent our men to investigate the northern region," she replied. "We need more time to assess the situation."

"Begging your pardon, Your Majesty," he started. "But we crossed the mountains to get here without an incident. I'm sure we'll be able to reach home safely."

"I won't stop you from leaving." Amicia frowned.

"Then it's settled." Gustav stood to his feet. The Erilian women looked to him surprised before following his lead. "We should start immediately and try for the highlands."

"I wish you would reconsider," the queen said, placing her teacup onto a small saucer with a soft clink.

"We've been away too long," Rhydra informed the other. "Our friends will get concerned if we tarry much longer."

"I understand." Amicia nodded. "I wish for you to stay, but I understand."

"May I suggest an alternate route?" Brondt asked. "Avoid the mountains and travel south. Take the twisted path through the southern ranges and go through the pasture lands of Woodmyst."

The four guests looked at one another thoughtfully.

"I don't think that's a wise idea," Sharek answered. "Someone could see us and inform the Seven. It would arouse suspicion what Alice might be up to."

"We have an agreement of sorts with Woodmyst," Akasati interjected. "A treaty, if you will. We supply stone to them. They provide stores and equipment. Seeing the four of us approaching from the south might be enough to break trust with us. We couldn't risk it."

"We'll stick to the route we took to come here," Gustav said to the commander.

"It must be exhausting." He shook his head. "Being so tentative. We've not had to worry ourselves with such things since the demise of the Mirikin."

"Neither did we until recently," Akasati replied. "I apologise for the abrupt manner in which we leave you, Your Majesty. And I thank you for your hospitality. But Gustav is right. We must return home."

Amicia moved around the table to the Erilian warrior, taking her hands into her own.

"All my best hopes go with you all," Amicia told them. "Let Alice know you have friends here in Newholt. You are all welcome here and no treaty is needed. My home is your home."

***

"I heard the quarry has reopened," Richard said, resting his hands against the guardrail of the centre bridge. The river swept by gently as he looked down upon the water's surface from the safety of the extensive structure made of stone and iron.

Waterfowl played noisily amongst the reeds near the edges as the morning sun warmed the back of the old man's neck. The market square to his right was already filled with patrons attempting to make a bargain and the streets about were busy with the comings and goings of horse, carriage and man.

"I didn't know that," Simon replied. He looked about momentarily, cautiously, to see who was passing by. "How did you find out?"

"They sent riders to watch the others," the other answered. "Some men still feel the need to inform me of what is happening."

"Be careful, Richard," the younger man warned. "You can't trust anyone."

"Can I trust you, Simon?"

Their eyes met.

"My wife is one of them," he whispered. "I love her wholeheartedly. But something isn't right."

Richard returned his gaze to the water.

"This will be the first time that someone born to Woodmyst is not seated upon the council," the old man frowned. "I held my tongue when the Seven took to the assembly hall, but I do not feel good about any of this."

"I didn't want to believe that they were capable of..." Simon turned to face the waterway. He peered along its path to where it passed beneath the western wall. "How could they do that to the little ones? She's my wife, Richard. I still don't want to believe it."

Richard saw the bodies of the Cunninghams, torn apart and strewn across their beds. Opened, as if from the inside.

"Truthfully," the old man said, "I considered leaving for the caverns myself. Not for my sake, but for Becka's. I'm afraid, Simon. I think Ruttger made the right decision. We have walls surrounding us. But it doesn't feel safe to me. The danger is already here. I don't think I can stay."

"If too many of us leave, others will follow." Simon lowered his voice as a small group of people passed by. "I already have concerns about those amongst our guards who came to us by Ruttger. They may still choose to pursue their commander, which would leave our defences rather thin."

"I can't stay," Richard repeated. "I simply cannot remain here. You should come, too."

"My wife is here," he replied. "My son is here. This is my home."

"I understand." The old man nodded slowly. "But I am going. I need my wife to be somewhere safe and it's not here. Not anymore."

***

Joanne stared blankly at the boots of the elderly man standing before the council. As he blathered on with numbers and equations, she felt herself drifting further and further away.

"Wheat stores are resting at one hundred and thirty-eight per cent compared to last year's quota," he said in a monotone murmur, ruffling the scroll in his hands as he moved on down the list. "Corn stores are set at a little over one hundred and fifty per cent. Oat stores are currently at one hundred and twenty-five per cent, based on last year's numbers. Moving on from the dried goods to the other produce from our plantations, we have potatoes sitting at over one hundred and twenty-nine per cent compared to last year's numbers, carrots at one hundred..."

"So, we had a good harvest?" Claire Staunton, robed in olive, interjected.

"Uh," the man stammered. "It... it... it... it would appear so."

"More than enough to get us through the winter, then?" she asked.

"I... I would think so," he said. "Yes. I could continue the report if you would like. We haven't reached the statements about livestock and timber supplies yet."

"Thank you, Master Drayton." Tricia Bell said. "We are certain you and the bookkeepers under your charge have been more than thorough in your calculations regarding our stores and supplies. Have you any word on the construction of our walls?"

Th... th... the walls?" he managed as he nervously rolled up the parchment in his hands.

"Yes," said the scarlet woman. "Will we see them completed before the snows fall?"

"I can't give you an answer, my lady," Drayton told her. "With the current supplies of stone, we may see the unfinished portion of the eastern wall built, but not the northern sector. We will need more stone blocks. We have seen most of the paving accomplished except for the roads by the north-eastern tower."

"Well!" Isabel Barnes, dressed in white, looked pleased as she peered along the line to the others seated with her. "That is good news. No more muddy boots."

Tricia shook her head slightly at the other's remark.

"Just one more question, Master Drayton." Christina Brocas, the woman in gold, held her index finger up. "Do we have enough to supply the community of people living at the caverns as well as our people within the city walls?"

"Without a doubt," the old man answered with a slight smile. "Our population has not increased since their departure. We should be able to make it through the winter and a little beyond with no issues or concerns to worry ourselves..."

"Thank you, Master Drayton." Tricia stood and bowed slightly to the old man. "We don't want to keep you from your busy schedule. I'm sure you have better things to do than to talk to us all day."

"Oh." The man bowed respectfully. "Thank you, my ladies."

With that, he turned and shuffled along the aisle to the large doors of the assembly hall.

The women watched him until the guards closed the doors behind him with a loud, resonating thud. The sound made Joanne jump slightly, bringing her back to reality.

"What's wrong with you?" Gilda asked, leaning forward in her seat to look the other in the eye.

Joanne looked to her left to meet those of the woman dressed in jade.

"What?" She furrowed her brow and looked to the others on either side of her. They were all peering at her questionably.

"You haven't been yourself since we returned to the city," Tricia said from her side. "You seem distracted."

"I'm troubled with thoughts of my family," she admitted. "I feel broken. It's as if I'm not whole."

"You miss them," the woman in lilac suggested. "Perhaps you should go to them."

"I don't think that would be wise, Sarah," Isabel replied. "I felt animosity between Joanne and Emily the last time they spoke with one another. Joanne belongs here. With us."

"Agreed." Tricia nodded. "The Seven must remain in the city. We can't leave now. The time of ascension approaches and we need to be together when it occurs. We can't risk losing any one of us."

"I'll be fine," Joanne assured them. "I just need to focus."

"We should hold coven by the great oak," Gilda offered. "We should channel our energy to protect our prime. She is vulnerable and we need her strength most of all."

Joanne felt a lump growing in her throat as her tears welled.

"Could this be an attack from some other entity?" she asked.

"Perhaps something unnatural is fighting the will of nature," Isabel said.

"I don't think so," Tricia replied before glancing at the woman in black. "I think it is just your emotions getting the better of you. You miss your sister and niece, and you're upset with them and yourself for the way you left each other."

Joanne wiped her eyes with the heels of her hands.

"We need to hold coven," she admitted. "And we should never speak of this to anyone. Especially Catherine."

Nine

As the sun-kissed the horizon to the west, the travellers set up camp once again. The towering mountains stretched as far as they could see to the north and south.

"A fire!" Arthur admired his handiwork as the flames lapped at the kindling in the hearth.

"Finally," his father snorted. David and the two male Agrodien warriors were erecting the tents while the young man busied himself with the fire.

"Kayl'sro," Nakra grunted, pointing his snout towards the treeline nearby.

They all turned to see Alice emerging through the trees with Nola'ee and the rukyul by her side. Both females were leading their horses on foot, walking them back to the campsite as each steed carried the slumped body of a deer over its back.

Liana, resting on the ground not too far from Arthur, chirped excitedly at the sight of the girl returning.

Leaving the fire, the young man dug into a satchel resting against his saddle on the ground by his side and retrieved a skillet. After rearranging the wood on the fire, he placed the flat pan over the flames.

"What are you doing?" David called. "She's got two full deer. They're not going to fit on that pan of yours."

"No," Arthur replied. "But we aren't going to be eating two full deer, are we?"

Alice pulled her stallion over to the dragon and rubbed the scaly beast's snout. She then turned back to her steed and pulled the carcass from its back to thump loudly on the ground.

The rukyul licked his lips with his long tongue as the girl dragged the deer by the hind legs, across the grass to the awaiting dragon.

"Not for you," Alice said to the dark creature as it pawed at the ground near the deer as it passed by. The girl pulled the body to the ground by the dragon's head. She released the legs of the deer and touched Liana on the jaw. "All yours, girl."

The magnificent creature didn't hesitate. It opened its massive jaws and lifted the carcass into its mouth. With a loud crunch, Liana clamped her teeth shut, breaking bone and flesh as she started consuming the deer.

In the meantime, Nola'ee continued to the edge of the camp and carefully lowered the carcass that her horse carried. She wheeled her horse away, leaving the dead deer on the ground so she could tie her steed to a fallen log where the others had also tethered their chargers.

Within moments, Alice had joined her and removed her saddle and equipment from her stallion before securing him to the same log. Together, Alice and Nola'ee returned to the fire.

"We'll take one of the hind legs," the girl told the others as she pulled a dagger from the small sheath on her belt. "It will be more than enough for one meal."

"What about the rest of the kill?" David asked as he stretched a tent cord out to be pegged into the ground.

"That goes to him." Alice pointed to the rukyul with her knife.

Bein glanced over to the creature, who was eyeing the deer intensely.

"He no like me," the Agrodien muttered.

"He doesn't like anyone," David replied. "Don't take it personally."

Slicing her knife through the pelt and plunging the blade into the deer's crotch, Alice started cutting the limb away from the body as cleanly as she could. A little blood slid over her hands as she sliced through the joint.

"Can you carve this up?" she asked Arthur.

"Steaks or chunks?" he asked, laying a canvas sheet onto the ground.

"Steaks, please." She smiled, holding the leg out for him to take.

He took the limb and placed it on the canvas. Lifting a knife from his own belt, Arthur skinned the leg and tossed the pelt onto the flames as Alice dragged the rest of the carcass away from the camp a short distance.

"Come," she called to the rukyul, who followed her eagerly. She gave the creature a pat on the shoulder. "Enjoy."

The rukyul buried its face into the stomach of the dead deer, piercing the skin with its large, pointed teeth. Alice could hear the crunch of bone and sickening wet sounds of raw flesh being torn from the kill as she returned to the fire.

Arthur had already thrown two steaks, roughly the size of her hand, onto the hot skillet, where they sizzled loudly. He was cutting a third away from the limb as his wife lowered herself by his side, kissing his cheek gently.

David shook his head slightly as he watched them.

"Why you do that?" Nakra asked.

The older man looked over to the reptilian questionably.

"I don't know," David replied, keeping his voice low. "I guess I can't believe that two people so young can be so adult. The both of them give me much to wonder about."

"You no like Kayl'sro Alice?" Nakra pulled another of the tent cords tight to peg it into the ground.

"Once," David acknowledged, "that was very true. But I was wrong about her. She is a good girl."

"Woman," the Agrodien told him. "She is woman."

David looked at the girl seated beside his son. She appeared as nothing more than a twelve-year-old adolescent female. But Nakra was right. She was anything but what she appeared to be.

She was powerful and wise. She was diplomatic and fearless. She was the wife of his son and he was proud to call her daughter.

Even so, he felt shame for the way he had treated her and knew he had so much to do in the hope to make it up to her.

Liana chirped.

She had finished eating her meal and was peering up at the mountains behind her.

"What is it?" Alice asked, looking over her shoulder to the dragon. It craned its neck back to look at her before returning its attention to the mountains.

The girl followed the dragon's stare to a bald place on the mountain's side some way to the south of their campsite. In the dying light, Alice recognised the rock face that had drawn Liana's attention.

"Something wrong?" Arthur asked, looking at the place of interest.

"It's the place where we met," she replied.

"Where who met?" David asked as he and the Agrodien took their places around the hearth.

"Liana and me," Alice said.

"I thought you met in the den back in the Haigok village," the older man said.

"Not the first time," she told him. "She tried to kill me up there."

Liana had edged towards the girl slowly, keeping her head low to the ground.

"This was when you battled them on the mountainside?"

"Yes," Alice answered as the dragon nuzzled her softly on her back. She reached around behind her and placed a reassuring hand on the beast's nose. "I guess it must bother her."

"She remembers it," Arthur opined.

"It's all right, girl." Alice turned on her knees and rubbed the creature's snout. Liana chirped softly in response.

***

Gustav erected the tent while Sharek tended to the horses, tethered to a fallen log, feeding them grain from a small hessian bag. The other two Erilian women kept the fire blazing as they roasted two rabbits over the flames, skewered on spits made of thin iron.

"It's getting dark earlier and earlier each night," Akasati said as she turned the spit. The sky was a deep crimson and a few stars were twinkling to life far above.

"Colder too," Rhydra replied, pulling her cloak around her tightly. "I can see my breath in the air.

"We're in the mountains." Sharek gestured around them as she approached. "It's always cold up here."

Gustav crouched beside one of the tent poles and pulled the cord taught before hammering the peg into the ground with a rock. He scanned the edge of the clearing they had chosen to camp in as he returned to his feet.

The forest was thick here, encircling them entirely. The shadows beneath the bare limbs of the trees were growing darker, concealing the landforms that were visible when they first dismounted their steeds.

There was a tall peak, jagged and rocky, not too far to the north of their position, that broke through the canopy like a tooth through the skin of one's gums. It loomed above them menacingly, causing Gustav to have second thoughts about their chosen spot for spending the night.

"How's supper coming?" he called out, placing the stone he'd used for a hammer by the tent's entrance before rising to his feet.

"Almost done," Rhydra replied.

He sat beside Sharek and placed his arm around her. She had been watching Gustav curiously, knowing something troubled him.

"What's the matter?" she asked.

"Nothing." He smiled, pushing his anxiety away.

She kept her eyes on his face, not believing his words, but not willing to question him in front of the others. Instead, she snuggled into him and rested her head on his shoulder.

As the shadows deepened and the air grew more chill, the troop feasted and talked of home and how they missed their beds. Akasati placed a small steel pot of water on the edge of the hearth as Rhydra set up mugs by her feet.

"Who has the tea?" Gustav asked, rifling through a satchel lying next to him.

"I thought you had it," Akasati said, reaching for her own bag and delving inside with her hand.

"I do," he replied suddenly, retrieving a tiny metal container roughly the size of his fist and cylindrical. "It was on the bottom."

"That was a close call." Sharek smiled.

A horse snorted loudly, causing Rhydra to peek over her shoulder. All steeds were munching on grass shoots by their feet, except one. It stood tensely with its head high, twitching and turning its ears in all directions.

"I'll say," Akasati chortled. "There could have been blood spilt over that."

The horse lowered its head and bit into the turf, relaxing its posture. Rhydra turned to face the flames again, stretching her fingers towards the heat.

"I miss my bed," Gustav said, repeating his words from moments earlier. "But I think I miss that monstrosity of a mattress in Newholt even more."

"Goose down pillows and quilts," Sharek said. "I think we were spoiled."

"We'll never have such luxuries in the caverns," Akasati said, peering into the flames as she thought about how warm and comfortable the beds were in the palace.

"Good," Rhydra told her. "You don't need the comforts of Newholt. Any of you. Soft beds and cotton sheets. If we remained there any longer, you would have grown fat and lazy."

"Yes, we would have," Sharek agreed with a cheeky grin. "And I could easily live with that."

"How do you think Amicia does it?" Akasati asked.

"Does what?" Gustav pressed.

"Remain so..." she pressed her hands against her sides. "Do you think it's all corset under her garments?"

"Amicia grew up with luxuries," Gustav answered. "I think she keeps herself in such condition by keeping a disciplined lifestyle."

"I couldn't do that." The other shook her head. "If I had people who served me breakfast and changed my sheets, I would lie down all day and have them feed me."

"And I guess they would carry you to the privy also?" Sharek laughed.

"They wouldn't be able to," Rhydra said, smugly. "She would be so fat that they would have to roll her through the palace."

The four laughed.

"That would be grand." Akasati grinned.

The horse snorted again. Rhydra turned to see three of the steeds turning their ears in all directions as they stared towards the northern edge of the clearing.

"How is that water coming?" Gustav asked.

"Not yet," Akasati replied, leaning forward to see a thin sliver of vapour circling over the water's surface. "It should be ready soo..."

"Shhh," Rhydra hissed. She turned her face towards the high peak, breaking through the forest to the north of their position.

The others turned to look at the monolithic shape silhouetted against the night sky. Darkness stared back at them, and the more they tried to listen, the more silent it seemed.

"What is it?" Gustav asked.

"I don't know," Rhydra replied. "But something has the horses spooked."

"Could be a rabbit," Akasati suggested.

CRACK!

Their heads snapped towards the east. Something was moving beneath the shadows of the trees. The sound of rustling leaves drew their attention momentarily.

Rhydra turned back to the steeds who kept their heads turned towards the north. Their ears continued to turn this way and that, picking up sounds all around them.

CRACK!

From the north.

CRACK!

A little to the west.

The four stood to their feet and picked their weapons from off the ground, unsheathing their swords, ready to defend themselves.

"Should we make for the horses?" Sharek asked.

"No time to saddle them," Gustav replied.

"Damn the saddles," Rhydra told him. "We should just go."

"Where?" Akasati asked. "To Newholt?"

CRACK! CRACK!

Their faces turned to the east again.

"That way is shut," Gustav said. "South and west is the only way."

"How many do you think there are?" Sharek scanned the treeline.

The sound of rustling undergrowth and breaking twigs resonated from the darkness.

"I don't really want to stay around to find out," Akasati told them, moving cautiously towards the horses.

"I agree," Gustav said, signalling to the others. "We should go now."

With her steed freed from the fallen log, Akasati leapt upon the beast's back. It stamped its hoof against the ground excitedly, eager to flee.

"Come on," she called to the others.

"Oh shit," Gustav whispered, as his eyes fell upon a shape standing at the eastern edge of the clearing.

Akasati turned to see a black form resembling a man. Even in the darkness, she could tell that it was not human. It appeared wet, lubricious, glistening in what little light the campfire provided. Long white needle-like teeth, twisted and contorted, grimaced at her as sharp claws expanded from the ends of rigid fingertips.

It emitted a long hiss, followed by a rhythmic clicking noise.

"What is it?" Akasati gasped.

"Go," Rhydra ordered, a desperate urgency in her voice.

Looking around at the others, Akasati felt confused. They were still some distance away from the steeds and had stopped in their tracks.

"Flee, stupid girl," Sharek hollered.

Akasati turned her face to the north to see a horde of dark creatures bursting from the treeline. They raced towards her on all fours like animals, bounding across the ground in haste, clawing and clambering over one another as they fell upon the open land.

Instinctively, she kicked into the sides of her horse and raced away to the southern edge of the clearing and into the woods.

With a quick look over her shoulder, she could see the clearing filling with a shadow that expanded from the northern and eastern edges of the campsite. Sharek, Rhydra and Gustav stood their ground with swords at the ready as the beings drew nearer and nearer.

The trees closed around her, obscuring her view of what was happening. She so wanted to turn back, but she knew she had no chance against such numbers.

Neither did her friends.

Behind her, she heard the piercing cries of the other steeds as they were attacked. The shouts of her friends echoed around her through the trees as they engaged the dark creatures.

Her eyes welled with tears as she leant against her steed's back, gripping the reins tightly in her hands as she held onto her sword.

The horse raced through the forest at a high pace, its hoofbeats rapidly smacking the turf in time with Akasati's heartbeat.

She knew her friends wouldn't last.

She knew they would meet their fate in the clearing.

She knew the creatures wouldn't be satisfied with Rhydra, Sharek, and Gustav.

They would come for her too.

They were most probably already coming.

She hoped her horse could run on and on.

She hoped they both would last the night.

Ten

Emily stood up and faced to the east, scanning the darkened mountain peaks in the distance. She knew she wouldn't be able to see anything, but something told something terrible, out there, caused her the pain in her heart.

She turned to look across the hearth to Karlena, who was leaning forward and holding her chest as if someone had pierced her with an icy blade. Jeremy placed his arm around her, his expression turning from jovial to a confused look of concern.

The others seated about the fire stopped laughing and paid attention to the two women who appeared preoccupied with something of which only they were aware.

"What is it?" Jeremy asked, leaning into Karlena.

"I don't know," she said as she cried, "but it hurts so much."

Tears streaked down Emily's cheeks, her chin quivered and her emotions hit a peak as she also wept.

"Our sisters," she murmured.

Karlena looked at her and broke down. She knew Emily's words were true. Something had happened to the others.

The bond between them had grown strong over the years since the trek to Blackrock Haven. They were not a powerful coven like the Seven, but they had a strong connection, nonetheless. And while blood did not relate them, as she and Joanne were, the Erilian women were the closest people to family that she had.

"Gustav?" Baldwyn asked, looking from Karlena to Emily for answers.

"I don't know," the auburn woman answered as Linet placed her arms around her sister-in-law for comfort. "I don't possess the ability to see. I'm sorry."

Feeling some shame, Baldwyn lowered his head and frowned, wishing he hadn't asked such a silly question.

Yuri moved his eyes around the gathering.

"Kayl'sro?" he asked, not truly understanding what was occurring. "Alice hurt?"

"No, mate," Glaun, the northerner, answered. "Your queen is fine."

Some relief swept over the Agrodien's face momentarily until he realised what the concern was.

"Erilian?" he blurted excitedly, turning to his wife.

Galonia motioned for him to settle down and spoke to him using their tongue. A soft conversation ensued between them before being interrupted by Gharnef. The two reptilian males discussed something together, using gestures and pointing to the mountains in the east as they spoke.

"What are you two chatting about then?" Kygra, Glaun's brother, queried.

"We go," Gharnef replied. "Agrodien take horses and search."

"No." Emily turned to them. "We don't know where they are. They could be on the other side of the ranges. You could be gone for days. Even worse, you could end up suffering the same fate they did."

Karlena sobbed uncontrollably.

"There is a darkness out there," the auburn woman continued. "I don't know what it is, but it is like a shadow in my mind. We need to stay together. We need to protect what is here."

She gestured to the children sitting by their mothers and fathers.

Yuri nodded, considering her words.

"We stay," he assured her, moving his gaze over his daughter and sons. He then locked eyes with his wife. "We not go."

She smiled gratefully.

***

Alice was on her feet, peering to the mountain range behind their campsite. She moved her gaze across the jagged ridge. The blackness of the mass seemed to swallow the immense stars in the eastern sky.

The rukyul lifted its head and eyed her as she scanned the trees carefully. She felt an unease in the pit of her stomach and couldn't explain its cause.

"Are you all right?" Arthur asked, moving to her side. The large beast lying near to her lost interest and lowered his head onto his front legs before closing his eyes.

"Something isn't right," she replied. "I don't know what it is."

"Well..." her husband looked over at the rukyul before turning his head to observe the dragon. Liana had been sleeping soundly for some time and didn't look as if anything alarmed her. He turned to see the horses nibbling at the grass, relaxed and at ease. One was even lying on its side. "The animals don't appear to be distressed. Are you feeling well?"

"I'm not ill," she told him. "It's something else. Something awful."

She lifted her hands to her brow and ran her fingers through her long hair, taking in a deep breath before lowering her arms by her sides.

Arthur wrapped his arms around her and pulled her to him tightly. He kissed her brow before touching his forehead to hers.

"Whatever it is," he said softly, "it isn't here. Come back to the fire. Sit with me a while."

She put her arms around him.

Together, they sat side-by-side and peered silently into the flames. The others gathered around the hearth looked over at the couple briefly, each wanting to ask her about her state of being. But Arthur had it under control and so they kept their tongues still.

Alice snuggled against Arthur, leaning into him. She felt contentment in his arms, a warmness on the inside that no fire could equal.

Still, the feeling of unease tickled the hairs on the back of her neck. There was something threatening, though distant, that drew her attention.

She tried to push the sensation away, but it wouldn't go.

Was this some new part of her, an ability she now needed to master?

She took a deep breath and gazed into the glowing embers.

Arthur kissed the top of her head.

It made her feel a little better.

Just a little.

***

The horse had slowed to a walk. It had been running as fast as it could for quite some time, and the terrain proved difficult in places, making the effort even more intense.

Akasati kept her ears pricked for any sounds coming from behind them. Her concern was that she hadn't heard the dark creatures when they attacked. It was as if they made almost no sound at all.

She watched the steed twist its ears around to detect the beings as it continued to plod along, making its way to the top of another rise. It struggled as it neared the top of the ridge, its body shaking with each step.

"All right," said Akasati, dropping to the ground and leading the beast by the reins. "Just a moment's rest."

Once they reached the crest, she peered back towards the way they had come. In her heart, she hoped that Rhydra, Sharek and Gustav had survived the onslaught.

Her head told her otherwise.

"We'll be fine," she said to the steed, rubbing its nose. It nickered, continuing to twitch its ears nervously.

Akasati felt her heart thumping in her chest, hearing it beat loudly in her ears.

The sudden feeling of nausea hit her hard as she buckled over and tasted bile and rabbit flow over her tongue. Her sword fell to the ground as her stomach relieved itself of its contents.

Emotions were next to strike as she felt tears stream down her cheeks and mucus drain from her nose.

The sensation of loneliness swept over her like a thick blanket as she gave her mind to her fallen friends.

Dropping to her knees, she gave herself some time to gather herself together again. She wiped her tears on the sleeve of her cloak before gathering the lower hem of the garment in her hands to wipe the mess away from her mouth.

After a few deep breaths, she lifted herself to her feet and picked up her sword.

The horse nuzzled her gently, reassuringly. It showed that it was ready to move on by padding the turf with its hoof.

"All right," Akasati said the beast, stroking its neck. She moved around to the side of the steed and leapt onto its back. "Let's go."

The horse trotted over the other side of the ridge and down the steep embankment towards a narrow valley.

The sound of night birds and flowing water grew as they moved on into the hollow.

The next stop, Akasati considered, would be to quench her thirst and wash the stinging taste of sourness from her mouth.

As she steered the horse from the steep slope to the floor of the valley, dodging thick shrubbery and bending her body beneath low limbs, she listened to the crickets chirping noisily by the stream's edge a short distance away. The steed instinctively and wearily made its way towards the bubbling noise of fresh, flowing water and singing insects.

The glistening ripples of the stream were inviting. Akasati felt a desperate urge to leap from the horse's back and dip her head into the liquid. Instead, she held her place and let the steed take her closer to the water's edge.

Once there, the horse lowered its head and drank. Dropping to the ground, keeping the reins in one hand and her sword in the other, Akasati knelt beside the horse and pressed her lips against the stream's surface.

The water was icy to the touch and sent a chill down her throat as she swallowed.

The sting of bile lingered.

She slushed the water around her mouth and spat, trying to clean any remaining filth that had escaped her stomach.

Once again, she swallowed a few more mouthfuls of water.

The horse lifted its head suddenly and peered across the thin stream.

Akasati followed its gaze and saw only shadow and darkness.

A soft rustle of foliage alarmed her once again.

Her heart pounded in her chest as her grip tightened on the hilt of her blade.

Her mind raced with thoughts of the creatures slinking silently through the undergrowth. Surrounding her. Enclosing.

The brush across the way shook as a large form moved by it.

She stood up, ready to fight until her last breath.

The large form moved to the river's edge directly across from them and gazed at her and the horse.

A buck.

Its posture was impressive, standing proud and tall with a crown of antlers that stuck out wide and high on the sides of its head.

It blew a wet snort of aloofness before lowering its head to drink from the stream.

Akasati relaxed as she allowed herself to breathe easier.

The horse returned its muzzle to the water, keeping an eye on the buck all the while.

She was about to do the same when she felt overwhelmed with emotion again.

The corners of her mouth fell as tears fell from her eyes.

Keeping as quiet as she could, Akasati sobbed in the darkness, overcome with grief and exhaustion.

Eleven

Arthur stretched his arm out to his wife, only to find that she was gone. He opened his eyes and peered at the slither of dim light emitting through the tent flaps.

The sound of Alice's distant laughing and calling enticed his curiosity, drawing him onto his elbow as he wiped the sleep away. Slowly, he lifted himself to his feet and dressed before exiting the warmth of the canvas shelter.

The fire had been rekindled, and a pot of water steamed silently at the edge of the embers. He glanced around and saw no others nearby, noticing the other tent flaps remained shut.

"Come on," he heard her shout, but it wasn't to him. He turned his head towards the grassland and saw the great dragon a short distance away, sitting on its rump and watching the girl dash across the grass at a high pace. The rukyul was chasing her and catching up.

He felt his heart leap to his throat, fearing the worst. The rukyul was attacking. Her enchantment over the beast was waning.

There was nothing he could do but watch.

Alice stopped suddenly and turned to face the creature.

It skidded to a halt and spun around, bounding like a clumsy pup.

The girl gave chase, laughing as she increased her speed, kicking up dust into a fine cloud behind her.

The rukyul realised she was gaining and bolted as fast as he could.

But he was no match for her.

She gained upon him within moments and slapped the creature's rump playfully.

It spun, almost tripping over its giant feet, and licked her over her entire face with one slobbery stroke of its tongue.

She fell onto her backside, laughing hysterically.

"Alice," Arthur called to her.

She peered over at him, still laughing.

"Good morning, Arthur." She got up and petted the rukyul on the shoulder as it moved to her side like a protector. Its demeanour instantly changed from playful to watchful.

"I woke up, and you were gone," he said, approaching. Liana lowered her head to him as he strode by, chirping softly. He stroked her snout and remained by the dragon as his wife moved towards his position.

"I was entertaining the rukyul," she explained, placing her arms around his neck. His eyes moved to the dark creature that was eyeing him.

"I don't trust it," he said. "You haven't even named it."

"It's not a pet," she replied, moving her face closer to his. She planted a kiss on his lips and held him.

Liana chirped.

"Jealous?" Alice chuckled as she reached over to the dragon, stroking it on the chin. It emitted a low rumble. She turned her attention back to her husband. "You trust her and you've known her for less time than him."

"The dragon likes me," he smiled. "I have a way with women."

"In your imagination, maybe," she quipped.

He moved his focus to the rukyul again. It sat upon its haunches and eyed the couple engaging in a moment of intimacy.

"It watches me every time I'm near you," Arthur grumbled.

"He watches for me," she clarified. "He won't hurt you, Arthur. You won't harm me, so he won't harm you."

"So, he's your guardian?"

"In a manner of speaking," she assented. "He protects the leader of the pack. Even against other members of the pack."

"And you're the leader?"

"Do you see him watching over any other?"

"No," he said, frowning. "I guess it must be in his nature to be distrusting."

"Wary," she corrected him. "Not distrusting."

"How do you know all this?" Arthur questioned, looking at her with curiosity and fondness.

"I don't know," she answered honestly, raising her brow. "I really don't."

He leant in to kiss her.

"It doesn't matter then," he told her before touching his lips to hers.

The creature groaned as it lowered itself to the ground, seemingly disappointed that the time of play was over.

"Maybe I should name him," Alice remarked.

"Not anything fancy, like Liana," Arthur replied.

"The dragon was named so before I took her."

"Shadow," her husband blurted.

"What?" She looked at him, bemused.

"It seems fitting," Arthur said, peering over to the beast lying on the ground. It moved its eyes back and forth, watching the couple as they conversed. "He's dark and quiet."

"Shadow," she said, looking at the rukyul. It lifted its head. "I like it. Shadow it is."

***

The tents were lowered and rolled into small bundles. The two Agrodien males loaded them upon the pack horses along with cooking utensils that were stored in canvas bags and hung high over the steeds' flanks.

Bein reached for the bundle containing the riding equipment made for the dragon. Alice moved her gaze to the reptilian as she finished stomping the hearth's flames out with her boots.

"Wait," she called abruptly.

He looked at her, baffled.

"You no want this, Kayl'sro?"

"I do," she replied, walking towards him. She lowered herself beside the bundle and started undoing the twine that held the covering material in place.

"We're packing to leave," Arthur reminded her. "Why are you opening that for now?"

"I think I should try it out," she said as she peeled the covering away.

A dark leather apparatus rested on the ground. It resembled a saddle, much like one used on a horse. The difference was a very noticeable strap that was set in place to loop around the thigh of the rider, and four large metal eyelets, two at the front and two at the rear of the seat.

A large leather piece was rolled underneath the saddle, along with four coiled straps that unfurled upon the open grass.

Liana chirped, moving her head up and down excitedly.

"No." Arthur waved a finger as he approached his wife. "No, no, no. No way. You're riding the stallion home, Alice. You do not know how to ride her. I don't want you to."

"If I don't do this now," she said, as she rose to face him, "I might not get the opportunity again."

"Excellent!" He raised his chin. "I don't want you up there. I want you down here with me."

"What if she is like a horse? What happens if I don't ride her, and she forgets what it's like to have a rider on her back?"

"I'm fine with that," he argued.

"I'm not," Alice told him. She peered over to the dragon, who was continuing to chirp and move her head about. "Look at her, Arthur. She needs this."

"What if you fall off?"

"I'll be strapped in," she answered.

"But what if the straps are loose?"

"Son," David called softly. "You're fighting a losing battle. You should know better than to tame your wife."

Arthur looked at his father and sighed. With a slow nod, he conceded.

"Please, be careful," he breathed.

She smiled and wrapped her arms around him.

"I promise," she whispered in his ear.

But he knew her too well. He grinned, understanding that she would push the limits as she always did.

"Liar," he said playfully, before kissing her cheek.

***

With a quick leap and downward thrust of her wings, Liana was airborne and climbing into the sky. She tucked her legs beneath her, curling her talons as she beat her wings in long strokes.

Alice listened to the sound of the air rushing around the membranous limbs. The noise was almost deafening, but the experience was exhilarating. She watched as the dragon's neck and shoulder muscles contracted and relaxed with each blow. The girl admired the power of the beast beneath her as the world below grew smaller and smaller from her perspective.

The others watched her from the backs of their steeds, craning their necks and shielding their eyes from the morning sun with their hands. Eventually, they grew so tiny that they reminded her of ants crawling on the ground.

Her heart raced with excitement, and her mouth stretched into a wide grin.

Suddenly, Liana turned to her right and dived for the ground.

Alice felt her stomach tighten.

The foothills raced towards her.

The windswept over her face, and her eyes watered from the sting of the speeding air.

Still, she could not rid herself of her overwhelming sense of joy.

As the girl and dragon rushed towards the surface, Alice saw individual blades of grass and wildflowers growing in patches.

The fear of the beast crashing into the dirt-filled her every sense.

Then, just before they met their doom, Liana swooped back into the sky.

Flapping her wings, she climbed upwards, turning in a tight spiral as Alice burst into uncontrollable laughter.

"By the gods," David gasped. "Your wife and her dragon are as twisted as each other."

Arthur shook his head and grinned. "Come Shadow," he called to rukyul who was peering longingly after the girl.

Shadow moved his gaze to the boy who was leading Alice's stallion by the reins from the back of his own horse.

With another quick look to the sky, he shook his hackles with a snort and followed the others.

The troop made their way into the woods that covered the slopes of the mountains, directing their mounts to the south as they climbed onto higher ground. All the while, they listened to the sound of the dragon tearing the sky open as the girl hooted and laughed high above them.

Liana levelled out, gliding above the mountain peaks. Alice took time to admire the view. It was a different way to see the land. An advantageous way.

She could see for miles and miles in all directions. The only down-fall was that she couldn't see into every trough and valley. To do that, she would need to fly over the areas of interest.

Still, she could see more benefits to having Liana during a time of conflict. It was no wonder the Haigok had used the creatures.

Alice felt the chill of the air enveloping her body. Even with her cloak wrapped tightly around her, the cold still bit into her skin.

She leant slightly to her left. Liana tilted her wings and made a wide turn, emitting a deep guttural call.

Eventually, they were facing the direction from which they had come.

Alice straightened herself upright, urging the dragon to level out again.

The girl searched the ground below, finding patches of open ground through the treetops.

It took her some time, but she found the others riding beneath a section of bare trees. They were nearing the ridge.

Arthur was looking up at her, waving.

She responded by raising her arm above her head before leaning to her left, turning Liana towards the south.

It was time to go home.

Twelve

The wagon rattled noisily as it moved across the glade towards the caverns. A lone horse pulled the heavily loaded cart, struggling slightly on the rise as it neared the little village by Alice's cottage.

A few of the Agrodien younglings raced out to meet the strangers, causing the driver to show some alarm as he steered the vehicle towards the auburn woman standing by the tiny hut.

"Emily," a woman seated by the man holding the reins called.

"Becka!" The other waved. "Richard. What brings you out here?"

"We're moving," the old man said, eyeing the reptilian children as they jogged alongside the cart. Their laughter sounded alien to him, but he recognised the look of innocence and play upon their faces. He squinted and leered at them. "Boo!"

The younglings squealed with delight, laughing as they turned away. With a swish of their tails, they raced off to their mothers watching nearby.

"What do you mean, *moving?*" Emily asked as Richard brought the wagon to a stop by the house.

"We don't feel that Woodmyst is our home any longer," Becka said as she climbed down. "Something doesn't feel right."

"We won't be too much trouble," the old man assured her as he looped the reins around a post jutting from the footrest.

"You're our family," Emily replied, offering him help as he carefully lowered himself to the ground. "You're allowed to be trouble."

She wrapped her arms around him when he was standing securely.

"Where is everyone?" he asked.

"Some are at the quarry," she answered. "Others are cleaning out the caverns and preparing to build huts and storage."

"And Alice?"

"She has gone to treat with the Night Demons," the auburn woman said. "Arthur and David went with her. She took three of the Agrodien warriors along."

"And you trust them?" he asked, peering back towards the reptilian children playing on the grass.

"They are a lost people," Emily told him. "But they are loyal to Alice. She trusts them and therefore, so do I."

The old man frowned. "Fair enough. Now," he said as he shuffled towards the porch, "how about a nice cup of tea then?"

***

A small pack of hounds trotted from out of the treeline and into the glade. Richard, seated beside his wife on the bench that ran the length of the veranda, counted seven rather healthy-looking dogs approaching the settlement as he sipped at his tea.

In his mind, he envisioned the livestock farther to the east being attacked by the group of canines. He was about to say something to Emily, who was sitting on the porch, resting her back against the house, peering at the tall peaks to the north.

A sharp whistle burst from the forest, calling the dogs to stop in their tracks. The hounds turned to see a group of people emerging from the forest, following the dogs.

The small troop consisted of five men and four reptilians. Some carried rabbits, tethered together and slung over their necks. The Agrodien males had two deer, one doe and a young buck, slung on crude poles and carried upon their shoulders.

"Emily," Richard muttered, watching the newcomers with interest. "You have visitors."

"No," she said, cheerfully. "These are our friends. They live with us."

"Your little community is growing well," Becka said.

"All Alice's doing," the auburn woman acknowledged as she rose to her feet and gave the hunters a wave. They returned the gesture, turning towards the tiny settlement and climbing the long rise to their homes.

"Looks like we'll eat well tonight," the other woman observed.

"Perhaps," Emily replied, sitting back down on the porch. "We have many mouths to feed here."

"So I see." Richard looked at the patch of grass where the reptilian younglings played. Some human children had joined the frivolity while their mothers sat with the Agrodien females to darn clothing and sew patches in garments by the entrance to one of the larger caverns. "Where are all their men? The Agrodien, I mean."

"Most are dead," Emily answered. "The Haigok killed many with their dragons. Before that, they experienced a coup. Many died then as well. Those remaining made themselves loyal to Yuri, who is off fishing at the moment, I think. You can see four of them returning from a hunt. The rest are scattered about, clearing the caverns. But their numbers are low. The women vastly outnumber the men. For every adult male, there are at least five adult females."

"Lucky for them," Becka quipped.

"Not so," Emily replied. "They are wed to one, and one only. Even in death, they are one."

Richard looked to the reptilians and felt a strange sense of respect.

"I knew it would only be a matter of time," said a voice to his left. Richard turned his head to see three familiar faces approaching. "What took you so long to get here?"

Ruttger was smiling as he strolled towards the cottage, holding Courtney's hand in his. Grinning beside them was Ewan Cunningham. The lines in his face were deeper, making him appear dismayed, not the man that Richard remembered.

"It was too quiet without you lot." Richard rose to his feet. His legs shook slightly.

"Careful," Becka pleaded, reminding him of his age.

"I'm fine, my love," he replied, lifting her hand to his lips. He shuffled to the edge of the porch. "What news have you?"

"Not much," Ewan answered. "Life is much simpler here. Better, in my opinion."

Ruttger nodded as his wife stepped upon the veranda, placing herself on the bench beside Becka.

"What do you make of these new folks?" Richard asked, peering back at the Agrodien and human hunters approaching from the woods.

"They are all good people, my friend," Ruttger assured. "You can relax your defences here."

***

Exhausted and hungry, Akasati steered the equally weary horse through the thick woods. She kept the animal as close to the watercourse as she could, allowing it to feed and drink from time to time.

Onward, the beast plodded. Its head hung low to the ground as it fought the urge to sleep. The rider found this a constant battle, too.

Holding her sword against her belly, she felt her head drop several times, quickly bringing herself back to reality, only to start the fight all over again. A few times, she snapped awake to find the steed had stopped moving.

With a soft jab from her heels, the animal started off again.

Slowly, wearily, the two of them moved on and on.

Occasionally, she lowered herself to the ground and walked beside the horse, leading it by its reins. She did this more for herself than for the animal. Stretching her legs allowed her the chance to wake up.

Even if it was only for a while.

Alternating between the steed's back and her own legs broke the monotony of the journey. Still, time seemed to drag on.

Peering up to the sky, seeing the sun high above her, she sensed that the day had passed noon. Fear of the dark suddenly swept over her. She didn't want to spend another night in these woods.

Not with those things behind her somewhere.

Urging her horse forward, she tried to muster as much as she could from the beast, always directing it southward and west.

The stream snaked its way into another, which eventually joined another.

It took her a good portion of the day to realise she had been following the early stages of the river that passed through Woodmyst.

This gave her some hope.

There was a goal she could aim for.

Home was not too far away, she hoped.

"Come on," she said to the steed, kicking her heels into its sides.

The horse trotted along the edge of the stream.

More and more tiny waterways spilled into the stream. Wider and wider, deeper and deeper, the river grew.

Eventually, Akasati recognised the surrounding land.

A moment of relief swept over her when she reached a place where the river moved around a bald hill.

Woodmyst was only a few miles away to the west.

The glade was on a path slightly to the north.

Turning the horse toward home, a sense of jubilation and rejuvenation filled her.

The steed must have experienced the same feeling of elation as it began galloping along the side of the hill.

Akasati could tell the beast was pushing itself a little too hard, but she had neither the energy to stop it, nor the will to hold it back.

Through more trees they ran, entering the thick growth of the forest that surrounded the caverns. The canopy suddenly shielded the light of day. Dry leaves flung into the air and crunched under hoof as the steed raced through the woods as fast as it could.

Her heart beat faster and faster as her emotions tangled into a wild mess of joy, sadness, and fury.

She was almost home, but she returned alone.

Sometime later, she and her steed burst into the glade, passing the livestock feeding on the wild pasture and feeling the sun upon her face again.

Instantly, the horse slowed its pace to a canter before decelerating to a walk. It made its way directly to the stream that ran through the open area.

There, it lowered its head to drink as Akasati slid from the steed's back and collapsed onto the grass.

She was home.

Thirteen

"I just found her by the stream," Oliver called as he carried Akasati into the cabin.

Emily guided him to the bedroom and gestured for him to lay her on Alice's bed. "Did you see the others?" she asked hopefully.

"Only her horse," the other replied as he lowered the woman onto the cot. "I don't know what's wrong with her. She has no fever."

"She's tired," Richard suggested, ducking his head past the others to peer in through the doorway.

"She's traumatised," Becka said, kneeling by the bed. "Look at her. She's covered in grit and so dead to the world that she doesn't even know we're here."

"Get me some warm water and a cloth," Emily ordered.

"I'll go," Lor said, dashing to the kitchen, where he found a small wooden pail. Before long, he returned to the bedroom and placed the vessel beside Emily and handed her a clean rag that he found in the other room.

"Thank you," she said, dipping the cloth into the bucket. "Now, all of you. Please leave and let me tend to her."

"You heard her, lads," Oliver said. "Let's go."

The gathering moved out of the room.

"Not you, ladies," Emily called softly. "I need you to help me get these clothes off her."

Agnes, Oliver's wife, and Linet took Akasati's clothing away to the stream where they attempted to clean away the muck that she had collected in her escape from the mountains. Emily, Becka and Courtney washed the woman as best as they could before covering her in a night-dress belonging to the owner of the hut.

"I wonder what happened to her." Courtney watched Akasati taking deep, slow breaths.

"Nothing good," Becka replied, observing rapid movement beneath the other's eyelids.

"I'll stay by her," Emily told the others. "Someone should be here when she wakes up."

"We'll all stay," Becka suggested. "I'll fetch chairs from the kitchen and make some tea."

***

Richard sat by the fire with others who shared his deep concerns. He poked at the embers with a long stick, occasionally peering over his shoulder to the front door of the cabin built into the cave.

There had been no movement from within for a long time. His wife and a handful of women remained inside, sitting by the bed where Akasati rested.

All were restless and worried, always asking the same questions and giving the same suppositions as answers.

"What happened out there?" one would say.

"Marauders must have attacked them," another would suggest.

"There is something out there," Kygra eventually shared with the others when he brought a stag, skinned and cleaned, to the fire and set it upon the spit.

"What do you mean?" Richard asked.

"It's one of the reasons we came here," the northerner replied. "People were disappearing. Our livestock were all taken. We assumed it was men, but we never saw any."

"Maybe they're coming south," Terix, Kygra's wife, proposed. "Maybe we're not safe here either."

"We're safe here," Glaun assured his people, looking around the hearth and meeting their fearful eyes. "We have each other. We have the brave Agrodien with us and we have Alice, the Kayl'sro, on our side."

Richard smiled at the simplicity of the man's words and admired the faith he had in them. Glaun believed what he said and was not about to hear anything to the contrary, whether true or not.

"Now," the northerner said, as he looked at the sky. "The sun sinks to the west and we need to prepare tonight's meal for everyone. Who will help me?"

"Aye!" Jeremy raised his hand. "Sitting here and fretting about my friend in there isn't going to help pass the time. What do you want me to do?"

"Potatoes," Glaun replied.

"Consider it done." The captain lifted himself from his chair and strolled away to the hut.

"I'll help," Oliver announced, following the other.

Richard jabbed at the embers again, sending a few tiny sparks skywards.

"What are you thinking, old man?" Ruttger asked, reaching for a pot of steaming water sitting to the side of the hearth.

"I'm thinking a nice cup of tea would be all right," he replied, holding out his cup. "If you're offering."

Ruttger reached for Richard's mug. Ewan stretched out his arm, thrusting his cup in Ruttger's direction.

"Yes please," he grinned.

Within moments, the three old men sat quietly, nursing their warm cups and staring into the flickering flames.

"Have either of you heard about any threats to the north?" Richard asked.

"Not since the time of the Sovereign," Ruttger replied.

"There are always tales of monsters in the frozen wastelands to the north," Ewan offered. "Some say there are giant creatures that look like men, covered in long white fur from head to toe. Others say there are giant spiders and flying asps that dwell in caves that tunnel deep into the ground, only ever seen by those who have not survived to tell the tale."

"Then how did you find out about it?" Richard asked.

"What?" the other asked, with a puzzled look.

"How can anyone have told you about it if they didn't survive to tell the tale?"

"I don't know." Ewan shrugged. "Drunken seafarers will tell stories of how they fought great sea serpents and made love to beautiful mermaids. I soon learnt not to question them after receiving a good beating over the face from one large quartermaster when I questioned his exploits."

"Why?" Ruttger chuckled. "What did you ask him, exactly?"

"I asked him just how he could make love to a mermaid when mermaids don't have any legs to wrap around a man," he replied. "I then got accused of calling him a liar, to which I accused him of putting his manhood in an ordinary fish. Next thing that I knew, I was lying on the floor of a dockside tavern."

The three men laughed.

Suddenly, a dark shadow swept over them, blocking out the sun momentarily.

A rapid gust of wind blew, causing the flames to flicker and bend.

Richard's gaze shot towards the sky as his heart raced excitedly.

His worst fears had returned to him as he spotted the creature swooping towards the livestock in the lower part of the glade.

The children playing by the caverns froze in place.

Richard was already on his feet and moving towards them. His legs weren't able to carry him as fast as he wanted, causing him to almost stumble.

"Move inside," he called to the younglings, waving his arms to get their attention. But they didn't see him, and his voice was not loud enough.

"By the gods," Ewan gasped, riveted to his seat.

The great dragon flapped its wings and landed softly by the stream, emitting a loud guttural call that echoed through the valley.

"Get the children inside," Richard called again, shuffling past the cottage.

A few of the Agrodien females risked being seen by the giant beast, lifting their offspring from the ground and racing back to the shelter of the cavern.

Ruttger ran past the other old man and towards the petrified younglings.

"Inside," he called. "Inside now."

He picked up a small child in one arm and urged the others towards the cave by turning them with his free hand and pushing them on. By this time, the other mothers had raced out from the shade of the cavern to collect their children.

The dragon lowered its head and dipped its snout into the stream to drink.

Richard watched the beast as a tight lump formed in his throat.

"What's going on?" Emily shouted from the door. Her gaze landed on the giant creature on the grass. "Oh, no."

"Back inside," Richard ordered her.

"They're back," Becka gasped. "They're back."

"Back inside," the old man repeated.

His eyes moved back to the dragon. He watched as something small slid from its back, landing on the grass before rubbing the great beast's neck.

"What's that?" Becka asked.

The tiny figure knelt beside the dragon's head and dipped low to the water.

"It's Alice," Emily whispered. Tears built up as she stepped from the porch and started across the open ground towards the stream.

"Emily," Richard called after her. "You can't tell from this distance."

"It's Alice," Becka told him. "It is her."

"How can you see that far?" he asked. "It could be a Night Demon for all we know."

"Your eyesight isn't as good as your wife's," Ewan said, placing a hand on the other's shoulder. "It's her. It's Alice."

Richard watched as Emily continued down the slope towards the stream. The little figure, Alice, started wading through the water towards the auburn woman. The two met on the closest side of the stream and embraced under the watchful eye of the dragon.

Richard nodded.

"It's Alice," he agreed, a wide smile growing on his face.

***

Bursting into the bedroom and falling to her knees beside the cot, Alice reached for the sleeping woman's hand and wept. She gazed into Akasati's face and noticed the rapid movement beneath her eyelids.

"Has she said anything?" the girl asked.

"Nothing," Becka replied.

"Has she opened her eyes?" Alice peered around the room to the others gathered about. "Made any movement?"

"She hasn't moved or made a sound," Emily answered, resting her hand on her daughter's shoulder.

"I felt it," Alice sobbed. "I knew something was wrong."

"As did we," Karlena said, kneeling beside the young girl. "Something terrible has happened to our sisters. But we don't know what."

The sleeping woman stirred slightly. Her brow furrowed and her mouth moved.

"Akasati?" Emily called softly.

"...coming," the woman managed. Her voice was hoarse and barely audible.

"Coming?" Becka queried. "Who's coming?"

The weary Erilian murmured something.

"What did she say?" Becka asked.

"Nonsense," Karlena replied. "She needs more time to recover."

"She said the dark ones are coming," Alice told them. She placed her hand on Akasati's forehead. "Tell me more."

Slowly, wearily, the Erilian woman's eyes opened and moved about in their sockets. Searching. Focusing. Eventually, her gaze met the gaze of the girl beside the bed.

"They are coming," Akasati murmured. "Hundreds and hundreds of them."

"Who?" Alice pressed.

"She needs rest," Becka urged.

"The dark ones," the other replied. "Black and slender creatures."

Akasati wept uncontrollably. Tears streamed down the sides of her face and soaked into the pillow beneath her head.

"They killed them," she sobbed. "They're all dead."

"Where?"

"Alice." Becka moved to the side of the bed, to where the girl could see her. "Please. This is enough."

Alice shot her a quick glance and returned her attention to the woman in the bed.

"Where?"

"North-east," Akasati mumbled, fighting through her tears. "High in the mountains. A day of riding at least."

"You're safe now," Alice assured her. She moved her hand from the other's brow and to her eyes. "Sleep."

Instantly, Akasati drifted away into slumber.

The others in the room watched on in amazement and disbelief as the girl lifted herself to her feet. She exited the room and returned to the kitchen where she set to making herself a cup of tea.

"So that's it?" Emily asked, following her through the cottage. "You can just do that in there and then come out here to make tea. Friends of ours... family are dead, Alice."

"My husband is on his way home," Alice said. "We have been gone for days and I just need some time to think. Tea helps me think."

"And then what will you do?"

"Feed Liana and Shadow," she answered as she poured hot water from a pot on the stove into a mug. "Spend the night with my husband

and wake early to take a fly over the mountains to see if I can find any trace of our missing family members."

"Liana and Shadow?" Emily gave her daughter a perplexed look.

"Come." Alice lifted her mug from the kitchen bench and crossed the room to the door. Emily followed her onto the veranda, where the girl pointed across the glade to the dragon resting upon the grass. "That's Liana. She was a gift from the Haigok."

"So, the talks went well?"

"You could say that," she replied, before sipping at the contents of her mug.

"And *Shadow?*"

"The rukyul," Alice said, stepping down from the porch and moving towards the hearth in the midst of the camp.

"And what does..." Emily started, her attention fixed upon the giant beast snoozing on the far side of the clearing. She turned to see her daughter walking away from her. "Alice, please. What does that thing... What does Liana eat?"

"Meat," the girl replied, lowering herself into a chair by the fire. "Don't worry. I'll butcher one of the sheep for her."

"Butcher one of the..." Emily stood beside her daughter, staring in disbelief at the dragon. "We barely have enough to get through the winter with what we've got and you want to feed that thing a sheep every day?"

"Honestly..." Alice looked across the glade to Liana. "I don't know how much or how often she eats."

"What were you thinking, bringing that beast here?"

The others seated about the hearth peered into the flames uncomfortably as mother continued to berate daughter.

"I went to treat with the Haigok," Alice explained. "I did just that. As a gesture of goodwill, they gave me Liana. To reject such a gift would have been an offence to them. That's what I was thinking, Mama. Now, please. Sit with me and wait with me for my husband to return."

Emily looked down at her daughter and felt ashamed for chastising her. It was so easy to think of her as her little girl and forget she was the leader of a community. The Kayl'sro of the Agrodien.

"I'm sorry," Emily muttered as she lowered herself beside Alice.

Alice reached over and took her mother's hand.

"I missed you, Mama," she admitted.

"I missed you too." Emily leant over and kissed her daughter's cheek. Both of them stared into the flames silently as Alice sipped her tea.

"Well," Richard finally said, breaking the silence. "I'm glad you two are all right. Just one thing. Is that dragon of yours a danger to any of us?"

Alice shook her head. "She obeys my commands," she informed the old man.

"And where do you intend to keep her?" Jeremy asked. "Surely, the open ground is no place for a dragon."

"She'll need a cave," Alice admitted. "The only one large enough is housing the Agrodien at the moment."

"That may be just a temporary hurdle," Ewan put in. "The men have been clearing the caves around about. Perhaps we can give the cleared caverns to the Agrodien first. That would free up the larger cavern for your new pet."

"We move now, Kayl'sro," Yuri offered.

"No." Alice smiled. "It's late in the day. She will be fine tonight. I may even pitch a tent out here and sleep by her. She might get frightened if she doesn't see where I am."

"Frightened?" Richard blurted. "That thing?"

"Believe it or not," she said as she looked over to the dragon, "Liana has a gentle spirit."

"I don't believe it." The old man frowned.

"Tell me…" Emily had been peering into the flames the whole while as the others conversed around her, but now she looked up. "How did you do that thing with Akasati?"

"What thing?" Alice asked, turning to face her mother.

"You made her wake up," the other commented. "You made her tell you what happened and then you made her fall to sleep again."

Alice thought about her mother's words, reliving the event in her head.

"She spoke to you?" Jeremy queried. "What did she say?"

"She said dark ones attacked them," Emily replied. "She said the others were killed and these dark ones are heading this way."

"I'll take Liana tomorrow and search for them," Alice informed them before turning back to her mother. "But to answer your question; I don't know how I did that. I just knew I could."

"What else can you do?" Richard gazed at the girl curiously.

"I don't know," Alice replied, shaking her head.

Fourteen

Simon lay on his back as his wife thrust herself upon him. Fear swept over him as he grew more and more concerned about the loud sounds of pleasure reverberating through their house.

He didn't care so much about what the neighbours would think. His mind was more troubled about his son, who was probably in the next room.

"We should be careful, Tricia," he said.

"Why?" she asked, not showing any sign of slowing down.

"Thedric might hear us," Simon told her.

"He won't hear us," she informed him through her heavy breathing. "I took care of him."

She grabbed his hands and placed them upon her breasts.

"Well!" He smiled. "Do your worst then, woman."

"I intend to," she replied, lowering herself over him.

She placed her lips upon his and reached above his head to beneath the pillow his head rested upon.

Like a flash, she was up again.

He watched her bare body writhe as her smooth arms stretched above her head.

She was too fast.

He didn't see the dagger in her hands.

He didn't understand what was happening when she thrust the blade through his throat.

He wasn't sure if it was a dream or a nightmare when the sound of steel grating against the bones in his neck filled his ears.

103

"I made it quick for him, Simon," she said soothingly, her thrusts slowing down. "Thedric didn't feel a thing. I promise."

Simon moved his mouth.

Why?

Why?

But no sound could be heard except that of gurgling blood filling his mouth.

"I love you so much." She frowned. "You were the best thing to happen to me, ever. But the time has come for greater things to happen. And I need to be with him for that to happen. We all do."

Simon tried to reach for her, to place his hands around her neck.

His mind finally came to its senses.

You killed my boy; you bitch!

But it was too late.

His muscles felt weak and his ability to move depleted.

Darker and darker it grew.

"I'll miss you, my love." She lowered herself and kissed him one last time.

Darker and darker.

He felt the blade slice into his chest before her fingers reached inside his flesh to peel back tissue.

There was no more pain.

Just a strange numbness that made him hope it was all a dream.

Darker and darker.

The faint sound of crunching bones in his ribcage grew more distant. He could just barely see her now. Her hands were deep in his chest.

With a great tug, she lifted his heart to her mouth.

Simon closed his eyes and waited for a new dream to begin.

Darkness.

***

"It has begun," Catherine said. Her eyes were on the red glow spanning the western horizon. The sun had already disappeared below the forest and the land about was darkening as the light in the sky slowly dimmed.

They stood upon the parapet walk above the western gate. Takmel moved his gaze over the city as the lanterns were lit along the paved streets by men on stilts, carrying torches. His hands rested upon the rail as he leant slightly forward, watching the people below.

The clock above the assembly hall told the city they were now in the sixth hour afternoon. Large oil lamps, encased in glass and hung from either side of the timekeeper, illuminated the clock face. The sight reminded Takmel of a full moon shining in the night sky.

"Do you feel it?" Catherine asked, turning away from the forest and moving slowly over to his side.

"I can feel it growing," he replied. "Do you think they will all partake?"

"They have to," she said, pressing herself against his back and wrapping her arms across his chest. "They've all complied so far."

"I'm not so certain about your aunt," he told her. "I think she had doubts."

"You knew she would be the most difficult," she said. "She is their prime, after all. Her will would be the strongest and most resilient. But she is still here. She didn't stay in the glade."

He took a deep breath and let out a sigh.

"Tonight will tell." His stomach tightened with nerves as he gave thought to what the others were urged to do.

"Don't worry, my love." She manoeuvred herself between him and the wall, placing her face near his. "Whereas you have one, soon there will be nine."

"Nine!" He smirked. "Such a shame about Alice though."

"We don't need her," Catherine assured him. Her countenance changed to disdain. "She can stay out in the wild. You have everything you need right here."

Takmel eyed her carefully before moving to kiss her.

"You're jealous of her," he observed.

"No." She frowned, turning slightly in his arms to gaze at the clock. "I don't really care about her at all."

"You hate her, then?"

"She's my sister," Catherine replied. "I hate her and love her all at the same time. Why are you so interested in her? Are you in love with her?"

"Maybe." He grinned cheekily.

She turned to face him again, searching his eyes for the true meaning of his words.

"You are," she murmured.

"And you are jealous of her," he affirmed. "I can sense it."

"Do you prefer her over me?"

"No." Takmel placed a gentle hand on his wife's cheek. "She would have served a purpose here that no other could. I needed her to help me fulfil my destiny."

"She won't join you," Catherine guaranteed. "Besides making herself betrothed to Arthur, she despises both of us."

"She despises your aunt," he pointed out. "She doesn't know what we have done. All she knows is that the Seven killed Henry Cunningham and Seamus Harling. Nothing more."

"She hates us because we returned to Woodmyst with the Seven." She wept. "My mother hates me too."

Takmel held her tighter and kissed her forehead.

"Don't cry," he whispered. "We don't need them. It might take some more time than planned without your sister here to take part. But, when all is done, and I have come to my full power, she and your mother will understand. All of this, the good and the bad, will make sense. They'll come around. They'll all see me as the true light of this world. I promise."

***

Joanne sat facing the fireplace, turned away so no one could see her face from anywhere else in the house. She had moved closer the chair to the stonework, so she was within touching distance of the flames.

Lucy kept looking over at her as she prepared dinner, putting corn and potatoes into pots for boiling.

The children were napping in the bedrooms.

"Any closer," Lucy said from the kitchen, "and you'll be sitting on the embers."

"Perhaps I should be," Joanne replied, leaning back into the cushioned seat, squeezing the ends of the armrest with her fingertips.

Lucy noticed the emotion in the other's voice. "What has got you in such a bad mood?"

"Nothing," the woman in black replied. "Everything."

Lucy put down the knife with which she was cutting potatoes and wiped her hands on her apron as she moved to her friend's side.

"Talk to me," she urged.

"You don't see it?" Joanne queried. "I thought you of all people would understand after what you have been through."

"Understand what?"

"He's bewitched everyone," she answered. "The officials. The commanders. The others of my coven. I think perhaps, even you. It's the Sovereign all over again."

"Bewitched?" Lucy furrowed her brow. "You're speaking of Takmel?"

"The Maji," Joanne corrected.

"He has bewitched no one," Lucy said. "Everything that is happening is for the better. There will be harmony amongst all when he reigns supreme."

"Blood has been spilt tonight," the other stated.

"Some sacrifices need to be made." Lucy returned to the kitchen.

"But you haven't even questioned why he needs you to—"

"Sacrifices need to be made," the other interrupted, pointing the blade towards the woman in black.

"He *has* bewitched you." Joanne felt tears stream down her cheeks.

"You'll think otherwise when it all comes to fruition. You'll see." She wiped the blade clean with a cloth sitting on the bench and started for the passage that led to the bedrooms. "Get up out of your chair. It's time."

Joanne felt the corners of her mouth pull down as tears blurred her vision. She lifted herself out of her seat and crossed the floor into the kitchen, where she retrieved another carving knife from a drawer.

"Come on," Lucy called softly as she entered the corridor.

Joanne wiped her eyes upon her sleeve and tried to compose herself.

A large knot tightened in her belly as she followed the other woman. Her chin quivered and her muscles felt tense as she walked along the passage towards her bedroom door.

Lucy waited by the entrance to her own room, softly placing one hand on the knob, ready to enter.

Staring down at the blade in her hand, Joanne slowly opened the door to her room. A soft squeak emitted from the hinges as she pushed the door in.

A quick look to her left and she saw Lucy had stepped into her room. Her knife raised above her head.

Joanne clenched her jaw and moved slowly towards the bed.

There he was.

Sleeping soundly on his stomach.

Little Antony.

Named after her father.

The only living gift from her departed husband she had to her name.

But it must be done.

She stepped closer to the bed, lifting the blade higher.

It is the only way.

A floorboard creaked under her feet.

The boy stirred.

"Morning, Mama?" he mumbled. He was still half asleep.

"No," she whispered soothingly. "Not yet."

She could not contain herself. An explosion of emotion burst from within, sending a flood of tears across her cheeks.

"I'm so sorry," she said. "I'm so, so sorry."

With every ounce of energy that she had left, she plunged the knife down.

And down.

And down.

Fifteen

Alice stood by her tent, facing towards the south. Facing towards Woodmyst.

A taut feeling gripped her in her stomach.

Something terrible had just happened.

The canvas of the shelter flapped softly in the gentle breeze flowing from the mountains as the stream bubbled by restfully. An orange glow emitted through the coverings, causing the shadow of another to appear on the tent's surface.

"Bedding's down," Arthur announced from within. "We could get some more blankets if you want. Just in case."

"All right," she answered, her face still fixed on something distant and unseen.

Her husband clambered into the open, almost tripping over the paws of the rukyul lying on the grass outside the opening. It responded with a soft grunt before stretching its long tongue to lick the boy's hand.

"Thank you, Shadow," Arthur said as he stood to his feet. He scratched the animal above its ear, to which the creature groaned gratifyingly.

"I see you two have become friends," Alice observed.

"I wouldn't go that far," he replied, moving to her side. "I think it's more of an acceptance of each other than a bond."

"He's not eating you," she said, smiling. "I think he likes you."

Arthur looked into his wife's eyes and noted the withdrawn stare.

"What's the matter?"

"I'm not certain," she replied. "I think they've done something."

"Who?" Arthur asked. "The Seven?"

"Yes."

The sound of wet flesh and cracking bones made him move his gaze to the dragon. It feasted upon one of the larger calves from the pasture.

Alice had slaughtered the animal for Liana while Arthur set up the tent. Blood still covered her hands from making the kill.

"What do you think they have done?"

"There is death on the wind," she explained. "I can feel it."

Arthur could tell her senses deeply troubled her. He searched for soothing words and found none.

"Wash your hands," he told her. "We'll see your mother and talk to her and Karlena about this."

Alice turned to face him.

"I love you," she said, holding his gaze a little longer before moving to the edge of the stream.

She rarely expressed her emotions so openly. She never needed to. Arthur could read her like one of the books he kept in the cabin.

But not tonight.

Not right now.

She was upset. He could see that.

Whatever it was that troubled her now troubled him.

For her to behave so strangely, it must be a strong magic brewing in Woodmyst.

"I love you too." He crouched beside her and ran his fingers through her dark hair.

She rubbed away the stains on her forearms and hands before drying them as best as she could on her leggings. The two of them stood together and embraced.

"I'm sorry," she told him.

"Why are you sorry?" Arthur asked, pulling her to him tightly.

"I just don't know what's wrong with me," she answered. The sound in her voice told him she was crying.

"There's nothing wrong with you," he assured her. "You are perfect to me."

She moved her head to look into his eyes and saw that tears were building in them.

He pressed his forehead gently against hers.

"Perfect," he said again. "Understand?"

She nodded and pressed her lips to his.

***

"I sensed it too," Emily said as she poured hot water into a teapot. "I'm not sure what. But I know it is bad."

Arthur took four mugs from the cupboard.

"Alice told me the same thing."

"I think blood has been shed." Alice dug her fingers into the armrests of her chair while she stared at the rug on the floor. Karlena sat across from her, listening intently for any sounds coming from the bedroom. Her mind was upon Akasati, who still slumbered behind a closed door at the far end of the corridor.

"Whose blood?" Arthur queried.

"I don't know," she replied. "Innocent blood, perhaps."

"Dark magic," Karlena muttered, looking over at Emily. "I feel something too. It reminds me of the time we were heading north to rescue your sister. It reminds me of when Ivo was taken from us."

"I saw him in a dream," Emily said suddenly. "I didn't remember it until now, when you mentioned his name."

Arthur poured tea into four mugs as Emily returned to the sitting room. She sat in a seat next to Karlena as the boy followed her with two mugs, handing one to her and the other woman before returning to the kitchen to retrieve the remaining two cups.

"I didn't give it much thought," Emily continued. "I just saw it as a stupid meaningless nightmare."

"Go on," Karlena urged.

Emily sipped her tea as Arthur handed her daughter a mug, taking his place in a seat by her side.

"It was in the fortress where he died," the auburn woman said. "He was naked. The way we found him, his chest opened and empty.

"She was there too. Sumaiyya. Dressed in white but hidden in shadow. She looked as if she was floating behind him.

"In her hand, she held his heart. It was beating and blood was being pumped down her arm.

"I wanted to wake up then," she continued. "But something held me there, against my will. Then he spoke."

She furrowed her brow as she took another sip from the steaming cup in her hands.

"Well," Arthur pleaded. "What did he say?"

"He just counted," she replied. "'One, two, three, four, five, six, seven, eight, nine. One, two, three, four, five, six, seven, eight, nine.' Over and over."

"What is that supposed to mean?" Karlena asked.

Emily frowned and shrugged.

"I don't know," she shook her head. "I woke up after that."

Alice shifted in her seat, feeling slightly uncomfortable in her spirit.

"It doesn't make sense," Arthur contributed. "Why nine?"

"The numbers are meaningless," the Erilian woman suggested. "It was just a silly dream, as you said."

"Nothing is meaningless," Alice put in. "We felt a disturbance. Something terrible is happening in Woodmyst."

"By the hands of the Seven," Karlena added.

"The dream could be a warning," Arthur put in. "I don't know what is so significant about the number nine. But we can make speculation why you saw Ivo and Sumaiyya in your dream."

"Takmel," Emily whispered.

"You think he is involved?" Karlena asked the boy.

"I have no doubts," Arthur replied.

Alice sipped her tea and peered at the rug again.

"Why nine?" she whispered.

A soft rattle at the bedroom door caused them to turn their heads.

Slowly, the door opened to reveal a very weary Akasati wiping her eyes. She stepped into the sitting room, groaning with each step.

"Here," Alice said, jumping to her feet and taking the other by the arm. She guided the sleepy woman to her chair and helped her sit.

"So bright," Akasati grumbled, shielding her sight against the light.

"I'll get you some water," Emily said, retreating to the kitchen.

"I smell tea," the woman told them. "That would be nice."

"Water first," Karlena ordered. "You've been sleeping for most of the day."

"Then I should have the use of a pisspot, too." The other smiled.

Arthur grinned and shook his head.

"I'll fix another pot of tea," he offered, standing up and moving into the adjacent room.

"There is a chamber pot under the bed," Alice informed the Erilian woman.

Akasati lifted herself from the chair, struggling as she pushed with her legs. The girl placed a hand under the other's elbow and hoisted her to her feet.

"Are you going to guide me all the way back in there too?"

"I think I must," Alice replied. "I don't need you messing my nice floorboards."

"Cheeky!" The Erilian smirked, peering over to Emily. "She's just like you."

"I have your water for when you return," the auburn woman said, holding up a mug for the other to see.

***

They had gathered around the fire.

Akasati was rugged up in blankets, covering her body from neck to toe. Only her head and hand holding a mug were exposed to the night. Her eyes flicked past the others gathered about and moved over the shadows beneath the trees lining the edge of the glade.

"What is it?" David asked.

"Darkness seems to move now," she told him. "Even if it isn't really so."

He understood.

She had seen something none of them could imagine.

Creatures of pitch-black attacked from the woods.

It was no wonder every shadow posed a threat to her.

"You safe now," Yuri growled.

She sighed. "I know."

Oliver peered across the fire to her, stroking his youngest son's hair. The boy sat on the ground by his father's feet, leaning his head against the man's leg.

"When you're ready to talk about it," he said, "we'll be ready to listen."

"I am ready," she told them. She looked at the children seated about. "I'm not so sure you are yet."

"What happened, Akasati?" Jeremy urged.

"We saw the Queen of Newholt," she began. "We told her of the Seven and the murdered councilmen. She told us of a threat from the north. She asked us to stay with her longer, just while her men investigated her concerns.

"Apparently, they had lost contact with settlements in the mountains. She said she believed a darkness was coming. I think we met that darkness."

"It could be the same darkness we encountered," Lilen said to her husband.

"Did you ever see them?" Akasati asked her.

"No," Glaun replied. "It was always dark. Perhaps they were too dark to see."

"Not too dark to see," the Erilian informed him. "We saw them."

She took a sip of her tea and looked at the flames.

"I made it to my horse," she continued. Tears slid over her cheeks. "The others were just a little too far away and there were too many shadows. Too many."

Emily reached over and placed a comforting hand on her friend's back.

"Sharek told me to flee." Akasati frowned. "She called me a stupid girl. I should have stayed to fight by her side."

"You would be lost to us also, my sister," Karlena said, wiping away her tears.

"By the gods, they were fast," the other continued. "So fast and so many. They took the horses first. I could hear them screaming as I rode away."

She bawled.

"It's all right." Emily moved closer and held the other against her.

"I'm such a coward," Akasati blubbered.

"I won't hear that," Alice said with a hint of anger. "You are no coward. Never say that again."

"Alice," Arthur hissed reprovingly.

"The Erilian warriors trained me," she explained. "They moulded me to be the best I could be. This woman spent more time with me than any other. She is the bravest person I know. I will not sit here and have her call herself a coward when I know she is not."

Alice leant forward, putting herself closer to Akasati.

"We lost family out there," the girl explained. "That's not your fault. I'll fly out tomorrow and search for the place where you say the attack happened. If I can, I'll bring them back."

"They won't be alive," Akasati sobbed.

"I know." Alice frowned. "But if anything of them remains, I can't leave them out there. They belong here with us."

"If you find them," the Erilian wept, "please place Sharek and Gustav on the same pyre."

"They were together?" Jeremy asked.

"They were in love," she answered.

The group fell silent, giving thought to Akasati's words. A deeper sense of lamentation filled them as they remembered their lost friends.

"Wait…" Akasati peered over at Alice with a bewildered look on her face. "Did you say fly?"

Sixteen

With her membranous wings spread wide, Liana followed the river upstream from far above. She altered her course occasionally at the will of her rider, who peered over the dragon's neck to the left and right at the many tributaries that bled into the major waterway.

Alice had tied her hair into a tight, neat braid from the crown of her head. She intended to keep it out of her eyes. The winds during her previous flight had tossed her locks over her face, obstructing her view from time to time.

But not this day.

She had donned an extra layer over her torso to shield herself from the chilly breeze. A thick, dark woollen scarf wrapped around her neck and covered her mouth and nose. Leather gloves tightened their grasp on the reins as she continued to search for any sign of the campsite Akasati had described.

Each time a jagged peak came into view, Alice turned the dragon towards it. She would circle the area to the south of each pointed landmark, looking for a clearing.

Many times, she had done this.

For hours, she had been searching.

The sun was high in the morning sky. She peered over her shoulder occasionally as they continued to the north and west.

They were a long way from home.

Liana flapped her gigantic wings, lifting them higher into the sky.

As she rose into the air, Alice moved her gaze to the north and saw a long line of jagged mountains. They were bare, black and brown rock with patches of snow already forming on their crests.

They reminded her of the teeth that lined her dragon's mouth, only they stretched on forever and ever into the distance.

On the edge of the southernmost peak was a thick wood. Most of the canopy had disappeared, but pine trees stretched their pointy green heads through the tangle of bare limbs of the surrounding plants.

A small patch of open ground grabbed her attention. Her stomach suddenly tightened, and a lump formed in her throat.

It was the first sign of a clearing near any landmark that matched Akasati's description.

Alice leaned towards the area of interest, urging the great dragon to turn.

"Down there, girl," the girl's muffled voice called over the breeze and through the garment covering her mouth.

Liana drifted lower towards the ground, circling to the left to allow her rider a fair view of the area.

There was a tangled mess of canvas and rope near the middle of the open ground. No sign of living or dead from what she could see.

"Down, Liana," Alice ordered.

The dragon moved over the clearing and hovered over the grassy area, flapping her wings as she slowly lowered herself to the ground.

Dust and silt blew up in a cloud as the dragon touched the ground before folding her wings to use them as forelimbs on the ground.

"Good girl." The girl gave the beast a hard pat on the neck as she unstrapped herself out of the saddle.

Sliding to the ground, Alice lifted one of her swords free of its sheath.

The canvas flapped gently in the breeze that swept down from the peaks behind her.

One of the tent poles still held part of the shelter erect. Alice could see that one of the tent flaps tied back to a fastener on the side of the canvas cover.

Something told her she shouldn't look inside.

Curiosity beckoned her.

Her eyes darted here and there over the ground where she could see freshly disturbed patches of ground.

Depressions from hooves, boot heels and claws had raked the grass open, exposing the soft dirt beneath.

She turned to see the dragon observing her. It didn't sense any danger nearby, and neither did she.

Still, her nerves were on edge as she returned her attention to the area surrounding her.

Pieces of leather strapping attached to a fallen log drew her attention. Here, she saw more signs of horse and strange creature. She guessed this was where the steeds had been tethered for the night.

The smell of blood filled her senses as she drew nearer to the log. She looked at the strapping, where she found dried splashes of red. The leather had been torn, but not by the horses.

Alice could see that only one steed had made it out of the clearing. The others made no tracks that led any further than the campsite.

More blood spatter littered the ground, sprinkling grass and soil in the area between where the horses were tethered and the fire by the tent.

A glint of silver drew Alice's attention to a thick patch of weeds.

She moved to the object and pushed back the grass to reveal a sword.

Blood and dark flesh stained the thin blade.

Alice recognised the sword. It belonged to Sharek.

A deep frown fell upon her face as she fought back tears of sorrow.

The Erilian woman would never leave her sword behind. It was a sure sign that she didn't survive the attack.

The canvas flapped again as a soft gust of wind flowed through the trees and over the clearing.

Alice moved her scrutiny to the structure.

It stood lopsided and seemed to call to her.

The one open tent flap on the right yawned an invitation for her to come and see.

It was only now, as she drew closer, that she saw the thick ribbon of blood along the bottom of the closed flap on the left.

The pungent, sour smell of death filled her nostrils as she stepped closer and closer.

Reaching with her blade, she lifted the left flap and pushed it over the canvas shelter, widening the opening to the tent.

The stench seemed to flood out and hit her in the face like an invisible flame bursting from a furnace.

Her stomach twisted as she bent her knees so that she could peer inside.

Eyeless sockets of three heads stared back at her, torn from their bodies and arranged in a rough triangle.

Gustav was the first that she saw, positioned closest to the door. His mouth was agape and deep claw marks stretched over his face from brow to chin.

Sharek was slightly behind him on the left and Rhydra on the right, both with similar scarring.

Alice dropped to her knees.

Her vision blurred as her eyes welled with water. Her mouth hung open as a cry escaped her.

A strange pain filled her, unlike anything that she had experienced before.

An uncontrollable howl burst from her lungs and filled the air, echoing through the trees and deep into the mountains.

***

Carefully, delicately, Alice lifted each of the severed heads into three blankets that she found inside the tent. After cutting some of the lines free, attached between the canvas shelter and pegs in the ground, she bundled the blankets over the remains of her friends and made three sacks to carry them home.

She used her hunting knife to remove two large, rectangular portions of the tent's roof. Laying one on the ground under the watchful attention of Liana, she placed the three crude sacks in the centre and bundled them all together into a neat package. With another length of rope, she tethered the bundle to her saddle, so it sat flush against the dragon's right side.

Liana gave a soft chirp.

"Not much longer, girl," Alice told her, rubbing the creature on the top of her head.

Moving about the area where most of the ground had been disturbed, Alice continued her search. She found the sword in the grass again and took it over to the other portion of canvas she had removed from the tent.

Laying the canvas out, Alice placed the weapon in the centre and resumed her search.

The sun was high in the sky by the time she found the other two blades. She also placed these on the canvas sheet beside the first. The girl peered around quickly for any of the other weapons carried by her friends.

There was no sign of their missing daggers.

Alice surmised they were still tucked in sheaths, which were probably still attached to their bodies at the time of their deaths.

The dragon chirped again.

Alice bundled the swords together tightly and fastened them to her saddle on the opposite side of Liana to where she placed the first package.

She climbed onto the seat and strapped herself in before taking the reins in her hands.

"Up," she ordered as she pulled her scarf over her mouth again.

The dragon jumped onto her hind legs and flapped her wings and long strokes.

Within moments, they were airborne and heading south.

Alice glanced down at the bundled canvas sitting behind her right knee.

Why leave the heads?

The package suddenly appeared small. She considered its size compared to the people that were carried within, to the people she remembered when she last saw them alive.

It didn't seem fair that only such small portions of them were being returned home.

But why leave the heads?

That thought circled around again and again during the journey, leaving her with only one solution to the question.

They were left there to be found.

***

The sound of pounding hammers and saws cutting through timber echoed from the forest surrounding the caverns.

Alice unhooked the saddle from Liana and set it on the ground. After giving the beast another pat, she hoisted the two canvas parcels and left the dragon by the stream.

Her mother was moving across the grass towards her, wiping her hands on a towel. The auburn woman peered to the area beyond the dragon before locking eyes with her daughter.

"Where are they?" she asked hopefully. "Are they alive? Are they still coming?"

Alice moved the package in her left hand.

"They're here," she replied. "It's all I could find of them."

Emily stopped in her tracks as the girl continued past, moving towards the campfire in the middle of the tiny makeshift village.

"By the gods," the woman gasped, holding a hand to her mouth as she peered at the canvas in Alice's hand.

"We need to set a pyre," the girl said. "And there are no gods. This is proof."

Shadow bounded towards her when he saw her approaching. His excited demeanour changed when he noticed she was not in a pleasant mood. He moved to her side and walked with her to the hearth.

Akasati was there, sitting with Richard and Becka.

"What have you there?" the old man asked.

"Our friends," Alice replied coldly.

The Erilian woman wept as Alice lowered the packages to the ground.

"How did you find them?" Becka queried as she reached her arms around the other woman.

Emily moved to her daughter's side as Shadow sniffed at the canvas.

"No," Alice told him. The rukyul backed away a short distance and rested upon his haunches, keeping his head low in submission.

"Are you all right?" the auburn woman asked her daughter.

Alice shook her head and fell upon her mother's chest, crying.

"Their heads were torn off," the girl managed. "They were placed inside the tent and arranged on the ground."

"Arranged?" Richard furrowed his brow. "Who are these beasts?"

"Not beasts." Alice frowned. "Beasts wouldn't do this."

"You're saying it was a calculated attack?" Arthur stepped off the porch and moved towards her.

She let go of Emily and fell into his arms.

"They were set like a spearhead," Alice told him. "Gustav at the tip and the others behind him and at the sides."

"Like a triangle." He pulled her closer to him and slid his hands beneath her sheaths to rub her lower back.

"Why would they do that?" Akasati wiped the tears from her eyes. "They're just mindless creatures."

"Not mindless," Arthur said. "They are moving towards us for a reason. You said that the Queen of Newholt told you they had no contact from the northern settlements. Perhaps these creatures are strategically moving to the south, taking out all men along the way one village at a time."

"We should prepare defences," Richard offered.

Arthur shook his head.

"We'd be wasting time," he replied. "The glade is too big to set traps, and we'd be risking the livestock. We don't have the manpower to build walls before they reach us. For all we know, we could be under their watch right now."

"So, we let them come?" Becka asked. A slight shaking in her voice drew Alice's attention. The others didn't notice it, but she sensed the heightened fear in the other.

"We let them come," the girl said coolly. "And we kill them all."

"There's too many," Akasati argued. "I only saw a portion before I fled, and there were too many then."

"For you," Alice told her, anger rising in her voice. "But I have Shadow and Liana. And I'll burn the entire Forest of Khun to ash before I let any of them into this glade. And if they get by the flames, they'll be torn to shreds by rukyul teeth and claw, and hacked to pieces by my blades. I won't let any here come to harm."

The Erilian woman stared at the young girl. She knew Alice meant what she said.

"You won't need to stand alone." Arthur pressed his forehead to hers. "I'll be by your side."

"I know." She wrapped her arms around his neck.

***

When the sun had lowered, and all had returned from their day's tasks, Alice moved to the western edge of the clearing where she prepared the pyre with Akasati, Karlena and the other crew members of the Adelandria. Their captain, Jeremy Shoenbach, placed Gustav's shrouded head carefully upon the wood heap. Karlena placed Sharek's head beside that of the old crew member as Akasati lowered Rhydra's remains next to them.

Alice reached her hand out, offering the flaming torch she held to the captain. He peered at the flame for an eternity. The girl saw the glint in his eyes as he fought tears back.

"They were your people," he said. "As we all are now. You should light the pyre."

"They were your people first," she replied. "It only seems fitting that their captain sends them on their way."

He agreed reluctantly and took the torch. Touching the flame to the kindling at the edge of the wood stack, he ignited the pyre.

It caught quickly, sending tongues of fire weaving through the timber. Before long, the remains caught alight and the sounds of lamentations could be heard coming from those who stood nearby.

Only Alice kept her composure.

Only she shed no tears.

She had cried enough today.

Now she felt angry.

Out of courtesy, she stayed to pay her respects. She would rather have been sharpening her blades and preparing for a fight.

When the pyre had burnt out and all had returned to the hearth near the cabin, Alice fetched her whetstone and got to work.

The others, seated by the flames, either watched her in silence or wondered if they should do the same.

"How goes the quarry today?" David asked, breaking the silence.

"Good," Baldwyn answered. "Good. We sent another twenty loads off to Woodmyst, which means they should have more than enough stone to complete those walls now."

"We might even get to close up before schedule," another man said, hopefully. "Don't you think, Boss?"

"We'll see," Baldwyn said. "We've still got to send another crate of pavers and clean up before we can call a break."

Alice continued scraping the stone slowly along the steel.

The noise wasn't irritating, but to David, the silence surrounding it was excruciating.

"We managed to clear quite a few caves out today," he said. "A couple of cabins have started construction. I'm hoping, with the manpower we have available, we could get at least three or four built before the snow arrives."

"We'd be glad to help once the quarry is closed," Baldwyn offered, trying to keep the conversation going so his ears didn't fill with the ringing of the blade. "Perhaps we could build more."

"You never know." David raised his brow. "It would be nice to get a few of us inside before everything freezes over."

"I need dwellings for the Agrodien," Alice informed them as she sheathed her sword. A look of relief came over David's face until he saw her reach for the other sword she carried. "Liana needs a cave, and the only one large enough is the one they occupy at the moment. Priority is for their shelters."

"That's almost two hundred bodies in that cave," Ewan pointed out.

"One hundred and eighty women and children," Alice specified. "Some of them would be more than happy to share a dwelling with another family. After all, they are all sharing one dwelling as we speak. At least we have tents and a cabin. They have nothing."

She turned to David. "Priority goes to them."

"Understood."

"Why do you sharpen your blades?" Richard asked, knowing the rest of the people were wondering the same thing.

"I'm preparing for an attack," Alice replied, running the stone over the steel so that it rang loudly.

"You know of one coming?" the old man queried.

"It's inevitable." She peered up quickly at him before returning her focus to the sword on her lap.

Yuri grunted something to Gharnef, who said something in his tongue to the other warriors. All of them suddenly lifted themselves to their feet and moved away into the darkness, leaving their women and children behind.

"And where are you lot going?" David stared after them.

"They go to fetch their weapons," Alice answered.

"You don't know those things are coming here for certain," Ruttger said. "No one could know that. Not unless your abilities allow you to see things, too. Do they?"

"I'm not able to see things yet to come," Alice assured him. "But my gut tells me this is far from over. A fight is coming. I know that much."

"Maybe those things will return to the north," one of the northern women offered.

Alice looked slowly over each of the faces surrounding her. She realised just how young she was compared to them. Only the younglings sitting by their parents' feet saw her as a senior, and even a few of them were her own age.

Yet, they all looked to her for answers. They all sought comfort and safety through her. She could read that on their faces.

"They won't turn around." She frowned. "They won't retreat. They won't just disappear. They are coming. They will move through the mountains and destroy every settlement and village they can, and then they will come here.

"Something drives them to the south. Perhaps something worse is on their tail. Whatever the reason, they are coming. And I plan to be ready to greet them when they arrive."

Seventeen

"And construction of the wall is almost complete," Master Book-keeper Lewis Drayton continued as he read from the parchment in his withered hands. "The overseer of the project predicts the last stone to be laid in place in three days. Final touches should be done a few days afterwards, weather permitting. All in all, we will have a wall surrounding the city before the snow arrives."

"That is good news," Joanne told him from her seat on the platform. The other six members of her coven sat beside her as they listened to the old man give his report. "What of our supplies?"

"There isn't much to tell," Drayton replied. "Stores are high. We harvested another crop of potatoes and pumpkins just yesterday. We will pick more corn tomorrow. There is still some wheat and oats to be collected from the fields. We will be in abundance to the point of overflowing."

"Good," the woman in black said, peering along the seats to other women. "It would appear that our meetings in the ruins have not been a waste after all."

"At least the others living by the caverns will have an abundance of supplies," Isabel, dressed in white, put forth.

"Our sacrifices have been well worthwhile," Christina, the gold woman, added.

Joanne moved her gaze to the edge of the platform. She wasn't so sure that she agreed with her fellow council member's opinion. Closing her eyes, she saw Antony's face staring at her from the darkness. He appeared confused. Scared.

131

"May I offer my condolences for your losses?" the old man offered, bowing slightly as he spoke.

Joanne looked at Drayton and smiled politely. "Thank you, Master Drayton. Your kind words are welcome."

Takmel shifted in his seat.

He and Catherine were in the back row of the assembly hall, watching the proceedings with interest. The boy's movement drew Joanne's attention away from the bookkeeper momentarily.

Did he move to remind her he was in the room?

Was it a way to communicate to her to take precautions with her words?

"Is there anything more, Master Drayton?"

"Only a question, my lady," he replied.

"Please?" She gestured for him to speak.

"Some of us were wondering if there were any plans to celebrate young Master Hamond's birthday?" Drayton enquired. He turned to look at the subject of his query, smiling happily at the boy. "I believe he is to become a man, traditionally speaking, of course. The bakers are wondering if they should prepare a cake."

"It isn't every year when a boy gets to celebrate his sixteenth birthday," Tricia agreed. "And he is becoming a man. It will be a monumental day for all of us."

Joanne shot her a sideways glance, quickly hiding her concerns by feigning a smile.

A monumental day for all of us.

"So it will be," she answered. "A cake would be a welcome addition to the day, Master Drayton. Please pass on the request to our fine bakers."

"Any particular flavour, my lady?"

"Why don't you tell the bakers to surprise us," she said cheerily.

"Of course." Drayton bowed again. "It can double as a celebration for the completion of the wall. How exciting. Unless there is something else required from me, I'll take my leave. Good night, ladies."

With that, he turned and started for the large doors to the back of the room, stopping briefly to bow to Takmel and Catherine before continuing on his way.

A monumental day for all of us.

Joanne felt her stomach tighten into a knot. In three days, Takmel would come of age. In three days, a ritual would begin.

It had already built inside them, bringing several climactic moments.

A sense of instinct guided them. It was never a simple choice.

A part of her wanted to turn and flee from this pull she felt.

But the chains that held her were too strong.

It guided her and held her, drawing upon the life force she carried within like a moth to the flame.

Perhaps it was because she was the strongest of the Seven, but she seemed to be the only one that held any trepidations. The others appeared compliant, happy.

The horrific actions they had all partaken in seemed to be trivial to each of them. Even Lucy acted as if it was just another day and that the murderous act she had committed was nothing more than a normal household chore, like cleaning the cutlery.

But the more Joanne felt the urge to fight, the stronger the chains would hold her.

She had to comply.

It was the natural progression of things.

Killing Antony was necessary.

Obeying the Maji was innate.

Loving Takmel was preordained.

Even if she didn't feel that way at present.

***

The rest of the stew was reheated. Plates were placed around the table and the four home dwellers sat to eat.

Fresh bread had been baked during the day and cut into thin slices before butter was spread to meet the edges.

Joanne eyed the steaming bowl placed before her. Her stomach turned as she stirred a spoon through the soupy mixture of corn, potatoes, and meat.

"I didn't expect it to last this long," Lucy said proudly as she sat next to the woman in black. "I don't know about you, but I think it smells better than it did last night."

"Improving with age," Catherine opined.

Joanne felt a cold shiver rush over her skin.

She peered across the table to see Takmel staring at her.

"Are you feeling all right?" he asked, sounding concerned. "You should eat some. Living on bread and tea alone cannot be healthy."

She watched silently as he dug his spoon into his bowl. Her eyes followed the portion as he lifted it to his lips.

A fatty piece of flesh balancing precariously on the lip of the spoon drew her attention as he placed his lips around the morsel.

With a loud slurp, he sucked the portion of stew into his mouth and swallowed hard.

She felt she was going to be sick.

"Are you sure you're fine?" he queried, lifting a slice of bread from a stack in the middle of the table.

"Mm-hmm." She smiled. She looked around at Lucy and Catherine, who were both devouring the mixture hungrily.

"Try some," Takmel urged her. "The taste has improved since last night."

I don't want to.

She dug out a tiny amount of the stew and lifted it slowly from the bowl.

Her throat seemed to tighten, and her stomach whirled with revulsion.

The brownish-grey liquid rippled around the yellow kernels and soft, white cubes of potato. The stringy dark meat threaded amongst it all reminded her of earthworms burrowing through the gardens.

I don't want to.

Forcing herself, she pushed the spoon past her lips and let the load drop upon her tongue.

She took a deep breath and held it as she let the stew swim inside her mouth.

It tastes so good.

She quickly dug the spoon into the bowl again, wilfully taking a second portion and a third.

It's really good.

"See?" Takmel grinned. "It's all better now."

She didn't understand why her temperament had changed, only that it had.

The idea of eating the stew had repulsed her only moments ago.

Now, she just wanted to get it inside of her as quickly as she could.

She looked over to Takmel, who was grinning at her, watching her admiringly.

She lifted the bowl from the table with one hand, drawing it closer to her chin as she continued to shovel the contents into her mouth.

She couldn't get enough.

She didn't care that it appeared sickening.

The greying mixture suddenly appeared appetising.

The aroma was inviting.

She didn't care that it contained the flesh of her son and Lucy's daughter.

She just wanted its warmth inside her.

Takmel continued to smile as he slowly sipped at the stew.

She wanted him inside her, too.

He had bewitched her.

He had won.

But what surprised her the most was that he didn't even appear to be trying.

She finished the bowl's contents, rubbing the insides of the dish with a slice of bread to soak what droplets remained before devouring them.

"There's more." He tilted his head towards the kitchen.

"What have you done to me?" she asked, as her hands shook.

"Aren't you hungry?" Takmel peered into her eyes. "Don't you want to finish it all?"

She tried to fight, but the instinct was stronger than her will.

"Yes," she answered sheepishly, lowering the bowl and spoon to the table. Her hands slid from the table and onto her lap. She rubbed her thighs, feeling a sudden urge to touch herself.

Takmel lifted her bowl and moved to the kitchen, where he ladled more of the stew into her bowl.

She looked at him ravenously as he placed the freshly topped dish before her. The others seemed oblivious to her transformation, continuing to feast.

"Eat," he told her, to which she lifted the whole bowl to her lips and tilted the contents into her mouth.

How has he made me succumb to his will? She wondered.

The questions rolled around inside her head, turning and twisting. But she didn't really care for the answers. With each spoonful she swallowed, she became his more and more.

The sheer act of submission was enough.

Pressing his hand to his mouth, concealing the wide smirk upon his face, Takmel looked over at the three women seated about him.

Eighteen

Amicia stood on the balcony above the main entrance to the palace. A disturbing feeling had been growing inside her heart.

Something terrible was happening.

She saw a shadow growing in the land, spreading like an invisible flood through the mountains, heading towards the south.

But something darker was making itself apparent.

Something ominous.

Something worse.

Brondt stepped from the door and moved to her back, sliding his arms around her waist.

"Beautiful night," he said, peering over the city to the harbour. The air was almost still and barely a cloud hung in the sky. The stars twinkled brightly, reflecting upon the clear water, so it was difficult to see where the ocean and the expanse above met.

"It is," she answered, leaning into him.

He sensed her mood.

"You didn't come out here to admire the scenery," he surmised. "Am I interrupting?"

"No." She shook her head. "There is something evil out there."

"In the ocean?" he asked, peering in the direction that she was looking.

"No, not the ocean," she replied.

"The shadow that you told me about." Brondt gently pressed the side of his face to hers. "Does it draw closer?"

"Yes, but there is something else emerging. Something with power at its command."

"Magic," he hissed. "Do we ready the soldiers?"

She shook her head. "I'm not entirely sure where it is."

"You have an idea, though," he inferred from the sound of her voice.

"It would be a guess," she explained. "I can't be certain."

"Where?"

"Woodmyst," she answered reluctantly.

"Do you think it's the girl?" he pressed, "Alice?"

"I don't know." She appeared slightly irritated, upset.

"It's all right." He kissed her cheek. "No more questions about it."

She turned to face him and slid her arms around his waist.

"I'm not as strong as I used to be," she admitted to him. "I don't see things as clearly and I can't do anything useful anymore. Ever since the rest of the Mirikin were destroyed, my powers have been depleting. I'm not fit to rule. If the people knew, they would..."

"Don't be ridiculous." He tightened his hold, drawing her closer to him. "You're the queen and the people love you. I love you, and I don't care about what abilities you once had. All I want is Amicia, not the Fuchsia Mistress. She can disappear completely for all I care, as long as I have you." He moved his regard to the city below them. "And all of them out there feel the same way as I do. They love you, not your magic."

She cried and pressed her head against his chest. He wasn't sure whether she was happy to hear his words or saddened by the concept of simply being as normal as he was. The only logical thing to do was hold her.

"The men heading north," she whispered suddenly. "Along the coast. Has there been any word?"

"None," he answered. "There's no need for concern yet. The ships are still moving to and from Blackrock Haven. If there was any trouble, surely they would have ceased their operations."

"The problem isn't on the coast." She pulled away from him a little, keeping her hold on him. "It's in the mountains."

"What would you have me do?" Brondt asked. "Should I take some men and ride the ridges?"

"No," she snapped, moving her face to lock onto his eyes. "I would not have you face the shadow on your own."

"You ordered others to go," he said, furrowing his brow.

"I won't lose you," the queen told him. "I won't."

"All right." He backed down, not wanting to upset her any more than she already was. She leant herself against him again.

"I need you here," she said. "I want you here."

"I'm not going anywhere, my love," he replied, wrapping his arms around her tightly.

***

The beacon light glowed over the rocks, warning ships upon the sea to stay clear of the area. The sound of waves breaking upon the rough, black surface was soothing to the eleven men who had been on the road for the most part of the day.

Now, with a full meal in their belly and a roaring fire to keep them warm, the men relaxed as the people of the reasonably new settlement began turning in for the night.

"Won't be long before I hit the bedroll," one man remarked. He glanced over his shoulder to the tent pitched a few yards away.

"I thought you'd be paying a visit to that young lass with the dark hair," another remarked. "You know the one, Edmond. She lives in that house just over there."

"The tiny house near the bakery?" another asked.

"I think it's part of the bakery, Morys," said another. "And I think she shares the room with her mother and father."

"I know the girl you speak of," the third man chuckled. "She still looks like she's the age of playing with dolls."

"She said she was seventeen," Edmond, the first man, replied.

"She said." The other continued to laugh.

"That's enough," a barrel-chested man wearing leather armour ordered. His voice was deep and husky, giving the man a menacing quality. "There'll be no cavorting with the locals on this assignment. Is that clear?"

"Yessir," the men chorused.

"It was just a bit of joking about, Captain Thornton," the third man stated.

"I don't care, Vawdrey." The officer glared at the soldier. "You can joke about all you want back at home. Hell, you can even do so during guard duty at the palace for all I care. But out here, you are mine and on duty at all times."

Thornton lifted himself to his feet and ambled around the campfire, eyeing the small village set between their camp and the beacon light upon the rocks. He then moved his gaze to a pile of rubble.

A long structure of stone lay toppled over and covered with years of growth. It was barely recognisable in the dark, but he remembered it for what it once was.

"Do you see that?" he asked the men. They all turned their heads to take in the sight. "That was once a great lighthouse. Right on this spot, a battle took place that saw the whole thing come crashing down.

"The men inside were dashed to pieces. In fact, this area was an outpost once. The people in the village there have reused most of the stones. But it was an impressive place to be.

"I was once posted here," he continued. "Before our queen came to her senses, she shared her forces with the White Mistress. The fortress here acted as a type of halfway house between Newholt and the White Keep.

"Do you know what destroyed it?" He looked sternly at the men seated by the flames.

"No, sir," one of them muttered.

"Unpreparedness," Thornton answered. "Whoring. Drinking. Gambling. Then a rag-tag band of men from Woodmyst comes riding in with a bunch of seafarers and they destroyed this place in one fell sweep.

"Even the White Witch's magic wasn't enough to stop them. She sent her own army of straw men against them. The men of Woodmyst simply used the flames that burnt this lighthouse down to wipe the straw men out."

He turned to face his men, a deep scowl worn into his furry face.

"You know what lesson there is to learn from all of this, don't you?" he grumbled.

The men stared at him blankly, waiting for him to answer his own question again.

"Don't be unpre-fuckin-pared!" he growled. "Second squad."

"Yes, sir!" A man jumped to his feet.

"Lieutenant Brook," Thornton said. "You and your men are on watch detail for four hours."

"Yessir," Brook replied with a salute.

"First Squad," he called.

"Sir." A second man lifted himself to his feet and saluted.

"Hit the sack, Lieutenant London," the captain said. "You will take the second watch."

"Yessir," London replied before turning to his soldiers. "Let's go lads. Four hours isn't very long when you need sleep."

"Aye, sir," said Edmond, slowly gathering himself before moving towards the tent with three other soldiers.

"And you, sir?" London asked.

"I plan to sleep right through, Lieutenant," Thornton told him. "One of the perks of being a senior officer. I can make you young bastards do all the hard work for me."

"Do you want a perimeter established, sir?" Brook asked. "I can post men on four corners of our campsite if you wish."

"Not necessary." Thornton shook his head. "Stay close to the fire. Send two men as sentries every ten or so minutes to walk the perimeter. Keep as warm as you can during the watch. The air has some bite in her tonight."

"Yessir," Brook replied, before turning to the remaining men seated by the fire. "Jendryng, you'll walk the perimeter with me first. Sparrow, you'll walk with Jendryng next. Bacon with Sparrow."

"Sounds like a dainty dish," Vawdrey chuckled.

"Sparrow with Vawdrey," Brook continued as the captain moved to the side of the camp, his eyes set upon the treeline to the west. "Vawdrey with me. Ten-minute intervals. That's the rotation, gentlemen. Any questions?"

No one spoke.

"Good." The lieutenant rubbed his gloved hands together. "Let's begin. Jendryng."

A younger man stood and started towards the officer.

"Your sword, idiot," Sparrow called after him, lifting the sheathed weapon and belt from the ground. "Just after the captain said to be prepared and all."

"Sorry," Jendryng offered as he collected his weapon from the other.

"No, sorry about it, boy." Vawdrey shook his head. "Where would you be if you got attacked out there?"

"Dead, I s'pose," he replied, strapping the belt around his waist.

"He got you there, Vawdrey," Bacon quipped.

"Come on," Brook ordered the young soldier, starting away from the warm hearth.

"Yessir." Jendryng jogged after him.

The two men started off to the right of the tent, moving a few yards into the darkness. Instinctively, their eyes moved to the open ground between the trees and themselves.

All appeared clear.

There was no sign of movement apart from a few cows standing motionless on the grass.

One horse, tethered to the back of the tent, snorted as they moved by. Jendryng moved his attention to the creature.

"You're looking the wrong way, soldier," Brook told him, maintaining his fix on the open area.

"Sorry, sir," the young man said. "This is my first assignment outside of Newholt."

"Don't let the others know that," the lieutenant instructed. "They'll treat you to some form of initiation, no doubt."

"Initiation?"

"Have you had your clothing stripped from you during the night, only to find them the next morning in the market square?"

"No, sir," Jendryng replied, his brow furrowing at the concept. "Why would anyone do such a thing?"

"To publicly embarrass young soldiers like yourself," the other answered. "I myself was a victim of such induction. My uniform, undergarments and any other clothing that I had was taken to the fountain in Newholt marketplace.

"The bastards in my unit tore my blankets from me in the morning and took off with everything that I could have covered myself with. So, off I set down the road from the palace, following them as they taunted me with my boots and pants.

"I ran for some of the ways, but the cobblestones were a little more than painful on the bare feet. So, I resorted to cupping my hands over my manhood and walking the rest of the way."

"Did anyone see you?"

"The entire city must have been out that day." Brook smiled. "The men in my unit got a good head start and had done such a lovely job by the time I reached the marketplace.

"Just imagine that statue of Gwendra, standing up there, dressed in my fatigues with those little stone fish spitting water at her feet. All I could hear was laughter all around me as I tried to undo my shirt with one hand without revealing too much more of myself."

"But surely the queen..."

"The queen was there, son," the lieutenant explained. "She and Commander Brondt just so happened to be in the marketplace at the time."

"By the gods!" Jendryng shook his head, shocked by the story. "I feel so sorry for you, sir."

"Why?" Brook asked. "It was an enjoyable experience for me. I learnt humility and how to take a joke. I also met four interesting young ladies, one of which is now my wife. Sometimes bad things turn out to be good."

"I don't know what I would do in such a situation, sir," the young man said.

"I understand that." The other nodded. "Which is why I'm telling you not to tell the others this is your first assignment."

The two men moved around the far side of the camp, where they approached a lone figure standing near the tent. It was Captain Thornton, still keeping a watch on the forest a good distance away.

"Captain," Brook said. "I thought you would be fast asleep by now."

"There's something out there," the older man grunted, glaring at the trees that ran along the feet of the mountains like a dark ribbon of shadow.

"Only cows, sir," Jendryng offered.

"Past the livestock, boy." The captain gave the young man a look of disdain. "Something hides in the darkness, watching us. I can feel it on the back of my neck."

Brook stared into the blackness.

He could make out the vertical lines forming the trunks of the pines. The gnarled, crooked branches of the oaks stretched like broken fingers to scratch at the air about them.

"Maybe rukyul," the lieutenant offered. "They have been seen venturing closer to some settlements recently."

"Perhaps." Thornton frowned. He kept his glare steady, searching the darkest places for longer. "I know something is there, lads. I know it. But this old man needs some sleep before he starts seeing things."

"Yes sir," Brook said, not really knowing what else to say to the old man.

The captain turned and started for the front of the tent.

"Keep an eye out there when you walk the perimeter," Thornton commanded.

"Yes sir," both men chorused as they watched their commander disappear into the canvas shelter.

Jendryng looked back to the treeline and searched the darkness carefully.

All he could see was shadow and more shadow.

"I have no doubt that the captain is right, soldier," Brook said quietly. "But I don't intend to spend the entire night watching the forest. Let's get back to the fire to warm up. You can take another look when you and Sparrow take the next walk."

"Yes sir," the young soldier acknowledged, following the officer back to the hearth.

Nineteen

"Hurry up, Cobham," Thornton growled from atop his steed.

Edmond Cobham was in the process of receiving a bundle of freshly baked loaves from the young baker's daughter. The other soldiers watched in silence, feeling a little envious of their comrade as the beautiful girl kissed him gingerly on the cheek. She smiled bashfully, shooting a quick look over to the other soldiers seated on their horses.

"Lucky bastard," Vawdrey murmured before turning to Jendryng beside him. "Did you see how she eyeballed all of us just now? That was on purpose, that was."

Symond Jendryng shook his head slightly, keeping his gaze fixed on his commander as he held the lead to the packhorse tightly in his hand, waiting for orders.

"Now I'm going to be thinking of those luscious eyes and her shapely body all day," the other continued as Cobham handed the bundle to another soldier so he could climb into his saddle.

"Let's go," Thornton commanded the troop, urging his mount forward.

"Just remember to practise self-control," Brook told the complaining soldier. "No touching your small bits."

"Very funny, Lieutenant," Vawdrey remarked sarcastically.

"You're a lucky man, Edmond," Jendryng called.

"I know." Cobham blew the young woman a kiss before following the officers away.

They travelled a well-worn road out of the tiny settlement and towards the north.

As with most mornings, the horses set off with enthusiasm, trotting along the path with their heads high. But it wasn't long before they resorted to a steady walk.

They spent a great bulk of the day crossing one open plateau after another. With each section of rising ground, hopes of seeing something different beyond the rise were dashed every time.

More grassland bordered with forest and mountains on the left and ocean on the right. Occasionally, a ship's sail could be seen on the horizon or a few deer dashing into the trees as they drew nearer to them.

It was so painstakingly monotonous that when something new appeared, they could hear Vawdrey remarking something like, "Ooh look! A deer," or "Over there, a ship."

Eventually, the quiet outbursts referred to more and more mundane objects like rocks and blades of grass.

Thornton growled once in a while in response to Vawdrey. But after some time, even he found the comments from the soldier a welcome break in the repetitious scenery.

By late afternoon, the troop had arrived at a thin stream. In the distance towered a mountain resembling a horn stretching into the sky.

"Is that what I think it is?" Jendryng asked.

"Your first time north, boy?" Sparrow looked to the other in question.

"Ah..." the young soldier peered at his lieutenant. Brook gave a blank look, showing that the lad was on his own. "First time north, yes."

"First assignment?" Cobham pressed.

"No," Jendryng answered. It wasn't a lie. Not entirely.

He had many assignments back in Newholt. This was just his first outside of the city.

"That is often called the Great Horn," informed Vawdrey.

"Often?" Lieutenant London creased his brow. "Why? What else is it known as?"

"Big fuckin' mountain," Thornton grunted. The others looked at him, surprised. "And yes, Vawdrey. I've heard that joke before."

"Can't blame a man for trying, sir," the other said.

"Yes, I can," the captain answered, lowering himself from his steed. "First squad, set up camp. Second squad, firewood and food duty."

***

With a couple of rabbits roasting over the flames, the troop settled back to relax before the last of the day's light disappeared for the evening. They could see a few ships far out to see as their lanterns were lit and posted on deck.

Jendryng kept moving his gaze to the peak of the Great Horn, far away to the north. His fascination for it was more than mere admiration for its appearance. It was menacing to look at. Steep and sharp.

But there was a history with the place that had sparked his interest since he was a child. Stories were told about the Great Horn that had made him fear the dark.

And now, here it was.

Within sight.

"What is it, boy?" Thornton asked, sitting beside the soldier.

Jendryng felt his stomach tighten as his nerves went into a frenzy. It was the first time the captain had shown any interest in him at all.

"That place has your fears." The old man looked at the mountain. "Doesn't it?"

"Yes sir," he replied.

"Why?" the captain questioned. "It's just a mountain."

Just a mountain?

"It's where she lived," Jendryng said.

"She?" Thornton scratched at his beard. "The White Bitch, you mean?"

"Yessir!"

"She's long gone," the captain assured him. "Dead on the fields of Woodmyst. I was there for that. I wouldn't worry yourself about the White Keep, boy. It's been empty since the liberation of Blackrock Haven.

"We'll be staying there tomorrow night," he continued. "There's another settlement there with a dock. We can send word back to the city from there and resume our patrol to the north."

"No one told us, sir," Jendryng ventured. "Just how far north are we going?"

"That's because you're a lowly soldier and not an officer, boy," Thornton answered. "But, so you know, we're riding all the way to Blackrock Haven. Then we are heading inland to seek the settlements in the mountains. We'll then ride back south to the Great Horn and come back to the road here. Then we go home.

"The question you should have asked is, why?" the captain finished.

"I don't understand," the young soldier said.

"And that's why you won't make an officer," Thornton told him. "Do any of you know why we're patrolling the north?"

A long silence ensued as the men looked at one another for the answer.

"I do, sir," Brook replied as he stoked the fire with a long stick.

"Please tell," the captain urged.

The lieutenant swept his gaze over all the men seated about. They were peering at him with interest.

"We've lost contact with some of the settlements in the mountains," he informed them. "A few of them have not been to the coastal communities to restock on supplies for some time. Our mission is to investigate why. We will, we hope, find that everything is fine and the inhabitants of the settlements are just becoming more self-sufficient. We just need to then return home and report our findings."

"And if we find everything is not fine?" Sparrow asked.

"We return home and report that instead," Brook answered.

"Precisely," Thornton said. "I personally believe there is foul play afoot, gentlemen. Something was watching the camp last night. Perhaps the settlement was their focus. But nevertheless, I felt eyes on us.

"After we eat, we take the same shifts as last night. I want careful attention paid to the treeline tonight. Understood?"

"Yessir," the men chorused.

***

"They've been there for hours," Andris Hill, the commander of the guards, commented as Takmel approached the gate to the ruins. "I don't think they've even moved an inch."

The boy leaned to peer through the iron bars towards the great oak. Some shrubbery partially blocked his view, but he could see them on the grass by the trunk of the giant tree.

They were in a circle, hands joined, eyes closed and on their knees. Their coloured cloaks pulled over their heads and their faces turned towards the sky. They spoke no words. They made no sound.

They remained motionless.

"It's getting dark, my lord," Andris offered. "Shouldn't someone go in there and take them home?"

"Never break the connection," Takmel told him. "If they remain like this by the time the light of day disappears, I want you to set guards at the gate here. No one interrupts them."

The commander nodded, looking to the women inside the old ruins of the Great Hall.

Takmel understood what was occurring.

It was a communion.

A joining of wills.

It was also the next step towards his ascension.

"Keep watch, Andris," he said, clasping a hand on the other's shoulder.

"Yes, my lord," the soldier replied.

Takmel started back along the road, returning towards his home.

The anticipation was almost too much to bear.

Tiny knots tightened and undid themselves in his stomach as he wondered what the Seven were experiencing.

The excitement was too thrilling, as he gave thought to the possibilities of what may come.

A wry smile crept upon his face as he drew nearer to the house.

The lanterns were alight inside, and the sound of discussion gripped his curiosity.

"...and some fresh butter," he heard Lucy remark.

"I might purchase some fish tomorrow," Catherine said. "Something different, for a change."

"That sounds good," the other replied.

It was idle chatter. Nothing of importance.

Takmel stepped upon the porch and opened the door.

"You're home already." Catherine sounded pleased as he stepped into the room. She looked at the space behind him as he closed the door. "Where's Aunt Joanne?"

"The Seven are still by the oak," he answered, moving across the floor to embrace his wife.

"Well..." Lucy glanced over to all the food that she and Catherine had been preparing. "For how long?"

"These things can't be rushed," he said, looking over at the boiling pots of corn and beans. "It does look appetising. Is that lamb I can smell in the oven?"

"Yes," Lucy replied. "I was hoping we could all sit down and enjoy this together."

Takmel took her gently by the shoulders. "I know it's hard to understand how this works. I'm not entirely sure myself. We're all learning as it happens. All I can tell you is that, right now for the Seven, it's like a natural urge. They can't fight it and it must take its course."

Lucy nodded, accepting what he said, but not comprehending it.

"I don't have powers," she said, a tear building in her eye. "I'm not the same as the rest of them. I don't deserve to be here, with you."

Takmel carefully wiped her tear away with his thumb.

"I chose you, Lucy," he said, holding her eyes with his. "Not for any magical qualities, but you have placed some charm over me. I want you more and more with each passing day. Perhaps there is power in you after all."

She smiled, content with his words.

Too easy.

He smiled again, causing her heart to melt with his boyish charm.

Catherine watched with interest, seeing the manipulation at work. She knew him better than all the others. She had been with him since the beginning.

She was there when it all started to manifest.

"Let's sit down." Takmel guided the other woman over to the table by the hand. "We'll enjoy this fine meal together. The three of us. All right?"

"All right," Lucy replied, moving towards the stove.

"No, no," he said, pulling her towards a chair. "You sit. I'll serve."

He kissed her hand as she took to the chair.

Catherine admired his serpentine nature. She moved to assist him.

"You too," he told her, pulling a chair out for her to sit in.

She planted a kiss on his lips.

As he moved to the stove, he gave her a long stare, full of amusement. It was only then that she realised he had been manipulating her, too. His interaction with Lucy had tugged her heartstrings as well.

She grinned, feeling aroused by the idea.

Has he been controlling me all this time?

She didn't care.

He was the Maji.

She was his.

And tonight, he belonged to her.

Twenty

"We move tonight," Yuri said stubbornly. "We take caves now. We live in worse before. We live in ghubahr."

"We live in what?" David asked, leaning over to Alice.

"Shit," she answered, translating the word.

"Caves good enough, Kayl'sro," Yuri continued. "We happy to go."

Alice offered tea to the Agrodien elder and his wife by gesturing to the pot on the table. Both assented, whereby the girl poured a mug for each of them.

"David?" she asked.

"Not for me, lass." He held up a hand. "I'll be up all night as it is."

They sat around the table in her cabin, discussing the development of the glade. She had just told the two reptilians that she intended to use the larger cavern as a den for the dragon. Before she had the chance to explain that David was going to build houses for them in the mouth of the other caverns, Yuri had made his offer.

"You won't be moving tonight," she explained. "I won't have the younglings moved from their cots at this late of an hour."

"Kayl'sro," Yuri interjected. "Our lives better because of you. We happy to move."

"No," Alice said. "The Agrodien have been through enough turmoil. No moving tonight. We'll reassess the situation in the morning, together."

"Your dragon needs shelter," Galonia reminded her.

155

"So do you," the girl replied. "I'm giving you an order as Kayl'sro. You are not to pack or even go anywhere near those caves until I have looked for myself."

Yuri looked restless.

Alice stared at him until he relented.

"Yes, Kayl'sro."

She reached across the table to pet his hand.

"You are a stubborn old lizard," Alice told him.

"With all available hands and materials," David started, "we should be able to build three or four structures like this pretty quickly."

"How long is *pretty quickly?*" Arthur asked from the sitting room.

"Four or five days," his father replied.

"Not like this." Yuri pointed around the room.

"What?" David quizzed, looking at the reptilian with a puzzled expression.

"Hokhtul dhu." Yuri was trying to explain with hand gestures.

"Simple?" Alice asked.

"Simple," the Agrodien clarified. "We no build like this."

"We like caves," Galonia tried to elaborate.

"Wait." Arthur stood to his feet and moved towards the table. "Do you want a door?"

"Yes, door," Galonia agreed. She started flapping her hands back and forth. "Window with little doors."

"Shutters," Arthur explained.

"Shutters, yes." She nodded before pointing to the front door. "And shelter."

"A porch with an awning," the boy explained.

"And what about the interior?" David asked, gesturing around the room.

"We look after that," Yuri replied.

David scratched his beard and raised his brow. "We'll have this done quicker than I thought."

"It might give you an opportunity to build more suitable shelters for those northerners bedding in the tents out there," Arthur offered.

Alice stared at the table, processing the conversation held between the Agrodien and the two men in the room.

"We might need to get some equipment from the mill," David said to his son. "Building an entire structure on open ground is a little different to building something like this. At least with this structure, you had the cave to help with the foundation."

"What if we did the same to all the caverns?" Alice asked.

"What?" the old man asked. "Build more cabins like this? I don't think we have enough resources available for that either."

"No," she replied. "Build more like what Yuri specified."

The Agrodien looked to her confusedly.

"Simple structures that would keep the winter chill out," she explained. "We build a stable door into the mouth of one of the larger caves for the horses. The others, we construct simple doors and windows."

"Just like the exterior of this hut?" Arthur queried.

"Exactly. We can work on the interiors later. The main objective is to get everyone inside where it is warm before the snow arrives."

"It's achievable," David acknowledged. "Some may have to share accommodation. Let's hope there won't be too many to protest about that."

"I hope not." Alice peered over at the giant. "Because my mother is already bedding in our second room."

"I understand." David frowned. "You're limited on space, and after what I did to you as chief..."

Alice sensed the emotion in his voice, even if he tried to hide it.

"Arthur and I can offer a space in the storage area behind the house," she explained. "It's as warm in there as it is in here. We just need to build something to keep you off the ground at night. At least, we'll have our family under one roof. That is if you want to."

"Thank you, yes!" He looked grateful, reaching over to her, taking her hand in his. "I don't think I can take much more of bunking with Ewan. He farts way too much in his sleep."

Yuri chuckled.

"So do you, Papa." Arthur smiled. "But you don't hear me complaining."

"Sound echo in cave." Yuri laughed before making the sound of flatulence by poking out his long tongue and blowing. Galonia shot him a stern look, to which he lowered his head bashfully. "Sorry."

***

Arnald Smyth stamped his feet on the ground, trying to warm his bones. His eyes fixed on the treeline as Edmond Cobham drained his bladder nearby.

"Too much ale tonight, Edmond?" the other asked, rubbing his arms as the chill wind swept down from the mountainside.

"Not enough," Cobham replied as he buttoned up his trousers. "I can still see your ugly face."

"Your mother seemed to like it the night before we came on this mission," Smyth taunted.

"And your mother takes it from behind," the other replied with a smirk.

"So, you're the one." He stamped his feet again.

"What are you doing?" asked Cobham. "Dancing a jig or something?"

"It's bloody cold," Smyth answered, watching the shadows beneath the trees. "Too cold for anything to be out there. That's for certain."

"Captain says to watch the trees, so we watch the trees."

"Watch the trees," the soldier mocked. "For what? More leaves falling?"

"Come on," Cobham called, walking towards the north. "We need to keep moving."

The tent was pitched a few yards to their right. The campfire had been set just to the side where the other members of the first squad sat, keeping warm by the flames.

"Would rather be back over there," Smyth grumbled as he followed his comrade along the well-worn road.

"Watch it there," Cobham called with a soft snigger. "Don't step in my puddle."

"Dirty bastard," the other hissed, glancing about on the ground. He couldn't see anything except light-coloured gravel and long grass on either side of the trail.

Movement.

His head snapped to the left.

"Wait," he called softly.

"What?"

"I think I just saw something," Smyth said, scanning the treeline carefully.

Cobham stopped in his tracks and peered in the general direction where the other was looking.

He saw only shadows and trees.

"What did it look like?"

"I don't know," Smyth replied. "I just saw something move."

"Big? Small?"

"I don't know."

Cobham shook his head.

"You're seeing things," he explained. "Not enough sleep. Come on."

Smyth continued to look towards the trees as he followed the other soldier. He tried to focus upon the dark regions between the pines, but he saw nothing.

Eventually, he gave up and accepted his comrade's words.

"You're right," he acknowledged, turning his head to face the other. "I just need slee..."

Cobham was gone.

Smyth turned on the spot, peering back towards the campsite to his right.

Nothing.

He looked back along the road in both directions.

The road was empty.

"Edmond," he called softly. "Edmond. This is no time to be jovial. Edmond."

There was no reply.

Smyth stepped carefully along the path to the north, following in the direction the other soldier had travelled.

"Edmond, please," he called. His stomach balled up and his legs shook. "Come on, Edmond."

"BLARRGH!"

A large form leapt out of the long grass beside the road.

Smyth jumped back in fright, feeling something escape him from his nether regions.

Sudden laughter from the other form gave him a small sense of relief as he came back to his senses.

There, in the middle of the road and quite pleased with himself, was Cobham.

"By the gods," Smyth gasped.

"That was brilliant," the other laughed.

"You bastard!"

"Edmond, please," Cobham mocked.

Smyth chuckled, his hand grasping his chest.

"I think I shat myself," he managed.

Both men laughed out loud.

"You're awake now," Cobham stated. "Aren't you?"

"You bet your mother's warm bed I'm..."

A dark figure leapt from the tall grass on the forest side of the road and tackled Smyth, taking him from the track and disappearing into the grass on the other side.

For a moment, all Cobham could do was stare at the place where his friend once stood.

Eventually, the movement just to the side of the road drew his attention.

He moved slowly, keeping his eye on the spot where the grass whipped about violently.

A black form, slender and sleek, hunched over Smyth's writhing body, tearing into his neck with long, white teeth.

"Oh shit," Cobham hissed.

The creature turned to peer at him.

Long shreds of flesh hung from its jaws, slapping against its neck as it tilted its head, curiously watching the man on the road.

It opened its mouth and hissed before emitting a strange clicking sound from its throat.

A reply came from the direction of the forest.

The creature returned to feasting upon Smyth, ignoring Cobham.

More hissing and clicks resounded across the pastureland behind him.

He turned to see the grass near the treeline moving.

Closer and closer, the tall vegetation seemed to part and shuffle as many unseen creatures made their way to the road.

"Oh shit," he murmured again, pulling his sword and forcing his legs to move. "Oh, shit! Oh, shit! Oh, shit!"

His voice grew louder and louder with each vocalisation.

His legs beat faster and faster.

"Oh, shit! Oh, shit!"

"What is it?" Lieutenant London hollered, pulling his sword free from its sheath.

"Oh, shit! Oh, shit! Oh, shit!" Cobham almost ran into the officer's arms.

"There sir," Gerard Sadler pointed to the road with his blade.

Twelve dark creatures, standing like men, lined themselves on the road.

"What are they?" John Cheyne, another soldier, asked.

"Oh, shit!" Cobham managed.

"Where's Smyth, Edmond?" London grabbed the frantic soldier by the collar.

"Oh, shit!" was all he could get out.

The tent flap suddenly burst outward as Captain Thornton stepped onto the scene with a sword in his hand.

"What's going on?" he barked.

"Intruders, sir." London gestured with his weapon.

Thornton made a quick evaluation of the situation and smacked the side of the tent with his blade.

"Get up boys," he hollered. "We're in for a fight."

***

The great oak seemed to move, stretching its roots through the ground to make the earth tremble slightly beneath them.

Its limbs bent and stretched, cracking open as if forced about by a strong wind.

Thick, red blood seeped from the wounds, dribbling down the wide trunk and onto the soil.

A whispering voice started calling through the air.

Death brings life.

Death brings life.

Another voice, dark and cruel, spoke from deep below, from within the earth.

The words were not of any language she recognised, but she understood.

A vision appeared. Unfocused bright light transformed into the form of someone she thought was familiar.

Flashing images of naked flesh writhing like snakes coiled together. Arms, legs, bodies, drenched in blood and filth.

The voice on the wind continued to chant.

Death brings life.

Death brings life.

An image appeared of nine unborn infants, still in the womb. Slowly, they turned to ash as the light of the sun appeared upon a dark, desolate horizon.

Thunder roared from the sky as the ground opened and fire spewed from the earth.

Fear gripped her, and she struggled to escape the horror transpiring.

Joanne opened her eyes.

The other women gathered about were as frightened as she. Their faces were pale and their breaths shallow.

All seven immediately looked at the tree.

It stood as it always had.

There was no blood draining from the limbs onto the ground.

There were no voices.

The night sky was still.

All was seemingly peaceful.

The other women turned their faces to Joanne.

She got up and calmly brushed her knees with her hands.

The others followed suit and followed her to the gate where Andris was still standing watch.

"You may return home, Commander," Joanne told him. "We'll be fine on our own."

"Yes, my lady." He bowed, remaining in place until all seven had exited the ruins so that he could close the gate behind them.

"Do we go to inform the Maji?" Tricia asked.

"You are all going home," Joanne replied. "And he isn't the Maji yet. There is something he must do before he can rightly lay claim to the title of *light of all*."

***

Thornton was first to move forward.

The twelve creatures leapt from the road and charged across the grass towards the troop.

The captain swung his sword in an upward arc as he ran. The edge of the blade was heading directly for one of the attacker's heads.

At the last moment, it dived to the side, avoiding the weapon.

Trapped in momentum, Thornton ignored the beast and focused his attention upon another, bringing his sword down again.

The first creature skidded to a halt and turned to pounce upon the captain from behind.

Just as its legs coiled to make the jump, Brook hacked through its neck with his sword. The black creature fell limp to the ground as its head bounced and rolled into the long grass nearby.

Thick, black liquid pumped from the wound and onto the lieutenant's boots.

His first impression was that its appearance reminded him of tar.

The smell was even worse. His thoughts ventured to times when rot and decay had infested a body, leaving maggots and worms to feed upon the remains.

Thornton hacked his blade through a creature's shoulder, slicing deep into its torso.

The dark figure screamed in agony as the captain retrieved his sword.

It fell, writhing and screeching.

With a plunge of his blade, Thornton finished the beast by piercing the chest.

"That's how it's done, boys," he laughed.

The troop didn't see the kill. They were all too engaged in their own skirmishes.

"Oh shit," Cobham continued to call as he swung his sword at his assailant.

It stretched its claws towards him, slashing and trying to grab his arms.

In desperation, it gripped his sword and pulled.

"Oh shit," the soldier yelled, yanking on his weapon as hard as he could.

The blade moved, slicing off three of the creature's fingers.

It recoiled, emitting an ear-piercing scream.

Cobham plunged the sword into the beast's neck, silencing the call.

"Shuttup," the soldier hollered. He stabbed again and again. "Shuttup. Shuttup."

It fell lifelessly onto the grass by his feet, where he continued to stick his blade into the dead beast.

"Shuttup. Shuttup. Shuttup."

"Seems Edmond has found a new word for the day." Vawdrey smiled as he lopped the arm off another creature. It screamed in reply. The soldier brought his sword around in a circle and lopped the animal's head off. "You can shut up too."

Another scream made him peer towards the camp.

Bacon pushed his weapon into a fallen creature not too far from the tent, silencing it.

"I think this was the last one," he said.

"One more." Cobham pointed back towards the road. "It got Smyth over there."

"Come on, lads," Thornton barked, jogging towards the road with his blade held high.

Working their way through the tall grass, the troop drew nearer to the sounds of wet crunches and slapping.

The beast growled as they came into view.

It hunched over the body of Smyth with its head buried in his chest.

"By the gods," London gasped.

Thornton didn't hesitate.

He drove his sword deep into the animal's side and twisted the blade.

It pulled away from the body and turned to face the swordsman. Thick blood oozed from the wound on its side as it swiped at the men standing about.

Thornton struck it again. He brought his blade down, chopping through the dark creature's skull.

Its arms fell loosely to its side before it crashed into a pile on the ground.

All eyes moved to Smyth.

The creature had torn his chest and stomach open.

"Gather his body," Thornton commanded. "We need to burn him."

"And the creatures, sir?" Brook asked.

"Let the fuckers rot," said the captain as he moved away towards the camp.

Twenty-One

By dawn's light, the troop had packed their camp and readied their horses to leave.

A pyre was set on the black rocks by the sea where they paid respects to their fallen comrade, Arnald Smyth.

No words were spoken.

No tears shed.

When the fire had burnt down and the pile of timber started falling apart, Thornton returned to the horses and mounted his steed.

"Time to go, lads," he called.

After climbing into the saddle, the riders made their way back to the road.

"Where are the bodies?" John Cheyne asked.

Brook's eyes darted about.

Sure enough, the bodies of all the creatures had disappeared. The only trace of them was the dark blood spatter over the grass.

"They can't have just got up and walked off," Jendryng queried. "Could they?"

"Of course not, boy," Thornton replied gruffly. "But that's what they want you to think."

"They?" the young soldier's eyes widened. "Who are *they?*"

"Others," the captain said, urging his horse along the road with a gentle kick. "You seriously don't believe that was their entire force, do you?"

Jendryng opened his mouth to ask another question.

"We need to move," Brook told him. "Keep your words for later."

The young man nodded compliantly.

Let's go," London hollered to the men, trotting after his commander.

The troop headed along the road, jogging their horses toward the Great Horn. Its stature became more and more menacing with each step taken by the steeds.

By mid-morning, the troop had travelled a good distance and were getting to the point where they needed to tilt their heads to see the pinnacle of the horn.

For Jendryng, it was almost like something from a dream. He moved his attention back to ground level and shook his head when he saw just how far the foot of the mountain was from their position.

There were still miles to go.

They could see small specks of white high upon the mountain, clinging to the tops of rocky crags and jutting pieces of stone. The forest seemed to hug the base of the massive structure, running up the sloping sides until the land became too steep for anything to cling onto.

A long tendril of land stuck from the Great Horn's side, stretching through the forest and trailing into the sea. The troop could see from a far distance that this mass was immense.

To help them get a better understanding of the sheer monstrosity of the mountain, a small village had been constructed by the seaside. Sticking from the end of the tendril of rock, and pointing into the sky, was a stone beacon.

A long dock ran from the village and over the water for a good distance. Moored at the end was a tall ship unloading supplies.

"With luck, we'll get there before that ship leaves port," Thornton said to Brook. "We need to send word to Newholt about our friends we encountered last night."

"We're not returning?"

"Our mission is clear," the captain replied. "We need to investigate the settlements in the mountains."

"I would have thought it pretty clear what happened to them," London offered.

"We don't know if anything happened to them," Thornton told him. "We're going farther north after a good night's rest here."

"Where is here, sir?" Jendryng asked curiously.

"Whitekeep, son," the commander replied. The young soldier seemed to freeze on his saddle. His muscles tensed and his eyes widened. "And yes, this is the place where the White Witch once lived."

"Good thing she's dead, eh?" Vawdrey smiled.

***

Following the road into the tiny community, the men counted five permanent structures positioned on either side of another track leading to the dock. Several temporary structures were located between these, with several small campfires sending thin ribbons of smoke into the sky.

The road they had been following led onward to the north. A narrow pass had been cut into the stone tendril stretching from the mountain's side to allow travellers to continue on their way.

Thornton steered his horse to the right and urged the animal slowly towards the dock. The troop passed the stable on their left, a large wooden building on the western edge of the settlement with a yard, encompassed by a timber fence, to the side. A couple of horses stuck their heads over the palings, watching the newcomers with curious gazes as they chewed on the grass they had torn from the ground.

The smell of fresh bread baking gripped the men's attention as they walked their horses by a stone building with a large chimney stack protruding from its side. Vawdrey sidled up to Cobham.

"Perhaps there's another little baker's daughter in there for you to get to know," he sniggered.

Cobham peered over to the building. His mind was still on the grass, peering at the remains of Smyth.

"Perhaps," he replied emotionlessly.

Vawdrey took the hint and backed off, allowing the other soldier to ride a little ahead of him. It was clear that his friend was in no mood to joke around.

Several people were moving about on the path ahead of them. There was a mix of men and women shifting supplies from the dock and into two buildings near the edge of the long wooden structure jutting over the water.

One building was the dock house. The other appeared to be a tavern with a second storey. Standing on the porch of the tavern were three young ladies waving to the men on horseback.

"Well, don't they look lovely?" Sparrow smiled.

"Don't get any ideas, boys," Thornton growled. "Three whores and ten men. The numbers just don't add up. Tonight, you sleep in beds, but you won't be sharing them with any women."

A groan of disappointment swept through the riders as they neared the tavern. The captain was first to drop from his horse, tying the reins to a supporting beam on the edge of the porch.

"Gentlemen," a voice called from across the path. All heads turned to see a burly man with a long moustache approaching. He was wearing a leather vest and a long sword sheathed to his hip. "What brings you to Whitekeep?"

"We're on orders from Her Majesty, Queen Amicia Elynbrigge, to scout the northern regions," Thornton replied gruffly. "Now, who the fuck are you?"

The man seemed taken aback by the sudden outburst of foul language.

"I'm, ah…" he blinked nervously. "I'm Sheriff Nathaniel Monteacute. Happy to make your acquaintance."

"I'm sure you are." Thornton stroked his horse's nose and was rewarded with a gentle nuzzle.

"Nathaniel Monteacute," Vawdrey whispered to Sparrow. "How many gold coins did his mother pay for that name, do you think?"

"Shut it," Brook hissed.

"Dismount, lads," Thornton commanded.

"There's plenty of room in the barn for your steeds, Commander." The sheriff pointed to the large building they had passed by moments earlier.

"Captain," the older man replied.

"Sorry." Monteacute gave him a perplexed look.

"I'm a captain," Thornton corrected the other. "Not a commander."

"Captain." The other smiled. "I apologise. As I was saying, the stable has more than enough room for your horses. I'm sure you'll find the accommodation for them more than adequate."

"I'm sure we will." The captain rubbed his buttocks before squatting down to stretch his muscles before returning to full height again. "Rooms for my men? Will this place suffice?"

"This place?" Monteacute glanced at the tavern. "There are beds inside, yes. But some are used for the clients of the, ah..."

"Whores." Thornton looked at the sheriff.

"Yes," the other replied sheepishly. "As you can see, we have just had a ship dock this morning and the young men on board will most likely want to spend some of their coin on such frivolities."

"Not tonight," the captain grumbled. "Lieutenant Brook."

"Yessir," Brook replied.

"Take men and all the horses back to the stable," the captain. "Get the animals fed and settled for the night before returning here. I'll be inside having a drink."

"Of course, sir." The lieutenant smiled before untying the reins of Thornton's horse and leading it away.

"Not tonight?" Monteacute furrowed his brow. He peered at the soldiers and back to the captain. A broad grin appeared on his face. "I see. You would like to procure such entertainment for yourselves. I fully understand. After all, have you ever seen such lovely ladies in all the realms?"

Thornton turned to look at the three young women standing on the porch of the tavern. They certainly were lovely and dressed for the part.

Their low-cut dresses, exposing more cleavage than he had ever seen any prostitute dare to show, got his blood pumping a little.

But only a little.

"Not tonight," he repeated to the sheriff. "My men will need rest. I have coin for the beds and a few jugs of ale."

"Ursula isn't going to like that, Monty," one woman said, placing a hand on her hip.

"Thank you, Rose," the burly man said. "I'm sure she can survive another night without customers."

"We got mouths to feed too, Monty," another of the three told him.

"Mouths to feed?" Thornton asked. "You have children?"

"No, they do not," the sheriff informed him. "She's talking about herself."

"Who's this Ursula the other one spoke of?"

"She's the madam," Rose replied. "And she ain't going to like it when she hears about you lot coming in here and not wanting any pokey-poke."

"I am so sorry, Captain," Monteacute held his hands up to the other. "I sincerely don't want to cause you any trouble."

"Where is this Ursula now?"

"She's inside," the second woman answered. "Probably behind the bar."

"I'll talk to her," Thornton said to the sheriff. He peered to the dock where the ship's men continued to unload. "You can give them the bad news."

With that, Thornton stepped onto the porch and strolled in through the door of the tavern.

Sheriff Nathaniel Monteacute stared at the ship moored to the dock.

With a deep sigh, he started towards it.

"Good luck, Monty," Rose quipped.

***

Thornton crossed the dimly lit room to the bar on the far side. Several round timber tables and chairs were positioned around the large space. An enormous fireplace blazed away to his left and an open door to the left of the room showed a hallway with a set of stairs to the side. Lanterns hung at intervals on the walls, shedding light on some tables positioned underneath.

A largish, middle-aged woman stood behind the bar, wiping a mug with a clean cloth. She placed the vessel on a shelf behind her before reaching for another, sitting on a wooden tray atop of the bench.

"Morning," she said as she stuffed the cloth inside the mug. "You'd be wanting ale; I suppose?"

"Ale," Thornton replied, "in three large jugs. I'll also be wanting eleven mugs for me and my men when they arrive."

"You'd be wanting beds for the night, too?"

"Beds." He nodded. "But no whores. I've got coin."

"No whores," the woman agreed.

Thornton looked at her curiously. He wasn't expecting the discussion to go so easily after hearing the way the women spoke about their madam.

"You don't want to know why?"

"Why?" She glared at him in question. Suddenly, a look of clarity swept over her face. "You think I'm Ursula."

"You're not?"

"I'm Maud." She placed the mug on the bar. "I'm the keeper of this establishment. Let me pour you one before I call her. You're going to need it."

The innkeeper carried the mug to a barrel tipped on its side, positioned in a cradle atop a bench behind her. She turned a tap on its side and dribbled a brownish liquid into the mug.

Moments later, she placed the vessel before the captain and pointed to the stool beside the bar.

"Pull up a seat," she said. "I'll get Ursula and then prepare the rooms for you and your men. It'll cost you eleven silver for the night. That's just for the beds. It's a copper for each mug. Three copper for meals."

"I've got gold only," he told her. "I'll give you six pieces for ale, beds and food."

"Six?" Maud raised her brows. "That's too much."

"It's what I'm going to pay."

"Ursula can pour more ale for you," she said, moving to a door at the side of the bar. "I'm going to fetch the clean linen for you."

"The linen you have on the beds already will be fine," he said.

"The linen I have on the beds is for the other customers." She grinned. "If you know what I mean?"

He did.

He sipped at the ale.

His face scrunched up in disgust.

It was old and turning sour.

But he didn't care.

It had been a long time since he had drunk a mug of ale.

"I hear you don't want the company of my ladies," a sweet, melodic voice said from the door.

Thornton peered over to see a young well-dressed woman, not all that far beyond her adolescent years, leaning against the doorframe as she wiped her hands upon a cloth.

"You're Ursula?" the captain growled.

"Ursula Wadham." She stepped forward, flicking her long dark hair over her shoulder with a toss of her head.

"They said that…" he shot a thumb over his shoulder, pointing to the door. "Well, they made you out to be…"

"You thought I would be older," she giggled.

"And meaner looking," he added.

"Don't I look mean?" she asked, pouting her lips and making a mock angry face.

She was beautiful.

He was lost in her deep blue eyes.

"No." He smiled.

"So tell me…" she leant on the bar with her elbows. His scrutiny wandered to the top button of her blouse, where he stared at her cleavage. Quickly, he averted his gaze, only to look deep into hers again. "Why don't you want the company of my ladies?"

He took another swig of his mug.

"We're on a mission," he replied. "I don't want my men distracted. We may need to be ready for an attack at any time."

"Attack?" she raised her eyebrows. "Are we at war?"

"No." Thornton shook his head. "I don't think so. But, we were attacked last night by some fell creatures from the forest."

"Deer?" she joked. "Rabbit. Rukyul perhaps?"

"No," he answered. "These creatures were similar in form to men. Dark skin. Large teeth. Thin. Very fast and agile."

She suddenly stood upright.

"Like shadows?" she said.

"Yes." The captain eyed her carefully.

"Others have said they saw shadows moving near the trees at night," she told him. "But they would not come near to the road. They would only linger in the darkness of the woods."

"Have you seen them?"

She shook her head.

"Has anyone seen them during the day?" he asked.

The door burst open.

Five men stepped into the room, directing their attention to Thornton.

"Who's the bastard that's stopping me and my mates from ravishing the ladies?" one man hollered. "Is it you, you old shit?"

"Yes," Thornton replied, lifting the mug to his lips again.

"Well, me and my mates have got to have some words with you then," the angry man yelled, moving across the room. "Haven't we?"

The other four were on his heels, ready to join in with what they thought was to follow.

The first man pulled his fist back, ready to strike the old man on the stool.

Quicker than a flash, Thornton had his dagger out of its sheath and pressed against the man's neck.

"You have a lot of questions," the captain growled. "Don't you, boy?"

"What?" the other replied nervously. He lowered his arms to his side and shivered with fear.

"I said you have a lot of questions. Don't you?"

"I don't..."

"Let me elaborate," Thornton started. "Who's the bastard? Is it you, old shit? We got to have some words. Haven't we?"

"Sir," a voice called from the door. Thornton took a quick glance over to see Brook and London across the way. "Is everything all right?"

"All under control, Lieutenant," the captain replied, returning his attention to the man before him. "Are you a dock worker or a crewman?"

"Crewmen," the other answered.

"And your friends here?"

"We're crewmen also, sir," one of them replied, holding his hands up in surrender. His eyes flickered from the men in the doorway to the captain holding a knife to his friend's throat.

"We just wanted some whores for the night after a long day's work," another man offered. "That's all. We weren't looking for trouble."

"Yes, you were," Thornton rumbled. "And you found it."

"Please?" the first man pleaded.

Thornton stared at him for what seemed a long time.

"I'll make you a bargain," he said before looking over his shoulder at Ursula. She had backed away to the doorway to the side of the bar, ready to escape if need be. "If the young madam here allows it, I will pay for your night of entertainment, but it cannot take place here."

"My ladies do not perform their duties outside of the tavern," she replied. "It's a matter of security."

Thornton inclined his head.

"You heard her," the captain relayed. "You'll need to use your hands tonight, lads. Or, I can let my men teach you a lesson about military discipline. You decide."

"Hands sound delightful," one man replied.

The others around him agreed wholeheartedly.

"What say you, crewman?" Thornton asked the first.

"I honestly don't know what I was thinking," he answered. "I've a wife and children. I don't need to partake in such disgraceful activities."

A smile stretched across the captain's face as he pulled the blade away from the man.

"Get out of here," he said. "Before I get cranky."

The five men rushed for the door and disappeared past the troop.

"Are you all right, Captain?" London asked as he approached the bar.

"Quite all right." He lifted the mug to his lips again.

"One for all?" Ursula asked, gesturing to the men with her chin.

"If you don't mind," Thornton replied.

She poured ale for all his men before returning to the end of the bar where he sat.

"I apologise," he told her.

"What for?"

"For behaving so undignified," he explained.

"You were defending yourself," she justified. "You don't need to apologise for that. Besides, I've seen worse. I'm a madam who works in a tavern on the edge of a dock, remember."

He grinned, getting lost in her eyes again.

"Then I apologise for taking business away from you tonight," he said.

"You didn't," she replied.

He looked at her, perplexed.

"Your six gold coins were more than enough to pay for accommodation, ale, food and my whores," she clarified. "The offer is still on the table if you want it."

He shook his head.

"Then forgive me if we take your money without supplying a service," she said cheerfully.

"It's not my money," he chuckled. "It's the queen's."

"Well, then!" She frowned. "We should have offered you the royal treatment first."

"The royal treatment?"

"You'll never know, now," she replied, offering a cheeky grin.

Twenty-Two

"When did she return?" Takmel asked.

He was standing near the door, removing his jacket. Catherine and Lucy sat by the fire, reading.

"Perhaps an hour ago," the younger answered. "Where have you been?"

"With Andris," he replied as he placed his coat on a hook by the door. "I've sent riders to Dweagan. Where is she?"

"Asleep." Lucy peered over at him. "She's very tired."

He moved away towards the bedrooms. Quietly, he opened her door and stepped into the darkened room.

The curtains had been pulled shut. The light seeping in through the door illuminated the area just enough for him to see her lying face down and naked on her bed.

He closed the door quietly behind him as he stepped softly towards her. His feet collected her cloak, which was left on the floor. Carefully, he moved it aside with his hands and continued to the edge of the bed, where he sat down.

He reached out and touched her skin with his fingertips, moving them across the small of her back and along her spine to her shoulders.

"Not yet," she murmured.

"So, you're awake," he whispered. He placed his hand on the nape of her neck and rubbed gently.

"Mm-hmm," she moaned. "And I said not yet."

She rolled away from him, onto her back.

His eyes moved straight to her breasts.

"Why not?" he asked, reaching his fingers towards her.

She intercepted his touch by grasping his wrist roughly.

"It isn't time for the Maji," she answered.

"When?" He sounded disappointed, recoiling his hand and placing it on the mattress beside him.

"Tomorrow," she replied lazily, closing her eyes. "After dusk. You must take all of us."

He smirked, liking the sound of such a proposition.

"All seven?" He almost laughed.

"All nine," she corrected him. "Your seed must be in all of us before dawn."

"My seed?" He creased his brow.

"You will need your rest," she mumbled. "You will need to perform well."

"And if not?" he asked concernedly. "If I can't perform?"

"Then we will not be yours," she answered. "Your hold on us will break and we will turn on you."

A deep pit formed in his stomach.

He lifted himself to his feet and moved to the door.

Catherine watched him from her seat as he reappeared within view. She expected him to come and sit by her near the fire. Instead, he took his coat from the hook and opened the door to leave.

"Where are you going now?" she asked. "You just got home."

"I need to speak to someone," he replied. "I won't be long."

Shutting the door behind him, he headed directly towards the centre of the city. Within a few minutes, he was entering the gate of the ruins and approaching the oak tree. There, he knelt at the base of the trunk and placed his hand upon the protruding roots.

Closing his eyes, he took a deep breath and whispered softly.

"Mother?"

***

Several more people ventured into the tavern as the day wore on. Most came for the ale, but a couple sat at a table or two to enjoy a finely cooked meal. Both Maud and Ursula were seen to scurry back and forth from the kitchen with bowls of stew and plates of fresh bread. Occasionally, one would stop long enough to pour a mug of ale for a customer before returning to the kitchen to fetch another's lunch.

Thornton placed himself in the corner by the fire and a window, looking into the street. From here, he could see all the way to the road leading north and monitor his men who were all stuffing themselves with casserole and toast.

His eye kept gravitating to Ursula every time she entered the room. There was something mesmerizing about her that continued to draw his attention.

She's too young for you, Georgie.

He sipped at his mug of ale and peered out the window, trying to distract himself with dust spinning in little clouds on the path, or flies buzzing around horse dung. Anything.

"Mind if I sit here?" a gruff voice asked.

Thornton turned his head to see a man about his age, holding a mug in one hand and a broad hat in the other. A long white beard dangled over his wiry frame and his clothes smelled of salt.

"Not at all." The captain gestured to an empty chair at the table.

"Thank you, kindly," the man replied. "I usually sit here before the night comes. Best spot in the house. Right by the fire. The name's Christopher, by the way."

"George," the other replied, extending his hand. The man took it with a smile as he lowered himself into the chair.

"You're an officer," Christopher said. "But you don't wear the uniforms of the city guards."

Thornton hadn't thought about it. The clothing his men wore was a little more casual than the regalia he would usually be required to display in Newholt.

"We're on a mission," the captain told him. "The uniform is not the most comfortable to move about in. We compromise by wearing the leather."

He knocked upon his breastplate with his fist to make a point.

"You come to kill the shadows?" asked Christopher, stroking his beard.

"Shadows?"

"Those beasts in the forest," he explained. "I've seen them at night. Me and Harry work up on that beacon from dusk until dawn, making sure the fire is lit and stays bright. We've seen them sneaking around on the edge of the road, creeping through the gap in the rock."

"Do you know where they come from?"

"Couldn't say that," he replied. "But I can say that the keep, way up in those woods by the feet of the horn, would be a place worth looking at."

"The White Keep?"

"Aye. They seem drawn to it." He leant back in his chair and gulped a mouthful of ale. "By the gods, this is the worst batch yet."

He thumped the mug onto the table.

"Not too bad when you haven't had any in a while." Thornton grinned, holding his mug up to the other man.

"I guess so." Christopher acknowledged. He moved his eye to Ursula and noticed her peering over at the captain in the corner. "Some other things are worth trying if you haven't had them in a while too."

Thornton watched the young woman as she crossed the room, holding a tray with more bowls of stew. She was looking at him. A smile flashed on her face before she turned away.

"Don't go there at night," the other man warned, leaning towards him.

The captain was puzzled.

"Why?" he asked. "What's wrong with her?"

"Her?" Christopher furrowed his brow and followed the officer's eyes to the young lady. "Not her. The damn keep, man. Don't go out there in the dark. Wait until it's light. Those buggers are too dark to see at night."

"What's stopping them from coming into the village here?"

"I don't know," he replied. "But something has them afraid. They come no farther than the road. At times, Harry and me watched them just standing there, all lined up on the road, watching us."

Thornton felt his heart beat a little faster.

"Did you tell the sheriff?"

"Monty?" Christopher almost laughed. "That poor bastard couldn't beat a dandelion. Monty. He's good with people. I'll give him that. A very friendly fellow. But put him in a fight? He'd be more help to the enemy than to you or me."

Thornton nodded.

"He seems like a nice fucker." The captain lifted his mug to his lips and swallowed hard.

"That's about the only other thing he's apparently good at," the other retorted. "He's been through those whores countless times."

"Must have some coin to spare?"

"Monty lives on the goodwill of the people here," Christopher informed the officer. "When business is booming, the dock is active. Monty does his best to keep everyone under control, and he's rather good at it.

"When business is slow, and there are no ships moored and no travellers on the road, Monty gets his reward from the madam of the village."

"Ursula?"

"No..." the man shook his head. "As far as I know, she's never been with anyone in her whole life. She is the madam, though. His reward is the three whores of White Keep. Rose, Audrey and Kateryn. The finest whores this side of Oakbeach."

"We came from that way," Thornton said. "And I didn't see any whores all the way from Newholt."

"I rest my case," Christopher replied, lifting his mug and taking a large swallow. "Gods, that's bad."

"Let me buy you a meal tonight, Christopher," Thornton offered.

"Thank you," the other man replied. "But that isn't necessary. As part of my rewards for my service to the community, I am given all my daily meals and other needs by the wonderful patron of this establishment. Have you met her yet?"

"Maud, you mean?"

"Aye." He leant back in his chair. "Maud. Isn't she a dish?"

Thornton chuckled.

"Don't tell my missus," Christopher pleaded. "She'll be in here later to sup with me."

"Have you and Maude ever..."

"Oh, gods no," he replied. "I wouldn't dare. If Mary was to ever find out how I feel for Maud, she'd string me up on that beacon by my ball sack."

"Your secret is safe with me," Thornton assured him.

He turned his gaze back out the window and peered towards the road. Farther away, the tips of the pines swayed gently in the breeze flowing from the mountains.

Somewhere, deep inside the forest, the White Keep stood.

As he watched the forest, he wondered if something in the shadows of the woods was watching him.

***

"We have five almost completed, and another three started," David reported to Alice. She was removing the innards from a sheep she had strung up in a tree and skinned. The sound of hammering echoed from the trees and through the glade.

"Will the five be ready for some of the Agrodien by tomorrow?" she asked.

"They're ready now," he replied. "All we need to do is finish the porches and awnings. The rest is done. Arthur's finishing the sealing up the gaps with that mud and wax mixture of yours on one of the caverns to the north."

"Does Yuri know?" She reached her hand into the cavity she had made in the sheep's belly and pulled the contents loose. They slapped onto the ground noisily.

Two dogs watching started forward to claim the discarded offal. A loud growl persuaded them to back off as Shadow, the rukyul, moved in slowly to devour the entrails.

"No," he answered the girl. "Do you wish for me to pass the news on to him?"

"Please," she said, cutting into the hip of the carcass, preparing to remove one leg.

"Who should I say gets to move into the new quarters?"

"Let him decide." She smiled. "He won't like it. But he'll need to make the call."

"You don't think he'll claim one for himself?"

"So, what if he does?" She slid her knife through the flesh with ease. It amazed David at how simple she made it look. "That's his decision."

She completed cutting around the hip joint and separated the limb from the body.

"Here." She held it out to the giant man. "Take this to him for me."

"Of course," he replied, grabbing the leg by the heel joint. "Do you want me to come back and help you with the rest?"

"No," she said, smiling. "But thank you. I'm only taking the other leg and one rack of ribs. The rest is for him." She shot a glance over at the rukyul who was lapping at the intestines on the ground.

"He's getting fussy about his food," Baldwyn called as he limped towards them, observing the massive creature. "You feed him too well."

"What's wrong with you?" Alice asked him.

"Old wound playing up." He slapped his thigh.

"I'd rather her feed him well than have him eyeball the younglings as potential prey," David told him.

"Aye," the other said, concurring. "I'm looking for Elka. Have you seen her?"

"She was in the field with my mother and Akasati, tending the livestock last I saw her," Alice answered as she started moving her blade through the flesh of the carcass.

"I'll look there, then," he replied, moving away. He looked over at the dragon lying on the grass nearby. "Good day, Liana."

The giant beast looked over at the man and chirped before emitting a deep, guttural rattle.

"I'll go see Yuri, then," David said, holding the leg up as if reminding himself that he had something to do. As he moved away, Shadow slunk to Alice's side and sat upon his haunches.

She moved her gaze to the entrails still lying on the ground before looking to the dogs waiting patiently a few yards away.

"Come on," she called to them.

They raced in and snatched up mouthfuls of the thick organs before tugging the mess away from the rukyul's stare to devour on the grass.

Shadow lowered his head, eyeing the girl as she continued to separate the leg from the body.

"If you wanted it," she told the creature, "you should have eaten it. Now you're just going to have to wait until I'm done."

He gave a disappointed grunt as he lowered himself to the ground and flopped his head onto his paws.

***

"I think we have already seen what has happened to the settlers in the mountains," London said to Brook. He kept his voice low so that others seated nearby couldn't hear.

The two officers occupied a table by the wall nearest the front door of the tavern. The rest of the troop were positioned at two tables pushed together near the middle of the room.

All except Captain Thornton, who was across the way at a table with another man. The two seemed to have a pleasant discussion.

It was the first time that either lieutenant had seen their commanding officer laugh so much at the one time.

"Our mission is to see for ourselves," Brook reminded the other. "We may still find some other reason for their missed appointments."

"Missed appointments?"

"I know," Brook said. "It sounded silly as I said it. I just meant that there could be another reason why no one has heard from them in a while."

"Like what exactly?" London raised his brows. "Do you seriously believe these things had nothing to do with why we're on this mission? Come on, Hugh."

Brook stared at his mug for a while.

"No, I do not," he replied slowly. "I think you're right, Ralf. But I hope to the gods you're not."

"Gentlemen," a deep growling voice announced from their side. They both looked over to see Thornton standing by their table. "Outside, please."

They quickly rose to their feet and followed the captain through the door and onto the veranda.

Thornton peered down the lane to the dock, where several men still moved about with cargo. He stepped off the porch and started towards the stable.

"Are we leaving, sir?" London asked.

"On the contrary," the captain replied. "I think our mission starts here. Or more to the point, over there." He gestured to the forest with his chin.

"Sir?" Brook asked.

"Those creatures have been seen here at night," he explained. "The man I've been talking to is one of the beacon operators. He told me he's seen them on the road up there, moving in and out of the woods, but never venturing into the settlement here."

"Why is that, sir?" Brook stared towards the woods nestled beneath the Great Horn.

"Why don't they come across the road?" Thornton asked, wanting clarification of the other's question.

"Yes, sir."

"I'm not sure," the captain replied. "I've got an idea, but I can't be certain. So I'm keeping that one to myself for now. The bigger question is, what is so special about here?"

London peered around and saw nothing out of the usual. He shook his head.

"I don't understand," he said. "It's just a little village in the middle of nowhere."

"Not in the middle of nowhere," Thornton told him, staring at the woods. "Do you know what's in there?"

"Trees," London quipped.

"Very funny, Lieutenant." The captain shot him a sideways glare of reproach. "In there, way up at the end of this stone wall stretching from the mountain, is the original White Keep. It was a place of death and torture in its glory days," he explained. "The lord of the keep was defeated here during the Realm War. He, his family, and his entire servitude were slaughtered inside its walls and left to rot.

"For years, it was left to its own devices until the White Witch claimed it for herself. Perhaps she fed upon the evil in that place. Perhaps a little of herself remains there. Perhaps it's all a coincidence. But for whatever reason, those dark creatures have been seen here.

"I'm not one who believes in coincidences, gentlemen. Something is drawing those fuckers here. Maybe this is where they spawn from and I intend to find out."

London fixed his gaze upon the treeline on the far side of the northern road. His eyes darted to the dark shadows beneath the pines and crooked, bare limbs of the oak. The wind blew through the under-growth, making the shadows move.

The shapes of men.

The shapes of trees.

It was difficult to tell from this distance.

"Should I ready the men, sir?" Brook asked.

"No," Thornton answered, peering up at the sun. The orb of light was almost touching the pinnacle of the Great Horn. "It'll be dark soon. The shadow of the mountain will cover all and we won't be able to tell the difference between man, beast or tree. We wait until the first light of the morning."

Twenty-Three

With the ship unloaded, all men working onboard and on the dock moved to the tavern. Most of the troop had moved upstairs to catch up on much-needed sleep.

Thornton, being the good leader, had gone upstairs to check on the accommodation. The bedding appeared comfortable and the rooms, each with four cots, were more than adequate for his men's needs.

"You two should get some rest, too," he said to his lieutenants as they returned down the stairs.

"I wouldn't mind some more ale," London replied. "If that's all right with you, sir?"

"Drink as much as you want," Thornton told him as he moved through the doorway and back into the main room of the tavern. "Just make sure you hide any headache you get in the morning. If I hear one complaint, I'll put you on report. Understood?"

"Yes, sir." London smiled.

"Same applies to you, Brook." He pointed his finger at the other.

"I stopped drinking an hour ago, sir," the lieutenant informed his commander.

"Then what's in your mug?"

"Green tea, sir."

"Green..." Thornton sniggered. "Well, look who's all trah-li-lah!" The three men chuckled. "All right then, lads. I'm going back to the table over by the fire if you need me. Enjoy your night and make sure the last of our men are upstairs and in their cots after supper."

"Yessir," the two chorused before Thornton moved away.

The captain returned to the table to see that Christopher had been joined by a plump woman and another man, dressed in dark clothing and similar in age.

"George." Christopher raised a hand as Thornton returned to his seat. "I was hoping you'd be back. This is my wife, Mary."

The captain took her hand and planted a soft kiss on her knuckles.

"My lady," he growled. "An absolute pleasure."

She smiled, revealing bare, blackened gum where her upper incisors should have been. She also had one lazy eye, making it hard for the captain to work out which one he should focus on when he looked at her. But all of that was minor compared to the mole growing upon her upper lip.

It was bulbous and dark, with long hairs sticking from the flesh. He now understood why Christopher found Maud so attractive.

"Pleasure's all mine," she cackled. Her voice almost made his ears ring from the high pitch that she emitted.

"And this is Captain Alington of the merchant vessel *Sophia*." Christopher gestured to the gentleman seated beside him.

"The ship moored to the dock, I presume," said Thornton.

"Aye," the man replied. "And you'd be the man who took my beds and women for the night?"

"It wasn't intentional," the old soldier replied.

"It's quite all right," Alington told him with a wry look. "You saved me from choosing who stayed on board the *Sophia* and who got to bed the girls. Three whores are just not enough for twelve men."

"Looks like they're a little busy at the moment anyway," Mary suggested, peering around the room.

Thornton glanced over to the bar and saw Maud and Ursula serving customers, but no sign of the three ladies he had met earlier.

"They're not upstairs," he informed her. "I can assure you of that."

Christopher snorted with a smile.

"Monty," he chortled. "I bet you anything, that bastard has them over there in his bed right now. And on your money too."

"Fine with me," Thornton replied.

"And me," Alington agreed, raising his mug to his lips. He drained the contents and pointed around the table. "Another round. On me."

"Make it on me," Thornton offered. "In fact..."

He raised his arm, waving to Maud.

It was Ursula who answered the call, however.

She moved around the edge of the bar, under the leering eyes of many of the men in the tavern. Thornton felt a hint of jealousy flare up. He had only just met the woman, and he already felt covetous.

Must be old age creeping up and desperation in.

"What would you like, Captain?" she asked, positioning herself between the soldier and Alington. The seafarer leant back in his chair to get an eyeful of the young lady as she spoke to Thornton.

"Another round," the older man told her. "And charge everyone's expenses over to me."

"I don't know if you would have enough gold coins for this lot," she joked.

"It'll be fine."

"Another round coming up, then." She gently placed her hand on his shoulder before returning to the bar.

"She likes you," Mary observed.

"She's just being friendly," Thornton replied, landing his gaze upon her mole.

By the gods, that's ugly.

He moved his gaze to her, but couldn't tell if she was looking at the fire to his left or out the window to his right.

"She has never touched a man in all the time I've known her," she assured him.

"So Christopher told me earlier."

"No." Mary leant forward and grabbed his hand. "I mean; she has never touched a man. Not even on his shoulder."

Thornton moved his gaze to her husband.

"She's right," Christopher agreed before taking a swig from his mug of ale. "She's always right."

"Bet your arse, I am," she chuckled.

***

Supper was another round of stew and bread, toasted if one pre-ferred. The timber creaked, and the wind offered a soft howl from time to time, seemingly louder when those gathered in the tavern allowed their voices to grow quiet. Thornton sat with his new friends for the duration until Christopher stood up to leave.

"Must be off," he said. He leant down and set a big kiss upon his wife's lips. Mary wrapped her large arm around the poor man's neck and kept him in place for what Thornton thought was longer than necessary. Both captains looked at each other uncomfortably until she released her hold.

"You take care up there," she told her husband as he started away. "That wind is getting stronger."

"I will, my love." He blew her a kiss. "I'll be thinking of you and only you. Goodnight, gentlemen. It was a pleasure to meet you both."

With that, he was out the door and gone.

Thornton looked out through the window. There was still some light in the sky, but the small village had grown darker.

The shadow of the mountain had fallen upon them.

"I must be off, too," Mary said. "I much prefer to be indoors before nightfall. Might I suggest, Captain Alington, that you get your men back on board your vessel before the full dark arrives."

"I might take you up on that," he replied. "I was intending to depart tonight, but I think there may be something more menacing behind this breeze. It could be a good idea to get my men back to the ship just in case."

"You're thinking a storm?" Mary asked.

"Aye," he answered. "Shall I see you safely home, my lady?"

"No need," she said as she rose to her feet. "I just live across the way. Goodnight, gentlemen."

Thornton stood and bowed slightly. "Night, my lady."

Both watched her leave before turning to one another.

"And I'll take my leave, as well." Alington reached out his hand to the other. "Pleasure making your acquaintance and hope to see you in the morning."

"Likewise," Thornton replied. "In fact, I hoped you could get a message back to Newholt for me."

"Of course," he agreed. "Write it down and I'll deliver it myself."

"Thank you." The soldier shook the seafarer's hand. "And breakfast is on me, for you and your crew."

"Much appreciated." Alington grinned. "Goodnight Captain."

"Goodnight Captain," Thornton retorted.

"Come on, men," called the captain of the *Sophia*. "Storm's coming. Time enough to tie down everything and shut ourselves in for the night. Skull the last of your ale and move your arses."

"Aye, Captain," a few hollered back.

Before long, they had emptied the room, except for a few locals milling about near the bar and the two lieutenants who sat by the doorway leading to the stairwell.

"Night ladies," Brook called to the two women behind the bar.

"Night!" London waved.

The ladies replied with a gesture and a smile before returning their attention to their regular customers.

"Night, sir," Brook called over to Thornton.

"Get the fuck to bed," the captain said.

"Yes sir," he replied, disappearing through the door to the stairs.

Thornton relaxed his posture and sipped at his mug of ale slowly. The firelight beside him seemed brighter as the environment outside the window grew darker.

He looked to the sky through the glass and saw dark clouds gathering above.

Alington was right.

A storm was coming.

"Bar's closed," Maud told the men gathered at the bench. "You should all get home before it gets too dark."

"One more round, please, Maud," an elderly man whined.

"Go home, Charlie," she ordered. "There'll be ale tomorrow. I promise."

"Fine," he grumbled, getting to his feet and shuffling towards the door. "I'll return tomorrow to make sure of that."

"I'm sure you will," she agreed.

Ursula moved to the door and waited for the men to leave, each bidding her goodnight as they strolled by.

Once the last of them had left the room, she closed the door and bolted it shut. She looked at the man beside the fireplace.

"So," she said, walking towards him. "You're still up?"

"Enjoying this fire," he replied.

"Want some company?"

His heart skipped a beat.

He fell into her deep blue eyes again.

"I won't say no."

"I'll get those mugs on the tables tomorrow," Maud said, peering at Ursula curiously.

"Tomorrow," the other replied with a smile.

Maud smiled back.

Ursula shot her a look. *Go away.*

Suddenly, the other woman understood and hastily moved through the door to the side of the bar, vanishing into the kitchen and out of sight.

Sitting beside him, Ursula placed her hand on Thornton's forearm.

"I know you've been hearing a lot about me," she said, locking eyes with his. "I've been asking your men about you too."

"Really?" Thornton raised his brows. "I don't know if I want to find out what you discovered."

"They told me you are a foul-mouthed, cranky bastard."

"Did they?"

"But they also said they would follow you through hell and back."

He frowned, looking down at the floor.

It wasn't unusual for most soldiers to say something disrespectful about their commanding officers. But to follow it up with something so reverential struck a chord with him.

"I hope it never comes to that," he said thoughtfully. "I've already lost one on this mission. I don't want to lose any more."

She placed a hand on his cheek and stroked his beard softly.

"There's something about you," she said. "You're the first man I've felt so drawn to. There's a kindness in there that you keep hidden. Why?"

A tear slid down his cheek as he looked into her eyes again.

It was then he saw the sadness that she held inside as well.

"The only person to ever know me was my wife," he shared.

"You're married?"

"Was," he answered. "She passed away from sickness twenty or so years ago. She couldn't have children, so we got to know one another pretty well.

"When she passed, I promised myself to never open up to anyone like that again. And I never have."

She wept.

"I was raped," she confessed. "My father and brother used to take turns with me since as far back as I can recall. My mother left when I was small. I don't even know if she is still alive.

"When I turned ten, something in me fought back. One night. The last night, they took me again. I wanted them to leave me alone. I wanted them to die.

"I don't know how," she continued, "but my father was holding me down while my brother was…"

"You don't need to tell me this." Thornton moved his arm around her shoulder, pulling her to him tightly.

"I made them both hit the wall across the room. I don't know how. They hit it so hard that their bones broke.

"I ran away. I ran for I don't know how long." Her cheeks streaked with tears flowing to her chin, dripping onto her. "Maud found me at the market in Barrowfield, begging for food, when I was twelve," she explained. "She had lost her husband at sea. We both moved to Newholt for some time before coming here to start a new life."

She wiped her tears on her sleeve. "I'm sorry."

He pressed his lips to hers.

She moved her hand to the back of his neck, caressing him, holding him against her.

"I think I've been searching my whole life for you," he whispered. She pulled him to her again and kissed him tenderly.

The window rattled slightly as droplets of water tapped against the pane.

Twenty-Four

Arthur sat upon the bench looking across to the other side of the campsite, to the treeline just beyond. Several small campfires had been lit near the new dwellings constructed over the past few days.

His hands were aching from the hard, arduous work. Yet, a wide smile had been resting upon his face for most of the afternoon and into the night.

The rewards for his effort were coming to fruition as Yuri and Gharnef escorted several females and their younglings into the caves. He watched as the large male reptilians, with flaming torches in their hands, led mothers and children to the incomplete structures that somewhat resembled the hut where he rested.

He glanced down to see the rukyul sitting on his haunches as he observed the proceedings with interest. Soft growls emitted from the beast as he tilted his head from side to side.

"What's the matter, boy?" Arthur asked.

Shadow turned his head and looked at the young man, grunting as if acknowledging, answering his question before turning to watch the Agrodien again.

Arthur chuckled quietly, amused at Shadow's reaction.

"Here," he heard Alice call from the door. She had a mug of tea in each hand, holding one out for him to take.

"Thank you," he said as he lifted it out of her grasp.

She sat down on the bench, sidling up to him and placing her head on his shoulder.

"I hope they like their new dwellings," she said.

"I do too," he replied, putting his arm around her shoulder. "I put a lot of work into those buildings."

She grinned.

"It's all about you, isn't it?"

"Yep." He sipped at his tea.

She scanned the area, counting the small fires lit outside each of the dwellings.

"We should have put stoves inside, rather than have fires outside," Alice mentioned."

"That's only temporary," he told her. "I've put chimney pipes into each of them, just like yours. They can build a fireplace around them or connect them to a stove later, if they wish."

She sat up and looked at him with a sense of wonder.

"And why did you go ahead and do something like that?"

"Just made sense," he answered. "Who wants to go outside to the freezing winter to try and get warm by a fire? Seems counterproductive to me."

She grinned and kissed his cheek.

"You are amazing," she said before putting her head on his shoulder again.

"I know."

The rukyul grunted, lowering himself prostrate to the ground, keeping his attention fixed on the movement just beyond the trees.

Alice thought back to when her little cabin was the only structure on the glade. Now, she was witnessing the beginnings of a community.

"We'll need to give our little village a name," she jested.

"Arthur Land," her husband quipped.

Both burst out laughing.

***

Christopher stoked the fire with a metal prodder before placing another large chock of wood in place. The hearth was set in a large iron cage sitting in front of sheets of polished steel to help reflect the light out to sea.

The flames bit into the timber as the strong wind worked its way around the stone wall behind him before sucking back into the little shelter he and the other man with him had.

The flames tossed about wildly as the storm raged around them. The cold air still got by the heat of the fire and his coverings, all the way to his skin.

"Surely," the other man said, hugging himself, "this must be an early winter."

"Don't know about that, Harry," Christopher replied. "But I do know it's bloody cold."

"I hope those poor bastards are all right out there." Harry peered out to the dark sea. White spray exploded upon the rocks beneath the beacon tower as he watched three lights bobbing slowly upon the tumultuous waves.

"I just hope they can see us through this rain." The other stuffed his beard into his coat, preventing it from flapping wildly in the breeze.

"Busy, out there," Harry mentioned, stepping away from the fire and onto the platform to avoid the glare of the light.

"What do you mean?" Christopher held his hands out to the heat of the flames.

"I count four," he replied. "No, five vessels."

"Which way are they going?"

"I think, south." Harry pointed a little to the north of their position. "Look, another. That's six."

"The only port to the north big enough for so many vessels is at Blackrock Haven." Christopher stepped away from the fire to see for himself. "They could be coming from the lands to the east."

"Heading here?"

"No, you fool. They might be heading for Blackrock Haven or Newholt. The storm might have taken them off course."

Harry watched for a while.

"No," he eventually said. "They're heading south. Look." He pointed to the light bobbing on the waves furthest to the right. "That one was back over there only moments ago."

"Must be blowing a gale out there." Christopher shook his head.

"Why risk the storm?" Harry queried. "I mean, the *Sophia* is still moored here for the night. They could have left before the storm hit us. But they didn't."

"Maybe they just got caught in it," the other guessed.

"Travelling at that speed?" Harry shook his head. "They would've left port only about two or three hours ago. The storm hit before that."

Christopher nodded. "That's if they are coming from Blackrock Haven. We don't know that for sure."

"Come on." Harry shot the other a questioning look. "I don't care how bad this storm is. No captain coming from the eastern lands would guide his ship this far north if he wanted to dock at Newholt."

"Well..." Christopher moved back to the fire, hugging his arms around his body. "They must have a damn good reason for risking their lives, then. Eh?"

"We should be ready to strike the bell in case any of them venture too close," Harry put forward. "Just in case the flames are too faint to signal them through this rain."

Christopher looked to the village side of the platform he stood upon. There was a ladder leading to the ground. Beside it, a tall stand bolted to the deck with a short arm of iron stretched towards him. Swinging in the breeze, fastened to a short length of chain, was a heavy iron bar.

"Where's the hammer?" he asked.

"On the floor, by the fire." Harry pointed to a short-handled mallet resting by the stone wall.

Christopher peered at the ocean and counted the lights rising and falling, disappearing momentarily behind dark waves before reappearing again.

There were eight.

A shrill scream broke the air around them, echoing from the northern road and over the village below the beacon tower.

Thornton sat up.

The call had broken his sleep, and for a moment he forgot where he was.

She moved her hand over his thigh, bringing him back to reality.

"It's not morning yet," she groaned.

He knew he had heard something.

Perhaps it was just part of a dream he was having.

He lowered himself beside her and wrapped his arms around her, closing his eyes.

The walls creaked as the wind howled outside. Loud, hard tapping against the windowpane signalled the continuing downpour. The breeze passing between the tavern and the natural rock formation to its side made a high whistle.

Maybe that's what I heard, he surmised.

It continued for some time, growing louder as the wind increased its speed before droning away as the draught backed off a little.

I'm sure that was what I heard.

He relaxed and snuggled against the young woman.

The shrill cry was closer this time.

He was up again.

So was she.

"You heard that?" he asked, assuring himself it wasn't a dream.

"Yes," she whispered.

He swung his legs over the side of the bed and searched for his clothes. She did the same, not wanting to be left alone in the room.

The two dressed quickly. Thornton slipped his boots on without doing the laces up. He grabbed his sword and moved to the door.

Ursula was on his heels the entire way, moving along the dark corridor towards the doorway into the main room of the tavern.

Jendryng and Sparrow were both on the stairs, weapons in hands and shirtless.

"Did you hear it too, Captain?" the younger man asked.

"Yes," he answered. "Where's your clothing, lads?"

"Sorry, sir," Sparrow replied. "I didn't expect to be seeing any ladies tonight."

"That's not what I meant." Thornton continued to the doorway. "It's fucking cold. You should be covered up."

Thornton crossed the room to a window by the door. Ursula was holding onto his shoulders so tightly he could feel her fingers digging into his flesh.

Sparrow and Jendryng moved to another window that looked out towards the stable. The wind rattled the frame and rain streaked the glass so much that it was hard to see more than a few yards.

"There," the younger soldier called.

"Where?" The captain peered along the street outside and saw nothing.

"Upon the road," the other replied.

Ursula pressed her head against Thornton's so she could see what he saw.

"How can you see anything out there?" she asked.

A great blast of light exploded in the sky, followed by a terrible roar of thunder.

At that moment, she saw several shadowy forms race along the northern road.

"It's them," she gasped. "They're coming."

Thornton watched as the figures lined up on the road, standing at full height like men. He couldn't tell if they were facing towards the woods beyond the road, or to the village.

"Why don't they attack?" Jendryng asked.

"I count eight," Sparrow informed them. "Perhaps they know we outnumber them."

"You really think those you can see are the only ones out there right now?" the captain questioned.

Sparrow pursed his lips and shook his head.

Another three appeared from the shadows and joined the line on the road.

"Why don't they attack?" Thornton whispered, repeating Jendryng's words.

The feeling of her fingers pressing against his shoulders, the warm touch of her skin against his face caused him to speculate a reason for the creatures' apprehension.

He kept his thoughts to himself, continuing to watch the figures on the road.

Another shrill scream caused a pit to form in his gut.

This is it.

He gripped his blade and prepared to move to the door.

In his mind, he saw the creatures scurrying down the street towards the tavern, attacking the inhabitants of the buildings between the stable and where he stood.

Instead, they vanished, running away towards the woods on the far side of the road.

Lightning flashed.

The creatures were gone.

The road was empty.

"With everyone in their beds, they had the best opportunity to attack," Sparrow said. "What game are they playing? Did they know we were watching?"

"No, they did not," Thornton answered. "And they're not playing any game. I think they're testing for defences."

"Defences?" Ursula hissed. "We have none here."

"Yes, you do," he replied, turning to face her. She looked at him, puzzled. "You, Ursula. You are what they fear."

"Me?" She shook her head. "I don't understand."

"You have magic in you." He placed his arm around her waist. The other two men looked on with interest, absorbing to the captain's words. "They seem to be attracted to it and fearful of it at the same time. You know who once dwelled in the White Keep, don't you?"

"Yes." She nodded nervously. "Sumaiya Tarkin, the White Witch. Everyone in these parts knows that."

"She's a witch," Sparrow gasped.

"No." She shook her head. "I'm not one of them."

"You are," Thornton assured her. "You told me what you did to your father and brother when you defended yourself against them. Only a witch could do such a thing."

"But, I don't want to hurt anyone." She wept.

"Not all witches have evil intent, Ursula." Thornton rested his sword against the wall and wrapped his other arm around her. "Our queen, Amicia Elynbrigge, was one of the Mirikin. The very coven of which the White Witch was prime. She fought against them, rebelled for the sake of humanity. She has no evil intent in her and we serve her gladly."

"A good witch?"

"I don't know about *good*." He smiled. "I'm not sure if anyone is truly good. But she is not evil. And neither are you, as far as I can tell."

He wiped her eyes.

"They fear you," Sparrow offered.

She looked over at the other two men.

"I've done nothing…" she searched for the correct word, "…*magical* ever since what I did to my father and brother. How could they know I possess this…?" She shrugged.

"I don't know," Thornton answered. "But it's the only thing that makes sense to me." He looked over at the two soldiers. "Get dressed, wake up the rest of second squad and Lieutenant Brook. I want some-one watching that road at all times."

"Yessir," the two men replied before moving away to the stairwell.

"And you, my lady," he said as he looked into her deep blue eyes, "are going to stay inside this building until I come back for you."

"Come back for me?"

"I'm taking my men to the White Keep at first light," he told her. "When I return, we are both getting on that ship and sailing to Newholt together."

"But your mission?"

"My priorities have changed somewhat," he explained. "You are my mission, now."

Twenty-Five

It was as if the sun hadn't risen.

Dark clouds covered the sky, and rain continued to fall steadily. The storm, however, had moved out to sea, making conditions a little more bearable as the troop moved towards the road.

Their boots splashed loudly in the small puddles and tiny tributaries formed by the deluge overnight. A very dull light that seemed to struggle through the clouds dimly lit the world around them.

Everything appeared grey, wet and bleak.

The men crouched in a line upon the northern road, peering into the forest ahead of them. Thornton slid his gaze over the trees, paying attention to the deep shadows under the pines and the small spaces between the thick patches of undergrowth.

"Are they afraid of the sun?" London asked.

"What sun?" Brook quipped.

"We hug the rock wall all the way in." Thornton pointed to the tendril extending from the mountain with his sword.

Jendryng peered up towards the tip of the Great Horn. A thick cloud skirted the monolithic landmass at its middle.

"We could get trapped with no escape if we do that, sir," London offered.

"We could get surrounded if we go straight in through the trees," the captain replied. "There's no tactical advantage in either case. We have an enemy we don't understand and a terrain we have not explored. At least we know we can follow that rock back to the road if we see any trouble."

"We going to sit here and talk about it all day, or go in there?" Vawdrey remarked.

Thornton smiled at the soldier before charging along the road towards the rock tendril. The troop followed closely.

They paused again where the rock had been cut open to allow the northern road to pass through. The captain waited until all his men had caught up before venturing off the road and across the grass, keeping the rock to his right.

It wasn't long before they were in the woods, running through low shrubbery and ducking beneath crooked limbs of deciduous trees.

It was hard going as they clambered over small rises and down shallow gullies, sliding across wet stones and slipping through the mud.

All the while, they tried to maintain their silence as they peered to their left, searching the shade under the trees for any sign of the dark creatures that may lurk about.

Eventually, they came to a black stone wall that extended from the tendril of rock, crossing their path and leading to the south.

Thick vines had claimed most of the structure, webbing across it in all directions like dark, protruding veins.

The extended section of the mountain was too perilous to climb. The rain had created several tiny waterfalls all over the exposed rock. These would pose a hindrance to the soldiers.

Thornton signalled to his men. He intended to follow the wall towards the forest.

The troop followed the structure a short distance, dodging around trees that had grown too close to the stonework before moving back to the right to hug the wall as they edged deeper and deeper into the woods.

The wall turned back towards the west. The captain noticed they were now following an overgrown path. Broken sections of the wall presented gaps wide enough to climb through.

Thornton signalled his men to halt before he hoisted his upper body through one of the larger holes.

He saw rocky ground and a steep incline on the other side. The terrain was too rough to cross, even though it was a shorter distance to a gigantic structure further within.

"What's in there?" Brook asked quietly as his commander lowered himself back to the ground.

"The keep," he replied. "I think we can get to it more easily if we keep on this trail."

With that, the troop continued, working their way along the wall until they came to a large gatehouse.

It had seen better days.

The gates had rotten away and part of the stonework had fallen, giving the appearance to the structure of having a great, yawning mouth.

"Keep your eyes peeled," Thornton told his men as he stepped cautiously into the building.

With their swords at the ready, the men placed their feet carefully, quietly, as they passed through the short corridor.

Beyond the gatehouse was a large, overgrown courtyard, surrounded by high walls.

A few trees and wild foliage had taken root, lifting pavers and breaking sections of the walls away.

The keep stood tall, brandishing scars of age. Thick cracks had formed in her walls, and one of her four towers had crumbled away.

Thornton's gaze moved directly to the large doors.

Black stains clung to the frame where fire had left its mark behind.

Staying close, the troop moved to the doorway and stepped inside.

The first thing they all noticed was the absence of a ceiling. Some sections of overhanging stone remained in place where stairwells once stood. But the roof, far above them, was gone.

"Fire did this," Cobham pointed out in a whisper. "The walls are all blackened with char."

His voice resonated around the room, bouncing off the walls and disappearing into the air above.

CLANG!

The sound of a bell clanging in the distance caused some alarm amongst them. The men looked to each other concernedly.

"What was that?" Vawdrey asked.

"Shhh," Thornton hissed, regretting it at the very moment he made the sound. It, too, echoed about.

They could hear several soft clicks coming from the shadows under a partly destroyed stairwell.

More echoed them from a fireplace across the way.

"They're here," Jendryng stated.

More clicks echoed from high above, in regions of the building the men couldn't see.

CLANG!

"They're everywhere," Brook said.

A shrill cry, from somewhere deep inside the keep, pierced their senses.

Rumblings and scratching sounds erupted around them.

They were moving.

"There's too many, sir," London suggested.

"I think you're right, Lieutenant," Thornton agreed. "Let's get the fuck out of here."

The troop turned and bolted back through the doorway as fast as they could.

The room filled with screams and sounds of movement as they ran across the courtyard and through the gatehouse.

CLANG!

They sped along the side of the wall, heading as quickly as they could toward the northern road.

Three creatures lunged over the stone barrier and landed on the ground before them. They emitted a loud cry, baring their long, white, needle-like teeth.

Thornton swung his sword and planted his blade into the top of one's head. Another creature lunged for the captain, only to meet the edge of Jendryng's blade.

CLANG!

The young soldier almost cut the creature in two, slicing deep into the abdomen and cutting through to the hip.

By the time it fell to the ground, losing its innards, Thornton was already hacking into the third figure.

"Go," he ordered his men.

They ran by him as he pulled his blade free from the fallen creature. He was now at the rear of the troop, listening to the hoots and screams of the horde pursuing them.

CLANG!

"Faster," he hollered.

London, at the front of the group, turned left to follow the wall back to the stone tendril.

"Forward," the captain commanded. "Don't turn. Keep going forward."

"The road's this way," Brook yelled, passing London as he skidded to a halt, correcting his direction.

"Oh, shit!" Cobham huffed as he pumped his legs as fast as they could go.

CLANG!

Another scream behind them signalled the creatures were still coming.

The men fanned out as they scurried through the woods, hacking at any growth that stood in their way.

Crunching twigs and rustling shrubbery filled the air behind Thornton as he put all his energy into running.

CLANG!

"Where's the damn road?" Bacon hollered.

Suddenly, they burst onto the open grass at the edge of the forest. The road was directly ahead of them.

CLANG!

Shrill screams and more hooting calls filled the woods behind them as they got through the thick grass and cross the road. They had come out of the woods a little to the south of the small village.

CLANG!

Thornton turned to see countless dark figures burst from the tree-line and race across the grass towards them.

CLANG!

"Get to the tavern," he called. "Get to the fucking tavern, now."

The troop sped along the road to the little street that stretched towards the dock.

CLANG!

As the other continued to the porch of the tavern, Thornton stopped near the stable and turned.

CLANG!

The creatures crowded along the road, snarling and clawing at the ground.

CLANG!

There were too many to count.

CLANG!

He knew his men wouldn't be able to hold them back.

CLANG!

"What is all that infernal ringing for?" Monteacute hollered, storming from his cabin as he tucked his shirt into his trousers.

CLANG!

"Ship coming in," a man called from the direction of the dock. "By the gods."

CLANG!

"What?" Monteacute asked.

CLANG!

The dockhand was staring along the street, past Thornton and to the crowd of dark figures standing on the road.

CLANG!

Monteacute followed the man's gaze and almost fell, weak at the knees.

CLANG!

"What's wrong, Monty?" Rose called from the doorway of his cabin. She was naked and trying to hide behind the doorframe.

CLANG!

"Get back inside with the others." The sheriff pointed to her, keeping his eyes on the horde. "Stay there until I come and get you."

CLANG!

"Harry," the dockhand hollered, cupping his hands around his mouth and facing the beacon on top of the rock tendril.

CLANG!

"Harry," he repeated. "Harry!"

"What?" came a faint reply.

"Shut that infernal racket," the dockhand yelled.

"Ship's coming." The other pointed to the sea.

"Look," the dockhand pointed to the road.

Harry poked his head around the edge of the platform.

"Keep quiet," Thornton barked.

Dead silence fell upon the little village.

Thornton's grasp tightened around the hilt of his sword as he prepared for the worst.

One creature started making the strange clicking sound he had heard earlier. Others joined in, one by one, until the entire horde was alive with the sound.

"What do you want to do now, you bastards?" the captain whispered.

"George," he heard Ursula call from the tavern.

The creatures moved; like a wave on the sea, they recoiled a small distance until they were standing on the far side of the road.

"Don't come out here," he replied, stepping backwards, watching the creatures. He continued his slow retreat down the street until he reached the bakery.

A woman was inside, frozen on the spot. Her hands were wrist-deep in dough and all colour had left her face.

"Go to the tavern," Thornton instructed her. "Slowly."

She nodded uncomfortably and moved, hesitating and turning to the oven behind her.

"There are loaves baking in there," she whimpered.

"Let them burn," he told her. "Move now."

She stepped out of the building and walked towards the other soldiers behind Thornton.

The clicking continued to resound from the roadside, mixing with the tapping of the rain falling upon the ground around them.

Thornton looked over to Monteacute.

"Get those men down from the tower," he ordered. "And tell that dockhand not to let anyone step off those ships. I'll come down and speak to the captains personally."

"Are they going to attack?" The sheriff watched the creatures with a growing fear in his eyes.

"I don't know what they're doing," the soldier replied. "And tell those girls to get back inside the tavern, now."

Monteacute assented uneasily and moved away to his cabin.

Thornton reached the porch and stepped up to the door.

The creatures hadn't moved since they retreated a short distance to the grass.

"George." Ursula stepped out through the door and wrapped her arms around him.

"I thought I told you to stay inside."

"I'm sorry," she said.

"I'm not." He leaned in and kissed her forehead.

"What do we do, sir?" Brook asked. "I don't think they'll give us much of a chance to continue with our mission."

"Mission's over," the captain replied. "Gather everyone you can and what belongings you can carry. We're hopping on those vessels and getting the fuck out of here."

Twenty-Six

The *Gypsy*, a three-mast schooner, docked to the left side of the port. The gangplank lowered and a young woman disembarked immediately.

She was tall and quite attractive, dressed in a long coat and leggings with a thin rapier on her hip. Her hair draped over her shoulder in a braid under a wide-brimmed cavalier hat.

Her attention fell directly on Thornton, the only man in any form of military attire, his leather armour and breastplate.

"You need to get yer people on board," she said.

"A woman?" the dockhand, an older man, gasped.

"Put yer eyes back in yer head," she scolded.

"I was about to ask you if you would allow us on board," he replied. "A few of the villagers are grabbing what valuables they have as we speak."

"Hoist the anchor," a call came from onboard the *Sophia*.

"We don't have much room," she explained. "I can't take livestock or horses."

Thornton peered back to the stable and gave a quick moment's thought to the steeds. The dark mass standing on the other side of the road caused him to evaluate the situation quickly.

"Fine," he said.

"Raise the sails," came the voice from the *Sophia*.

"Dear me," the woman murmured. "Those bastards are here already?"

"Those bastards have been here the whole time," the soldier replied.

215

"Why aren't they attacking?"

"That's a long story that I don't think we have time for," he answered. He extended his hand to her. "Captain George Thornton of the Newholt guard."

She kept her attention on the creatures as she introduced herself. "Captain Davine Staiger. My ship, the *Gypsy*. Have you spoken to the commander of this other ship yet?"

"Yes," he replied. "Captain Alington is leaving. He has already taken most of the townsfolk on board. There are only my men, William here," Thornton gestured to the dockhand, "the sheriff and four ladies in the tavern."

"How many men are you in yer troop?"

"Ten, including myself," he replied.

"That's sixteen." Staiger frowned. She peered back at the road. "Are you sure you have everyone else on board the *Sophia*?"

"We checked all the buildings," Thornton grunted. "There's no one else."

"Then we best get moving," she said, turning back to the ship. "I'll see you onboard."

"I'll need to get the horses," he told her.

"I said, no horses." She glared at him.

"I understand," he replied. "But I need to set them free. Give them a chance against these things."

She moved her gaze to the barn and back to the soldier.

"Get yer people to the ship," she told him. "We'll wait for you. But be quick about it."

"Get ready to release the moorings, William," Thornton told the dockhand.

"Aye sir," the other replied with a salute.

Returning hastily to the tavern, Thornton approached Lieutenants Brook and London, who were both watching the horde from the porch.

"Escort everyone to the *Gypsy*," he ordered. "Captain Staiger has agreed to take us."

"To where, sir?"

"Who gives a shit?" he replied, stepping through the door. "Anywhere but here would be nice."

Thornton peered around and saw his men, Monteacute, and the three whores. But there was no sign of Ursula.

"Where is she?"

"She went back there, sir," Sparrow answered, pointing to the doorway at the side of the room.

"Get to the ship," he told them as he moved into the corridor. He quickly passed by the stairwell and into Ursula's room at the end of the passage.

She was there, foraging through a chest of drawers.

"What are you doing?" he asked. "It's time to leave."

She turned and held up a small hessian bag.

"Money," she explained. "I almost left without it."

"You're more important than that." He took her by the arm. "Come on."

"It's not mine," she told him as they moved back into the corridor. "It belongs to the girls."

He nodded, understanding.

"You have it now," he said. "So, let's get you to the ship."

The tavern was empty.

Thornton led Ursula through the room and outside. He turned to see the troop moving along the road towards the dock.

The *Sophia* was already pulling away with the wind filling her sails.

"Vawdrey," Thornton called.

The soldier turned and jogged back to his captain, splashing water with each step.

"Sir?"

"Escort Miss Wadham to the *Gypsy*."

"Yessir," he assented, before gesturing to the dock. "This way, my lady."

"Where are you going?" she asked, her eyes wide with terror.

He was already walking along the street towards the stable.

"I need to set the horses free," he called back.

"George, no," she cried.

"My lady, please," Vawdrey urged.

"Go with him, Ursula," Thornton yelled over the rain. "I'll be right there."

Reluctantly, she followed Vawdrey to the dock, peering back to see the old soldier disappear into the barn.

The creatures followed him with their stares until he was out of their sight. Then, one by one, they turned their gaze upon her.

Leering at her.

Grinning with their long, white teeth.

The maddening clicking sound continued to resound through the air.

"My lady," Vawdrey called from the gangplank.

"I need to make sure he is safe," she told him as she stood upon the dock.

William loosened the stern rope attached to the mooring. He tossed it up to a crewman on board the *Gypsy*.

"I'm sure he'll be fine," the dockhand told her.

"I need to see," she replied.

Thornton moved to the far stall in the stable and opened the pen's gate. He checked to make sure the horse wasn't tethered before moving to its hindquarters, where he gave it a slap on the rump.

The steed whinnied in protest and bolted through the stable and out through the doors.

Thornton repeated the process, moving along to each stall, some housing two beasts to save space.

With the last horse outside, Thornton jogged back into the rain and onto the street.

The horses were milling about at the edge of the road, seemingly unsure of what to do.

The dark creatures flexed their claws and opened their jaws, moving their regard from the animals to the lone man standing a few yards away.

"Yah!" Thornton bellowed, raising his arms and waving his sword.

The horses flinched but didn't run.

He shook his head.

"You're on your own," he said, turning his attention to the dark creatures. They seemed to be all watching him.

"There he is," Vawdrey pointed. "Now, come aboard."

"I should wait for him," she replied.

"Come on, Ursula," William appealed. "Please, get on board. Don't make an old fart like me beg."

She looked at the old man and felt pity. Water had soaked through her clothing and dribbled over her skin. He had been in the elements for far longer than her.

"All right," she conceded, hugging the hessian bag to her chest.

Reluctantly, she stepped upon the gangplank.

One of the dark creatures edged forward slowly.

The horses trotted away to the south, moving amongst the tents and temporary structures near the side of the street.

Thornton stepped back, keeping the horde in view.

The one creature, moving towards him slowly, lowered itself to all fours and started crossing the well-worn road that continued to the north.

Ursula took Vawdrey's hand as she moved along the gangplank.

It felt unsteady, wobbling with each step that she took.

"Almost there," he said as he tried to steady her ascend to the deck.

She placed her boot upon the deck of the *Gypsy*, sensing a sturdier surface beneath her.

"There you are." The soldier steadied her as she placed both feet on board.

"Welcome aboard the *Gypsy*," Staiger called from the quarterdeck. "Now, where's yer captain?"

Thornton continued moving backwards along the road. He reached the baker's house, staring at the creature that slunk towards him.

It crawled across the road, scraping at the soggy ground with each stride.

Pausing at the road's edge, it reached its claws to the ground on the street leading into the small village.

Testing the territory, Thornton thought.

It edged forward a little more.

Apprehensively.

Touching the ground, sniffing the air.

A little further.

A little more.

Thornton was level with the tavern now.

He gripped his sword tightly in his hand.

The creature reached the stable and stood at full height.

It expanded its chest, sucking in air.

A long, ear-splitting scream pierced the air, drowning out all other noises around about.

The horses squealed and raced away towards the south, keeping between the road and the sea.

The horde moved as one, like a flowing tide, towards the tiny village.

"Fuck me," Thornton spat as he turned and ran for the dock.

William saw the oncoming wave of terror.

He hastily untied the mooring line and raced for the gangplank.

"Go," he hollered. "Go. Go. Get out of here."

"George?" Ursula screamed, racing to the side of the ship to peer back along the dock.

He was running as fast as he could along the wooden structure, past the dock house and nearing the ship.

The horde split into two groups.

One chased the horses that were racing away.

The other scrambled down the street and flowed past the baker's house, across the tavern's porch and towards the dock.

"Raise the sails," Staiger called. "Hoist the anchor. Let's go!"

The crew acted immediately.

The *Gypsy* was already moving as Thornton started up the gangplank.

"Come on, sir," Vawdrey stretched his hand out to his captain.

The gangplank tilted to the right as the ship pulled away from the dock.

The old soldier thought he was going to end up in the drink and, therefore, fodder for the creatures on his tail.

He reached out and grasped the younger man's arm just as the plank splashed into the water.

The creatures crowded upon the dock, racing along its surface, pushing those on the sides into the sea in their overzealous attempt to get to Thornton.

Vawdrey pulled the captain safely onto the deck.

As the ship pulled away, heading towards the open ocean, the passengers on board the *Gypsy* peered back to shore, the creatures standing where the land met the sea.

Thornton got up and leant against the railing, moving his gaze to the south. The dark figures were engaged in a savage flurry, tearing into the steeds he had let free only moments ago.

Suddenly, the creatures turned and fled on all fours, leaving the village and racing away towards the south.

"Where are they going?" Ursula asked.

"The only places left for them to continue with their ghastly deed," Captain Staiger replied, sidling up to them. "They've destroyed everything north of here. Blackrock Haven is empty and the mountain men are no more."

"You know this?" Thornton asked. "That the settlers in the mountains are gone?"

"Aye," she said. "Men from Blackrock Haven searched and found no trace of anyone, except blood."

"They attacked Blackrock Haven yesterday," one crewman offered. "Tore through the town in less than an hour."

"We have a few people on board down below," Staiger told them. "Most of the other ships loaded up with passengers and left during the night. We were the last to leave."

"Did you get everyone out?" Jendryng asked.

"Only the living, boy," she said as she turned and started towards the wheelhouse. "And the living are few."

Twenty-Seven

The chestnut stallion was tethered to a small wagon, loaded with bundles of goods being moved from the larger cavern to the new Agrodien homes. Alice led the beast by the reins, walking along a track the continuous traffic had worn into the ground over the past few days.

"We should level this out a bit," said Arthur, walking beside her. He had a large pack filled with blankets strapped to his back, causing him to struggle with each step as they traversed a slight incline to the dwellings. "Make the path wider and line it with logs to prevent the surface from washing away in the rain."

"Let's wait until we have everyone indoors first," she replied, looking out to the clearing where the encampment of temporary housing stood. "We'll have plenty of time to beautify the place, then."

"I know," he agreed. "But I can see it all clearly in my head right at this moment."

"Whoa," she said to the horse, pulling up outside of a newly constructed dwelling. Lor and one of the Agrodien warriors were working on a veranda for the structure. The porch's frame had been completed, and the two were now hammering planks of wood into place for the floor.

"Kayl'sro," the reptilian said as he stood and bowed slightly.

"No, Nakrah." She held her hand up. "That's not necessary. I could use some help taking this load inside."

"I help." He placed his hammer onto the completed section of the veranda, next to a box of nails, and stepped towards the cart.

"As will I," Lor offered. "I can't let my favourite niece do everything on her own."

He walked to her and kissed her on the head before moving to assist Nakrah with the goods.

"Someone could help me get this thing off my back," Arthur suggested as he flailed his arms in an attempt to drop the pack from his shoulders.

"Here." Alice let the reins go and stepped in front of him, using her thumbs to flick the straps from him. The pack flopped heavily to the ground.

Arthur instantly felt twelve feet taller and a hundred pounds lighter as he sighed a deep breath of relief.

"Thank the gods," he said, crouching low and standing upright, stretching his legs.

"No thanking me?" Alice asked.

He wrapped his arms around her waist.

"Thank you," he said before planting a kiss on her cheek. "Thank you," he pecked her on her nose. "Thank you," he kissed her forehead. "Thank you," his lips pressed into her eye. "Thank you."

"All right," she giggled. "All right. No more."

"But I haven't even covered your face yet." Arthur frowned playfully. "And there is so much more of you I would like to kiss."

"Steady on, now," Lor called. "There are people watching. No one needs to see this."

"Sorry, Uncle." Alice grinned.

"You know," he said. "The two of you could be helping."

"We could?" Arthur chuckled.

Alice smacked him in the arm friskily and moved to assist with unloading the cart.

"Ow." The young man rubbed his arm.

"Get over here and help," she laughed.

Arthur started towards the cart.

Something tapped him on the head.

"That better not have been a bird," he said, peering up at the trees.

A drop of water landed on his cheek.

The rain was coming.

***

Takmel sat at the table eating a hearty breakfast of eggs, sausage, and toast.

"Anything else, birthday boy?" Catherine asked.

"Nothing more," he said, holding up a hand. "I'll be too full to move soon."

"Don't overdo it today," Joanne grinned. She was tidying up in the kitchen after helping to cook the meal. "You know what tonight holds for you."

He knew.

How could he forget?

"What do you have planned for the day?" Lucy asked as she cleared the table.

"Not too much," he answered. "I may go for a walk in the fields later."

"Shouldn't you spend the day resting?" Joanne asked.

He locked eyes with her and read some flare rising behind them.

His influence upon her was waning already.

She was fighting him from within.

The night couldn't come soon enough.

"I'll be more than ready when the time arrives," he told her. "Don't worry about me."

She couldn't hold her stare, moving her gaze away to look at anything but him.

The other two women seemed oblivious to her condition.

He placed his knife and fork on the empty plate sitting before him.

"I think I'll take that walk now," he said, standing up from the table.

"Should we accompany you?" Catherine asked hopefully.

"No," he replied. "I think I need to be alone for a little while. I'll be back soon."

*****

The wind carried them southward with great speed.

Staiger stood upon the quarterdeck of the *Gypsy*, scanning the horizon with a long spyglass.

"The *Sophia* sails ahead of us," she called to Thornton. "There is smoke coming from the shore."

"How can you tell?" Bacon asked, holding his hand up to the rain. "The sky is grey, and the world is thick with this misery."

"Smoke is black," she answered, folding the spyglass away.

"What could be burning?" Ursula moved to the banister. She held a canvas sheet over her head to keep the rain away from her already soaked skin.

Thornton squinted, peering to the land on their right, trying to work out how far they had travelled.

"It's the lighthouse," he growled.

"The lighthouse?" Cobham gasped. "You mean the village near that ruin?"

The old soldier nodded.

Cobham's face dropped. He shook his head slowly and shuffled away.

"Oh no," Brook murmured.

"What is it?" Thornton asked.

"The baker's daughter," the lieutenant replied. "He had a brief romance with her."

The older man looked over at Ursula and wiped the rain from his face, or at least that's what he told himself.

"What do you think caused the fire?" Jendryng asked, squinting into the weather to see the smoke for himself.

"Those things," Monteacute suggested. "Maybe they set the place aflame."

"I don't think so," Sparrow replied. "We didn't see them strike fire back at White Keep. Did you see anything of the like at Blackrock Haven?"

"No." Captain Staiger shook her head. "We saw animals tearing at the flesh of men. There was no fire. Either the villagers set torches to the place themselves or it resulted from an accident."

"It matters not," Thornton told them, turning to see Cobham sobbing on the deck with his back against the railing at port bow. "The creatures are ahead of us. That's all that matters now."

***

Brondt stood upon a balcony overlooking the northern sector of the city. Below, he could see people bustling about, buying and selling in the streets, racing from one awning to another in the hope to avoid getting wet.

His eyes moved to the horizon, where the ocean met the sky. Both appeared a dull grey, and with the rain falling steadily, it was hard to see where the two met.

But several dark forms had appeared in the haze, riding upon the sea from the north. It wasn't unusual to see ships on the horizon. After all, Newholt was a city of commerce and trade. Many vessels came from lands far away.

But it was odd to see so many coming from the north at the same time.

Something in his guts told him to be alarmed.

He turned and stepped from the balcony and through the large double door leading back into the palace. He started down a long corridor, passing several doors on either side of him, before descending a large stairwell to the lower floor.

"Commander," the guards would acknowledge, standing at attention as he walked by.

He entered a large sitting room where a fire roared in a massive stone recess set against the wall to the right.

Amicia was there, sitting in a deep seat to the left, reading. He moved towards her gingerly.

"The ships are coming," she said, not looking away from the pages of the book she read.

"They are," he replied.

"The people on board will need blankets, food and shelter." She closed the book and looked at him. "We should also inform the generals to set their garrisons on all sides of the city."

"Of course." He was about to turn, but felt she may still need him. "Is there anything else, my love?"

"If you could build a wall around our city before nightfall..." She smiled nervously.

"I don't think so, my love." He furrowed his brow.

She put the book on a side table and walked to him, placing her hands on his shoulders.

"Be careful," she told him. "The shadow is coming."

He nodded, planting a kiss on her forehead. "I will."

Soon, Brondt was in the barracks, standing around a table with the generals of Newholt. A large map of the city stretched out before them.

"Is this the latest plan?" Brondt asked the surrounding men.

"I fetched it from the Magistrate's office, sir," a soldier replied. "It should be up-to-date."

"All right." The commander scrutinized the layout of the city. "We should set catapults here, here and here," he said, pointing to locations along the northern edge of the city, close to the sea. "Another three here, here and here."

"Why there, sir, if I may ask?" one general queried.

"They are more likely to attack from the north," Brondt explained. "We should concentrate our defences in that region. I will want some of our catapults spread along the western edge, just in case they try to flank us."

"And to the south?" another general enquired.

"We'll put one garrison," the commander replied. "We can't let the enemy get that far around us though, gentlemen."

"What do we know of this threat?" another asked. "Who are they? What do they want?"

"I can't answer that." Brondt looked to the other before moving his gaze over all gathered about. "I'm running on instinct and feeling here. The queen has sensed a darkness approaching."

"Permission to speak freely, sir?" a general asked.

"Speak."

"From experience," he began, "I've seen our queen react to visions and feelings she has had before. I've not seen her ever be wrong about any of them. So, if Queen Amicia has concerns, then we all should pay careful attention."

"Aye," the generals chorused.

"And the reserves, sir?" asked a lieutenant standing behind his superiors.

"Are you in command of our reserve force, Lieutenant?" Brondt asked, sizing the man up.

The officer was robust and a little well-aged to be such a low-ranking officer. A leather patch sat over his left eye and a deep scar stretched over his forehead above and cheek beneath.

"Yessir," he replied proudly, standing up straight.

"I need the reserve forces at the docks," the commander explained. "Ships are coming from the north with people in need. Blankets, warm food, bread, shelter. You will need to organise all of that. Are you up to it, Lieutenant?"

"Yessir." He saluted.

"All right, gentlemen." Brondt peered back to the map. "Let's coordinate our forces."

Some time later, the military leaders broke their meeting and departed to get things underway.

Brondt jogged across the palace courtyard to catch up with the leader of the reserve forces.

"Lieutenant," he called.

The other turned to face the commander, saluting and standing to attention.

"At ease," Brondt commanded. "I think I remember you. You fought at Woodmyst?"

"Yessir," the other replied, pointing to his eyepatch. "I got this souvenir fighting on the field."

"You were a lieutenant then, yes?"

"Yessir," he confirmed.

"What is your name?"

"Landon Wake, sir."

"Why didn't you apply for promotion?" the commander asked. "Why didn't anyone else promote you?"

"I didn't want it, sir," Wake answered. "After Woodmyst, I would have rather retired from the service than have continued on. But I don't know how to be anything but a soldier. And, as commander of the reserves, I can help people without having to use my sword. Handing out blankets and seeing mouths fed is far more rewarding to me than wielding any weapon. I apologise if I sound cowardly, sir."

"Not at all," Brondt replied, clasping a hand onto the man's arm. "Do your duty and stay safe."

"Thank you, sir." He saluted again and was rewarded with acknowledgment from his commander.

With that, Lieutenant Landon Wake turned and walked away through the rain.

Twenty-Eight

The light of day had dimmed as the sun, veiled by thick clouds, moved low in the western sky. The *Gypsy* continued to tail the *Sophia*, racing with the wind as a new storm front chased them over the sea.

Rising and falling over each wave, Thornton kept his eye on the ship in the distance. His stomach was swirling, and he was using every ounce of energy that he could muster to control the urge to throw up.

White spray exploded over the deck with each long crash to the surface. The vessel lurched back up again as they hit the next wave, rising to its crest, where the ship seemed to linger for a long time. Then down she came, sliding over the water's surface at an immense speed before another explosion of sea and salt swept over them.

"Oakbeach." Captain Staiger pointed towards the shore.

The soldiers peered over the rail, trying to see the port town.

The land was dark and there was no sign of life in or near the buildings they could make out in the haze.

"Do you think the creatures got to them?" Rose asked from the shelter of the galley, near the front of the ship. She stood in the doorway, poking her head out to view the town.

"Either that or they fled," said Sparrow. "There'd be light in the windows if there were anyone home."

"How long until we reach Newholt?" Thornton called to the captain.

"Within the hour at this speed," she answered, turning to see lightning flashing through the clouds far behind them. "Perhaps sooner if the wind picks up. Which I think it will."

231

"Why the rush to get home, sir?" London asked.

"I hate the ocean," the older soldier replied. "And I think we'll be safer there."

"What makes one city like Newholt safer than any of the other towns and villages we've passed?" William, the dockhand, queried.

Thornton looked to the galley, where Ursula and the three ladies she supervised were now located.

"Just a hunch," he said, looking towards the shore as Oakbeach moved away from them.

Thornton moved his eyes back to the ship sailing far ahead of them.

White spray hit the deck again.

Silently, he prayed they would get to Newholt sooner than the captain predicted.

With luck, they wouldn't have seen the horde approaching them yet.

With luck, his intuition about the creatures was correct.

***

Takmel was crossing the centre bridge through the town.

The rain was teeming down and his coat, lifted over his head, offered little shelter from the onslaught. There was no one else in the street, save for a few packing their stores away and closing shutters over their windows.

He heard footprints racing towards him from ahead.

"My lord," a voice called. Takmel saw a guard jogging down the paved street.

"Yes," he answered.

"You have been summoned to the assembly hall," the guard informed him.

"Thank you," Takmel replied, starting towards the centre of the city.

Moments later, he walked past two guards and through the giant doors of the building. Seated on the platform were all seven members of the council with Catherine and Lucy positioned at either end of the line of chairs.

The doors thudded closed behind him as he moved along the aisle.

Takmel turned to see the guards were now gone.

"We are alone," Joanne told him. Her voice reverberated through the room so it lingered, almost an echo. "I've sent the guards to the wall for their night duties."

Distant thunder called from far away.

"The sun is almost gone for the day," said Tricia, dressed in scarlet and seated by her prime's side.

"Do you bring the storm?" Isabel, the white woman, asked.

"I do," he replied, moving towards the platform slowly.

"So!" Joanne got up. "You are powerful after all."

"I will be," he said confidently, "after tonight."

"Do you remember what you must do?" Joanne started down the stairs, descending from the stage and onto the floor.

"Yes," he answered, peeling off his wet coat and shirt and dropping them to the floor.

"All of us or none at all," she said. "Part of us does not want you to succeed, Maji."

"I know." He started untying the cords on his trousers.

Joanne dropped her black cloak to the stone floor, baring her flesh to him.

"Dusk has come," Gilda, the jade woman, announced.

"Then we begin," Joanne whispered.

He took her in his arms and pressed his lips to hers.

She pulled him to the floor and wrapped her thighs around his waist, receiving him.

Isabel disrobed, discarding her scarlet clothes to the floor, as the sounds of pleasure filled the auditorium.

Thunder called again as she slowly made her way down the stairs.

A sinister smile stretched upon her face.

***

Thunder and lightning raged above Newholt as the soldiers waited with their generals for the enemy to arrive.

They hadn't seen hide or hair of anyone on the northern road, and no sign of life flanking their positions to the west of the city.

Ships had moored to the docks, and soldiers on the docks redirected the passengers to empty warehouses where Lieutenant Wake had set up cots, blankets, and a kitchen that had large pots of stew over small campfires.

"How many more out there?" Wake asked the captain of the last vessel to dock.

They were standing at the edge of the pier near the large door of the warehouse.

"The *Gypsy* was the only ship behind me at Blackrock Haven," the man replied. "I'm not sure if she made it out or not."

"All right." The lieutenant clasped the captain's shoulder. "Get inside out of this weather and get warm."

"Thank you, sir," the other replied, moving into the building.

Wake peered out to the ocean and to the north.

It was too dark to see any vessels in the rough sea.

***

"The darkness is growing," Amicia said from her throne. She was watching Brondt pace back and forth across the floor, biting his nails nervously.

"We haven't seen battle here for centuries," he told her. "The last conflict we were involved in took place far from here. Most of those soldiers have retired to farming and shop-keeping. Our forces are made up of mere boys. Younger than I was when I first picked up a sword. I should be out there."

"No," she snapped. "You're my husba... You're my commander. I need you here to make tactical decisions. Not down there where you can get killed."

"Are you sure they're coming?" he asked, hoping she was wrong.

"Something is heading towards us," she replied, closing her eyes. "But I sense something else too."

"Something else?"

She shook her head.

"I don't know," she answered. "Something powerful. Something happening now."

Lightning flashed, and a great clasp of thunder boomed from the sky.

Amicia opened her eyes and looked at the commander.

"This has been summoned," she said.

"The storm?"

She sighed. "The shadow is upon us tonight."

***

Joanne wrapped her black cloak around her tightly as she watched Takmel and Tricia embracing on the floor.

Isabel let her white garments fall to the floor as she descended the stairs.

The auburn woman peered up to see a grimace on Isabel's face.

Am I the only one hoping he fails?

A sudden inner turmoil began as she struggled with the idea of being under his spell forever.

Part of her wanted to be rid of him. But something bigger, a larger portion, wanted him to have her again. This part longed for his power and ached for him to control her.

She didn't understand where it came from, only that it was there.

Every time she tried to fight it, she saw flashing images of Yasmeen Svoboda and Sumaiyya Tarkin.

The thunder rolled far away as Tricia let out a call of pleasure. Joanne felt sickened and excited at the same time.

Takmel pulled away from Tricia.

She giggled as Isabel lowered herself into Takmel's awaiting arms.

"He's an animal," Tricia sniggered, peering over to Joanne. "I want more."

The images of the Sovereign and the White Mistress flashed into Joanne's thoughts again as thunder resounded far above.

"Another time," Joanne said to the other. "Find your cloak."

***

"Lower the sails," Alington called as the *Sophia* made for the port. "Prepare to dock."

"Who are you?" a voice called from the pier. The captain looked across the way to see a man with an eyepatch calling to him.

"Captain Geoffrey Alington," he yelled back, "of the merchant vessel the *Sophia*. We sail from White Keep and have passengers in need of shelter."

"Were you attacked?"

"Not quite," Alington replied. "But we saw countless dark creatures on the northern road."

"Countless," Wake muttered before returning his attention to the captain of the *Sophia*. "Were they heading this way?"

"If you mean south, then yes," the other hollered.

"Guard," the lieutenant called.

A man standing nearby ran over to the officer.

"Sir?"

"Run to the palace and inform Commander Brondt that dark creatures have been spotted at White Keep and are heading south."

"Yessir," the young soldier replied, before racing away.

"Tie yourself on where you can," Wake yelled to Alington. "There's food, blankets and a place to lie down in the warehouse there."

"Will do," the captain called back with a wave. "Thank you, sir."

***

Lights onshore gave Staiger a target to aim for.

"Newholt," she called.

"Thank the gods," Thornton growled, gripping the railing tightly, hoping the contents of his stomach were going to stay in place.

"Are we safe?" Ursula called from the galley.

"We're not docked yet," the captain answered. "But we're almost there."

"It doesn't look as if they've been here yet," Kateryn said, peering through the galley window. "Maybe it's safe?"

"One could only hope." Monteacute squinted, trying to keep the rain out of his eyes.

It appeared as if the city was untouched.

Lights were burning in windows.

The palace was still standing.

Ships were moored at the docks.

"Perhaps the creatures have gone into the mountains," Jendryng offered.

"What's that?" A crewman pointed to the northern edge of the city.

Orange balls of light ignited a small distance away from the community.

"Fire!" Rose gasped. "There's another fire. Just like what happened at that settlement we passed."

"I don't think so," Thornton growled, moving across the deck to starboard beam.

Suddenly, the orange balls of light started arching through the air, flying from the city and to the north.

The passengers on the *Gypsy* watched with interest as the fireballs started falling through the sky and crashed to the ground.

The flames spread explosively, engulfing moving figures in their path.

Thornton saw masses of dark figures in the light of the flames.

They were here.

As another barrage of fireballs flung into the air from the line of catapults, Thornton pursed his lips and frowned.

It appeared they weren't any safer going to Newholt than they would have been back in White Keep.

"I was wrong," he whispered.

Twenty-Nine

With the larger cavern emptied of all supplies, and the Agrodien refugees moved to other caves, Alice led the great dragon out of the rain.

Liana sniffed at the rock walls and floor as she crawled after the girl, chirping and rumbling with her throat.

"Come on," Alice called to her, holding a flaming torch high above her head as she moved on into the cavern. She felt a growing un-easiness in her stomach, pressing a hand against her abdomen as she moved on.

Arthur, Emily and Shadow were walking ahead of them, searching the area with their own torches. The rukyul sniffed the ground and trotted a short distance beyond the firelight.

"How far inside does she need to go?" Emily asked, peering into the darkness ahead.

"I'm not sure," Alice answered.

"She was a fair distance inside the cave back in the Haigok village," Arthur stated. "Almost at the very end, I would say. How far does this cavern go?"

"A long way," Alice replied. "It narrows out a little towards the end. Too small for her to fit."

The dragon chirped again, sniffing the ceiling and the floor.

Lightning flashed outside, causing the beast to turn her head. She let out a deep growl before quickening her pace, following Alice farther inside.

"Hey," Alice called as the dragon nudged her insistently with her muzzle. She moved to the side of the cavern, pressing herself against the wall. "You want to go in so badly, there you go."

Liana moved by Alice, crawling with some urgency to get deeper into the cave.

"What's going on?" Arthur called as he saw the dragon approaching on her own.

"She's scared of the storm, I think," Alice called, holding her stomach again.

Thunder roared outside the cavern.

Liana chirped as she neared the boy.

"Best move," Emily told him, stepping aside to allow the beast through.

Shadow grunted his disapproval as he bounded to the side, watching the dragon crawl away into the darkness.

Alice followed her into the cavern.

Eventually, Liana stopped moving and turned about in a circle, wrapping her tail around her body before lying down in the dust. She looked over at the girl and chirped.

"She's frightened," Alice whispered, pressing her hand against the dragon's cheek.

"How can you tell?" Emily asked, peering at the long, protruding teeth. "She looks so menacing."

"Sometimes," her daughter explained, "the most menacing creatures are the most afraid. Their appearance scares others. But they are just as scared too."

"Did you read that in one of my books?" Arthur questioned.

"No," she replied, rubbing the dragon's neck. "I learnt it myself."

Liana closed her eyes and let a low rattle emit from deep in her throat. It reminded Arthur of a cat purring.

"Kayl'sro," a familiar voice called from the cavern's mouth. The sound of the Agrodien female's voice reverberated through the cave. "Are you here?"

Liana suddenly opened her eyes, alarmed by the intrusion. She chirped loudly.

"Shhh," Alice whispered to the dragon. She continued rubbing the beast's neck, turning her attention to the source of the voice. "I'm in here, Nola'ee."

"You need to come and see," the other called. There was a sense of urgency in her voice.

"What now?" Emily headed back to the cavern's entrance.

"Sleep, Liana," Alice whispered to the dragon. The creature closed her eyes and started purring again. The girl turned to the rukyul who was sitting on his haunches watching with interest. "You stay here, too. Watch her."

Shadow grumbled and lowered himself prostrate to the cave floor.

Nola'ee was standing just inside the mouth of the cave. Her leathery skin was dripping with water.

Lightning flashed again.

"That's getting worse, that is," Arthur observed.

"Yes," the Agrodien assented. "Much worse. Come, look."

"You want us to go out in that?" Emily pointed to the torrential rain.

Another flash of lightning revealed that others were standing in the field, peering back towards the cave. Yuri, Gharnef, Bein and Mralner were staring at the sky behind the cavern.

Alice strolled by her mother and husband, holding the torch high with one hand and pressing the palm of the other against her gut, moving into the rain without hesitation. She crossed the open pasture, approaching the awaiting Agrodien party.

Nola'ee was on her heels in an instant, leaving Arthur and Emily in the cave. The two humans glanced at each other, silently agreeing they should follow.

"Yuri," Alice called. "What troubles you?"

"Look, Kayl'sro!" He pointed to the sky behind her.

She turned to face the cavern and saw Nola'ee being followed by her mother and husband. But that wasn't what grabbed her attention. High above the mountain to which the enormous cavern belonged, farther to the south, a strange anomaly was occurring in the sky.

Lightning flashed again, revealing a swirling whirlpool of mist and cloud.

It was as if all the vapour in the air was being drawn to that one position.

Lightning flashed inside the vortex.

Thunder rolled.

"What is that?" Emily asked.

Alice felt something tighten in her stomach.

"Woodmyst," Arthur told her. "That's directly over Woodmyst."

"All darkness is being drawn together." Alice frowned. She dropped the torch to the ground, where it snuffed out in the damp grass. Her hands clutched at her stomach. "I don't feel well."

She fell to her knees hard and started falling to her side.

Arthur dropped his torch and wrapped his arms under hers, lifting her from the ground before pulling her away towards the cabin.

"Inside with you," he said. He was struggling with her as he moved, making very slow progress over the field.

"Arthur." Yuri offered his services, stepping in to lift Alice gently into his arms. He cradled her against his chest as he hurried to the hut.

Within moments, he lowered the girl onto her bed.

Emily fetched towels and started drying her daughter off.

"Thank you, Yuri," she said to the reptilian. "I'll take it from here."

"We wait?" he asked.

"No," Arthur replied, grabbing his hands in a gesture of gratitude. "I am so thankful to you, Yuri. You're a good friend. Please, go home and be with your family. I'm sure she'll be all right."

Yuri got the sense that Arthur's words were more for himself than for the Agrodien.

"I'm sure she will be," he soothed. Yuri turned to the other reptilians and ordered them out of the cabin in their tongue.

"I stay with the Kayl'sro," Nola'ee said.

"We go," Yuri told her.

"I stay," she insisted, standing defiantly by the door.

Yuri looked over at Arthur.

The boy nodded.

"She can stay," he replied, unbuttoning his wife's shirt.

"We will go," Yuri said to the others in their tongue. He turned to Nola'ee, "You guard her with your life."

She lifted her chin. "Always."

✱✱

Fireballs arced through the sky, lighting up the world below, revealing countless dark forms with grimacing smiles of sharp teeth.

They were speeding forwards, ignoring the fire in the sky and getting a large proportion of their force under the barrage from the catapults.

"Send in the troops," a general hollered.

Lieutenants along the line, set just in front of the giant timber slings, shouted the command to their men.

"Advance!"

A great roar shook the air as the men charged, holding their swords high.

"Archers," a general bellowed.

They echoed the order along the line.

Arrows filled the night sky, speeding into the wind and rain, over the advancing troops and deep into the bodies of hundreds of creatures.

"Again," the general called.

"We'll hit our men," an officer argued.

"Again, now," the other barked.

The archers let another volley loose, avoiding hitting their comrades and piercing the flesh of more dark figures.

The troops hit them next.

Swords and axes swung wildly at the beasts.

Claws swiped, and teeth gnashed at flesh.

Blood spilt.

Bones broke.

Bodies were slain.

The soldiers continued to roar with courage, cry in fear.

The creatures screamed and clicked with their throats as they leapt high into the air to attack.

Others writhed over the wet earth like worms, snapping at the ankles of men with their jaws.

***

"They'll breach the defensive line," Brondt spat, standing on the balcony of the palace where he observed the attack from the north. "I should be down there."

"I demand that you remain here," Amicia said from his side, watching on in horror. Lightning flashed above them, illuminating the scene. The horde stretched back as far as she could see in the limited time she had. "There's so many of them."

"Tell the generals to keep firing their catapults to the north," the commander called to a guard standing just inside the door.

"Yessir," the young man replied, turning to run along the corridor.

"There may be more of them than people in this city," the queen wept.

Brondt looked at her compassionately.

"Don't give up so easily, my love." He put his arms around her. "This battle has only just begun and my men have been itching for a fight for years. They are trained for this."

He was lying, and she knew it.

But it was what she needed to hear.

She pressed herself against him and peered into the darkness, watching the glints of steel in the distance as men put their lives at risk for her city.

Brave men she didn't even know.

Tears streamed down her cheeks.

***

"There's food and shelter in the warehouse." Lieutenant Wake pointed to the building at the end of the long, broad pier. "Your passengers and crew should head over there."

"Aye." Captain Davine Staiger tipped her hat to the officer. "That sounds more than appealing. Let the ladies go first, lads."

"Not fair, Captain," one crewman quipped. "You being a lady and all."

"Don't ya' ever call me such a vile thing, ya' bastard!" she spat.

Thornton assisted Ursula and the three whores along the gangplank.

"You're coming, too?" she asked the older soldier. "Aren't you, George?"

"I need to report in," he informed her. "My duty is to this city. My men and I will be required to help defend it."

"You can't leave us," Kateryn contended, looking at the men that had travelled with her. "Not now. We need you."

"Lieutenant Wake's men will take care of you," Thornton assured the four women. "And there will be quite a few seafarers in there with weapons on their hips, I would say."

He gestured to Captain Staiger and her men, all carrying rapiers on their belts.

"You'll be safe with us," the captain of the *Gypsy* agreed.

"I don't want you to leave," Ursula pleaded.

"Go inside." Thornton placed his hand upon her cheek. "Get out of this rain. I'll be back for you as soon as I can. I promise."

She placed her lips against his and held him for an eternity.

"Captain," Brook called.

He didn't want to let her go.

"Captain," the lieutenant shouted again, with desperation in his expression.

"What?" Thornton snapped, turning his head to the other, who was standing at the end of the dock.

"Look." He pointed to the water a short distance to the north.

"Go inside," the captain of the troop told Ursula, letting her go so he could investigate.

As the women and other passengers of the *Gypsy* moved away with Lieutenant Wake, Thornton looked to the dark water for whatever Brook was signalling to.

At first, he saw the rise and fall of the tide. There were countless tiny splashes as raindrops pelted the water's surface.

Then he saw it.

A little further away than he thought Brook was pointing at.

Large ripples, as if invisible boats were moving through the water, drew closer and closer.

"What is that, sir?" Jendryng asked.

Thornton turned his head and peered at the others clustering around behind him.

"How the fuck would I know?" the captain growled. "I'm guessing it's nothing good. Get back and prepare for the worst, gentlemen."

The troop moved, giving themselves some distance from the end of the dock as they pulled their blades free from their sheaths.

"They don't get past us," Thornton ordered. "Wake's men are the last resort. You're trained for this. Fight until you can't fight anymore."

"Yessir," they chorused as they watched a large ripple move across the water to the end of the pier.

"Here they come," London shouted.

Slick, black forms appeared at the end of the wooden structure, clawing up the timber pylons, crawling from the sea.

Wide white grins taunted the men.

Thornton counted twenty with more still snaking their way through the water.

Splashes under the dock brought a sense of alarm to the captain.

"London," he barked.

"Sir?"

"Run to the warehouse," Thornton commanded. "Tell Wake to shut that door and get his men ready to defend the entrance."

"Sir." London bolted along the pier as fast as he could.

"Watch the sides, men," the old soldier said, gripping his sword tightly in both hands. His eyes were on the twenty slender figures slinking on all fours towards him.

Thirty

"Bolt the doors shut behind us," Wake hollered as he and ten armed men ran back out into the rain on London's heels.

"Wait!" Ursula ran after them, dropping a bowl of stew onto the floor.

Audrey called after her, but the other ignored the calls, racing into the darkness.

"My lady," London called to her, grabbing her by the arm before she ran past him.

"I need to be with him," she cried.

"You silly girl!" The lieutenant shook his head. "You'll distract him from what he does best."

"I can't stay in there," she argued as a few men scrambled from the kitchen area, leaving the steaming stew and long line of people awaiting their fill, to push the large timber doors closed.

The immense hinges holding the panels screeched noisily as they swung closed. A thud resounded through the warehouse as the doors shut into place.

The men immediately ran to the wall to the side of the door and hoisted a large, heavy timber beam to lower into two metal brackets, securing the door.

It was too late for her to return to the shelter.

"All right." London shook his head. "You stay behind me and do exactly as I tell you to. Understood?"

She nodded.

She turned to face the pier, seeing the rest of the troop some distance away.

Dark figures were advancing along the dock before them. More were climbing up the hulls of the ships moored on either side of them.

They were rising from out of the sea.

Her heart suddenly felt as if a thin sliver of ice pierced it through.

Thornton watched the creatures as they edged closer and closer.

Their claws dug into the timber of the wharf's deck.

Their long teeth grimaced menacingly and mouths opened wide.

Their dark tongues lolled out of their mouths like thin asps.

One beast let out a shrill cry as it leapt through the air.

With a quick step forward, Thornton used both hands to bring his sword around his back and over his head.

It connected with the figure in the air.

The blade sliced into the beast's shoulder and cut through the rib cage.

It dropped to the deck, where it writhed and kicked madly as black ooze spurted from the wound.

There was no time to celebrate as more creatures suddenly advanced.

A flurry of blades and blood ensued as the troop hacked into the approaching horde.

"Oh shit," Cobham gasped again and again as he slew one beast, only to see another taking its place.

And another.

Dark arms and legs, heads and discarded flesh dropped to the floor as screams of agony mixed with the terrifying cries of the creatures during their continued attack.

More and more clambered from the water, moving onto the dock or climbing the sides of the ships nearby.

Several beasts lunged from the vessels, dropping from a higher place of attack.

"Heads up," Bacon hollered, meeting one of the beast's faces with the sharp end of his weapon. It squealed like a pig as he pulled his blade free, kicking the beast in the abdomen, sending it to the gap between the dock and the *Gypsy*.

The soldier couldn't tell if his victim had splashed into the water below as the deafening din of screeching creatures filled his ears. His blade was already hacking into another beast before he had time to contemplate what had happened.

It was almost instinctive.

One beast was down, but then there was another to destroy.

As more dark figures rose from the sea, dropped from the ships, clawed at the troops, Brook quickly glanced out to the ocean just beyond the docks and saw an increasing number of large ripples in the water.

"There's more coming," he hollered as he stuck his blade into the mouth of a screaming beast.

A loud sickening crunch ensued as he retrieved his weapon.

Lightning flashed above them.

The blinding light momentarily revealed a horrific sight on the pier.

Blood and limbs laid askew over the dock, dropping into the water below as the two forces engaged in battle shoved or kicked them aside.

Ursula watched, petrified, as the men chopped the beasts down, one after another, only to see more and more climbing into view.

Her stomach tightened and her heart seemed to sting as she noticed more waves, caused by the advancing horde beneath the water's surface, moving into view.

The appearance on Wake's face told her that the troop wasn't going to make it out alive.

But she knew this deep inside already.

Her head started to pound.

Pain in her temples increased to the point where she believed her skull would explode.

Thunder roared as the sky ignited again.

And again.

With each flash, more pain built inside.

She dropped to her knees, shaking, shivering.

Her hands moved to her eyes.

"My lady?" Wake crouched beside her. "Are you all right?"

"Step back, Lieutenant," she said calmly. It was as if control was no longer hers.

The pain was immense, but it fed her. Empowered her.

She pulled her hands away from her face as she lifted herself to her feet.

"By the gods," the soldier gasped, stepping back.

The orbs in her sockets were pitch black with tendrils of darkness expanding from the sockets beneath the skin.

She stepped forward slowly, reaching towards the sky with her hands.

The dark creatures on the dock stopped attacking, suddenly frozen in place. The ones climbing the sides of the ship held their positions.

"Illuminate," Ursula whispered.

Streaks of lightning flared from the sky, touching her fingertips before being redirected outward.

"What is that?" Brondt stared towards the docks, where lightning from many points in the sky was being combined into one thick beam.

"There is one amongst us." Amicia held her hand to her chest. "I can feel her power."

The light bent around the troop on the pier, striking each of the dark creatures surrounding them.

On the sides of the ship, the figures smoked before falling into the water with a loud hiss.

Beams of electricity struck the water's surface around the dock, spreading its influence on the advancing creatures under the surface.

Suddenly, the light disappeared, and Ursula fell to her side on the pier.

"By the gods," Wake managed, as he raced over to her.

"What in blazes was that?" Jendryng hollered.

Thornton pushed past them and raced along the dock to the fallen women.

He dropped beside her, releasing his grasp on his sword to pull her to his chest.

"Ursula," he called softly.

"She's still breathing," Wake told him. "How did she...?"

"We need to get her inside," Thornton told him.

"Of course," the other said, turning to his men behind him. They were all staring in awe at what had occurred. "Get the doors opened."

One of them raced to the doors and thumped against the panels, calling for someone inside to let them in.

It wasn't long before the group was inside and Thornton was placing Ursula into a cot.

"What happened to her?" Maud asked, dropping to her side.

Thornton shook his head.

"We all saw it," he said. "But I do not know how to explain it."

"She's a witch," Vawdrey announced. "And a bloody good one, at that."

***

Alice was suddenly sitting up rigid in her bed.

Her eyes were black as pitch, and she was staring at the wall past her feet.

"Alice?" Arthur placed his hand on her arm.

Emily stepped back from the bed, her heart thumping wildly in her chest.

"Kayl'sro?" Nola'ee tilted her head, confused.

"Another rises," Alice muttered in a monotone voice.

"Another rises?" Arthur asked. "What is it? What other?"

She turned to face him.

His stomach tightened as he stared into her dark eyes.

She grinned and placed her hand on his cheek gently.

"A new power," she replied.

"A new...?" The boy creased his forehead. "Good or evil?"

"What is good?" Alice blinked. "What is evil?"

She dropped her hand as her head lolled.

"Alice?" He placed his hand under her chin. "Alice, are you there?"

She was gone.

Sleeping again.

He lowered her onto her back and covered her with blankets.

"A new power," he repeated.

"Do you think she's speaking of something in Woodmyst?" Emily queried.

He shook his head and frowned. "I don't know."

"Have you ever seen her eyes like that before?" the auburn woman asked.

"Once," he answered.

***

Six women gathered by the edge of the platform. One was still dressing as the others watched the event taking place before them.

Takmel was now embracing Gilda, the last of the Seven. Sweat covered him from head to toe as he moved into her. His body ached as if some force was trying to prevent his success.

He peered over at Joanne, who was smiling wryly.

"Are we tired, Maji?" she asked. "Do we need to rest?"

"I'll succeed," he managed. "Why do you contend with me? I am more powerful. I am supreme."

"Your power relies upon ours," she corrected him. "Without us, you are nothing, Maji."

"I am the Heir of Darkness," he said, writhing, thrusting, moving. "I am the ruler of all."

"Not yet, little one," she murmured, leering at him. "After this one, you have two more to place your seed into. You're getting tired, Takmel. You need rest. But time won't wait for you."

She was trying to put him off.

She wanted him to fail.

The part of her he had conquered was fighting back and was winning.

There was only one way for him to get her back.

He needed to complete his task.

He looked away from the black witch and to the naked flesh of the woman he coupled with.

She was beautiful, enchanting. He didn't need to look at Joanne. His focus needed to be upon Gilda, the here and now. She was moaning sounds of pleasure and calling his name over and over. Joanne's words could not cause him any doubts in his abilities.

His eyes, his ears, his mind focused on the naked woman with her arms and legs wrapped around him.

Her breath fell upon his neck and ear as he put her solely in his mind, blocking out everything else around him.

She was all that mattered.

She was all there was.

She was…

His abdomen tightened as his body convulsed.

The uncontrollable release caused a deep tremor over his flesh.

A wide smile spread over his face as he moved his regard to Joanne.

She was glaring at him.

"Two more," he murmured. "Then you are all mine forever."

Thirty-One

A volley of heavy ammunition, stone and rock blazing with fire fuelled by a coating of tar, arced through the sky towards the horde still massing on the northern front.

"Watch that trajectory," a general called to a catapult team nearby. "We have men out there."

Archers fired, again and again, piercing hundreds of the black figures with each shower of arrows.

But still, they came.

Thousands moved towards the city in a single, pulsating form. There was no structure to their approach. No organisation.

They just moved as if with one mind.

The soldiers in amongst the carnage continued to slash with sword and axe, taking down a multitude of the attacking creatures, losing quite a few of their own.

The constant screams of men and beast carried on through the night, building terror in the hearts of the troopers manning the machines along the line.

The battle was drawing closer to them as the dark figures from the north pushed the soldiers back towards the city.

The general checked the catapults from his position, moving his gaze along the line to see them loaded.

"Torches," he called, ordering loads of tar-covered rocks to be ignited. "Volley."

Tails of flames filled the sky as lightning burst in the clouds far above.

The blazing ammunition crashed into the horde, ploughing through them violently, pulverising their flesh and setting them ablaze.

"Reload," the general hollered as he watched the gaps in the enemy force caused by the barrage of catapult fire suddenly close up as more and more creatures moved in.

***

"How is she?" Wake asked, standing to the side of the group assembled around Ursula.

"She sleeps," Monteacute replied. "Whatever it was she did, it took it out of her."

"I've never seen such a thing in my life." The lieutenant shook his head. "And I fought on the fields of Woodmyst."

"I would say you saw a fair bit then, eh?" Captain Staiger said from the other side of the cot where the girl was lying.

"About half of what I should have seen," he replied, pointing at the patch over his left eye.

Staiger grinned, then suddenly felt guilt for expressing herself in such a manner. She peered at the young woman slumbering in the bed.

"I remember seeing the dead rise," Thornton said from Ursula's side. He was kneeling next to the cot and wiping droplets of moisture from her face and neck. She was soaked through from the rain.

The others listened intently, looking at him as he moved the towel in his hand slowly over her skin.

"We had a victory," he went on. "The battle was ours. The forces of the Mirikin were defeated, dead mostly. But so many of ours were lying next to theirs, just as lifeless.

"I had friends there; many friends staring up at me with their dead eyes. We had a victory, but I had never felt so alone and defeated in my life.

"Then that bitch, Tarkin, made them all move. She wasn't done.

"Her dead soldiers walked and crawled again. My friends, our own men, joined with them.

"If it wasn't for that one man who rode onto that field to take her down..." Thornton felt a tear slide over his cheek.

"Tomas Warde," Lieutenant Wake said. "I remember. She got him."

"Yeah." Thornton wiped his face. "But he got her too."

Wake frowned, peering at the floor.

"That he did," he whispered.

"All of that..." Thornton gazed at Ursula. "Every bit of it pales on what she did out there."

He leant over and kissed her on the forehead.

A great thud against the door caused all to look around at the giant timber panels.

"Now what?" a reserve guard called as he approached the door. "Who's out there?"

There was no reply.

The guard looked over to his commander.

Wake held a finger to his lips, urging everyone to be silent.

It was a useless gesture, as children, unable to contain themselves, sobbed as desperate parents tried to hush them.

The doors thudded again.

They could hear scratching sounds moving up the walls on either side of the panels.

Climbing.

Climbing.

THUD!

The doors rattled.

Several jumped, emitting small outbursts of gasps.

"Dear gods," someone shouted. "They've come for us."

A shrill scream resounded from the other side of the doors.

"Unarmed people to the middle of the room," Wake commanded. "Women and children to the centre. Her too." He pointed to Ursula, still slumbering.

"Help me," Thornton called, moving to the head of the cot, lifting it by the legs. Jendryng took the feet and hoisted it so they could carry the bed away from the doors and farther into the building.

The rest of the troop moved closer to the panels, pulling their weapons free of their sheaths.

Small puffs of dust floated down from far above as the invaders clawed at the building from the outside.

THUD!

The doors shook again, followed by another terribly high-pitched cry.

"Watch the roof," Wake called, pointing his blade to the rafters.

His reserve forces, all of twenty men, gathered closer to the doors, setting their gaze on the dark void above them.

Larger pieces of rubble fell to the floor as the creatures peeled the roof open.

Brook pointed. "There."

Dark, thin fingers gripped at the thatching and ripped at the material, keeping the weather out. Bit by bit, the hole grew until one beast could stick its head through.

A great, white smile beamed from the darkness, causing alarm to spread through the room.

Some sobbed.

Others screamed.

THUD!

The soldiers' eyes moved to the door as it rattled again.

More debris tumbled to the floor with drops of rain close behind.

A scream sounded from above, echoed by another just behind the large panels of the door.

"Here they come," a reserve guard called.

One creature dropped through the hole in the roof, leaping to a nearby rafter.

It crawled along the wooden beam a short distance before dropping to the floor.

Cobham's blade met it, slicing through the beast's stomach and sending its entrails over the ground as it fell.

Another beast appeared beside Sparrow and found a similar fate.

Then another dropped.

And another.

Wake swung his blade in controlled arcs, contacting creature after creature with each swing.

His men were not as disciplined as he, chopping wildly with their swords. Sometimes they hit their target. Sometimes they didn't.

"Get in there, ya bastards!" Staiger called, pulling her rapier from her belt. She charged in and joined the conflict, grinning madly as she sliced into a creature's neck.

"Come on," Alington called to his own crew as more dark figures dropped from the roof.

The creatures tumbled in, one after the other. Too many to count.

Before long, the area between the door and the refugees from the northern communities filled with soldiers and armed seafarers battling with dark creatures.

Swords versus claws and blade against teeth.

The calls of men yelling as they attacked, creatures screaming with each approach, filled the room to the point of deafening.

THUD!

The doors continued to rumble as more beasts gathered outside.

Monteacute pulled the blade from his sheath, preparing to race into the fray.

"No," Thornton told him. "I need you to stay here. Watch her for me. Please."

The sheriff looked the captain in the eye and nodded.

"All right," he replied. "But only until I think I'm needed in there with you lot."

Thornton clasped his hand on the sheriff's shoulder and turned his attention to Maud and the three ladies under Ursula's care, all kneeling beside the cot.

"Look after her." He turned to see more dark creatures dropping in through the hole in the ceiling. "And try to wake her up. She may be able to help."

With that, he and Jendryng raced across the warehouse floor, leaping over upturned cots and discarded bowls of food, towards the conflict.

Swinging his blade upwards, Jendryng chopped into the crotch of an unsuspecting creature.

It screamed in agony, falling to the ground in a writhing, twisting heap.

Jendryng stabbed into the ribcage of the beast, causing it to stop moving.

He recoiled his weapon and turned just in time to see Thornton lop the head off another dark figure. Continuing to run forward, the older soldier brought his blade around and sliced through the leg of another.

The floor was a mess from redundant limbs, disembowelled bodies of both man and beast, and blood.

Staiger jabbed her thin blade deep into the flesh of one beast as another came rushing towards her from the side, screaming, with its arms flailing. Closer and closer.

She retracted her rapier and quickly thrust it into the advancing beast's mouth.

It penetrated tissue and bone, poking out the back of its head.

Its arms dropped to its sides lifelessly before it fell to the floor.

She didn't have time to observe her handiwork as another creature dropped down from the rafters, landing on the floor close to her.

Her blade swiped across the beast's chest, ploughing a deep wound where dark, thick fluid seeped out. It dropped to its knees and placed a hand against the cut, screaming.

She silenced it by piercing the throat of the beast.

With a smile, she turned to see yet another racing towards her.

"Slow learners," she muttered as she raised her weapon again.

London kicked one beast away with his boot as he hacked into the arm of another.

He found himself in the worst place imaginable.

Directly beneath the growing hole in the roof.

In a wide arc, he swung his blade around his body and connected with the side of a creature's head.

It screamed but suddenly fell silent as London retrieved his blade and chopped into the beast's head again.

As it fell, he turned to see another behind him, a little too close for comfort.

With just enough room to manoeuvre, he stabbed the blade straight ahead and pierced the other's chest.

Sudden pain down his spine caused him to turn.

A dark figure smiled at him. Its pointed fingers dripped with blood.

His blood.

He jabbed his weapon into the stomach of the attacker, feeling the blade break through bone as its tip popped out through the creature's left shoulder.

Another sharp sting on his side caused him to look down.

A creature had got in too close.

Its long teeth pierced his hip.

With a great tug, it closed its mouth tightly and tore a sizeable chunk of his flesh from his body.

London could see bright red flesh along with white sinew and bone.

There didn't seem to be much blood.

At least, not as much as he thought there would be.

Another set of long teeth sank into his shoulder as he dropped his weapon.

He fell to his knees as he felt the strange sensation of his arm popping out of its joint.

Another attacked him, biting his across his thigh.

The feeling of pain flowed back.

Throbbing.

Aching.

Stinging.

He screamed as another creature hit him across the back of the neck.

Blood flowed over his chest as the beast shook him violently.

The sound of tearing flesh and crunching bones filled his ears.

"No," Brook hollered as he witnessed dark figures tearing his comrade apart to devour his body. He edged his way over to the frenzy, hacking and chopping into every dark object that moved.

In the periphery of his vision, the glint of blades continued to sparkle as he stabbed and sliced his way through the horde.

Several creatures backed away, holding their claws up defensively, only to have them hacked off by the furious soldier.

"Kill 'em all," Thornton growled, moving to Brook's side. "Kill every last one of the fuckers."

It was only then that the lieutenant realised that a line of swordsmen had been beside him, moving with him towards the door.

They were pushing the creatures back.

Some had even climbed back through the hole in the roof.

They were retreating.

"What the hell?" Sparrow gasped, eyeing several of the figures cowering against the doors.

Thornton turned to see Ursula standing across the floor.

She was leaning against Monteacute and walking towards them.

"They fear her," Captain Staiger observed.

One creature clawed its way up the timber doors.

"No, you don't," one of the reserve guards said, throwing his sword at the beast.

The edge of the blade hit the figure, causing it to fall back to the floor.

It wasn't wounded, but it cowered with the others against the door.

"Destroy them," Thornton commanded.

His men hacked into the creatures, slicing limbs from their bodies and leaving a thick pool of blood on the floor and spattered over the door.

***

The horde raced towards the foothills to the west of the city.

"They're trying to flank us," Brondt said, watching the event transpire.

The mass moved towards the trees as one.

Thousands of creatures disappeared into the forest.

"Is this some trick?" he asked, looking at his wife.

She stared in disbelief.

"I don't know," she answered. "I don't know what this means."

"Tell the catapults and archers to keep firing," the commander hollered to a guard.

The soldier bolted away as the two on the balcony kept careful watch of the army of fiends.

"They're moving on," she said. "They're going elsewhere."

"Yes," he acknowledged. "But where? Nothing lies in that direction except..."

"Oh, no!" Amicia shook her head.

Thirty-Two

He laughed as he pulled himself away from Lucy, the last of the nine. The sound reverberated around the auditorium as he rolled onto his back.

As Catherine finished clothing herself, Joanne draped a cloak around the blonde woman's shoulders.

Takmel reached for his trousers as the Seven gathered by the steps leading up to the platform.

"What now, Maji?" Joanne asked. Her demeanour suddenly withdrew, becoming seemingly compliant. "Light of all."

"Maji," a deep, thunderous voice called softly from somewhere near the ceiling. "We have arrived as you instructed."

"All of you?" he asked, standing up as he tied the cords on his pants.

"All of us," the voice replied.

Twenty dark vaporous forms descended into the room, positioning themselves a short distance in a circle around the young man.

"Why are the Gomatha here, my lord?" Joanne queried.

"To see my destiny fulfilled," he said.

"You have the nine." She bowed her head. "This is all that is required."

"But it is not enough," he hissed malevolently. He stretched his arms out wide and extended his fingers as far as he could.

Thin strands extended from the smoky figures surrounding him, stretching towards the young man as if being pulled by some strange, unseen, unfelt wind.

"Maji," one being called. "What are you doing?"

Takmel laughed as the wisps of smoke touching his chest absorbed into his skin.

Lucy stood next to Catherine, observing the strange event unfolding.

Joanne watched on with the other women, unable to intervene, unwilling to act.

She belonged to the Maji.

She had no right to protest his actions.

She couldn't fight him, even if she wanted to.

So, she watched as he absorbed their power, draining them of their life force.

"Takmel," one called. "Please."

"Goodbye, Vonavo," he said as the last of the Gomatha vanished.

The young man fell to his knees. A shimmer of darkness enveloped his body.

He felt exhausted and filled with energy at the same time.

Slowly, he lifted himself to his feet and sighed.

His eyes had turned black, with a shadowy haze drifting around them like mist.

Lightning flared, and thunder cracked far above.

"Now," he sneered, "I am ascended."

The nine women stared at him blank-faced, eagerly waiting for his instruction.

He reached his hands out to them. "Come to me, my queens."

Smiling excitedly, they rushed into his embrace.

Their hands stroked his bare chest and back, touching him all over. He felt their lips on his skin.

Joanne moved to his face, pressing her lips to his.

There was no struggle. No biting words.

She was his.

They were all his now.

"We have so much to do," he said.

"It can wait," she told him as he felt the cords of his trousers loosen again.

***

"Are you all right?" Thornton took Ursula into his arms. She leant into him and rested her head against his chest.

"I feel tired," she replied.

"Perhaps you should lie down a while," he suggested, starting towards a nearby cot.

"No," she replied. "I don't want to lie down. This will sound strange." She peered around at the torn bodies of men and creatures nearby and listened to the sound of others sobbing further in the room. "But, I'm hungry."

"Well," one of the reserve soldiers began, "we've got plenty of..." He turned to see Lieutenant Wake pointing to a mess of overturned pots, blood-soaked bread and spilt stew. "Bloody heck!"

"I apologise for his outburst, my lady." Wake bowed to Ursula.

"I've heard worse," she said, smiling, moving her gaze to Thornton.

"Is there anything left that she can eat?" the captain asked.

"Not here, by the looks of it," Wake replied.

"I think I know where we can go, sir," Brook offered. "It's a bit of a hike, but we could probably take everyone if they're willing to come."

"Where?"

"The barracks, sir."

***

"I'm hungry," Alice murmured, crawling upon the bed. She stretched her arms out to the side.

"Open your eyes," Arthur told her, taking her by the hand.

She blinked them open and peered around the room, confusedly. Three faces stared back at her. Her husband, mother and Nola'ee.

"Thank the gods," Arthur murmured.

"What?"

"The last time you opened your eyes," he replied, "they didn't appear normal."

"Black," Nola'ee blurted. "Kayl'sro Alice eyes were black."

"Do you remember?" Emily questioned.

"I remember waking for a moment," she answered. "I think I saw lightning near some boats. And a woman with dark hair in the rain."

"You said that *another rises*," Arthur pressed. "What did you mean?"

"I think I meant the woman." Alice placed a hand on her forehead. Her head was throbbing. "I need water and I'm so hungry."

"I'll get you something." Emily moved to the door.

"I need to get up," the girl said, kicking the covers away.

She sat up quickly. Too quickly.

The room spun a little, forcing her to put her hands on Arthur's shoulders.

"You should lie down," he said.

"No." She put her weight on him, lifting herself to her feet. "I just need to take it slowly. Where are my clothes?"

"They are wet," Nola'ee informed her.

"I have other garments." She looked at Arthur and gestured to her nakedness. "Unless you want me to walk around like this."

"Of course not!" He blushed. "I'll fetch you something."

***

The last of the horde disappeared, vanishing into the treeline that ran along the foothills to the west.

Brondt and Amicia watched from the balcony. The sound of erupting cheers and cries of joy spread along the northern line.

"This isn't finished," the queen told her husband. "They're being summoned. That's all."

"What do you mean?"

"The darkness is spreading," she replied. "Not retreating."

"They'll be back, then?"

"I don't know." Amicia moved her shoulders as if a chill slid down her spine. "But something will."

The commander turned to the east.

A faint purple glow stretched across the horizon.

The clouds had broken apart, allowing the last of the starlight to shine through.

"The sun will be up soon," he told her.

"I'm famished." She took his hand.

"The creatures?" He gestured towards the mountains.

"Send some scouts to track them," she ordered. "I don't want them to engage with them. Only observe."

He assented.

"There's not much else we can do," she told him. "We were very fortunate to survive."

"I know," he replied. "It's just that the others in their path will not be so lucky."

She sensed his deep concern and shared it.

"Come," she said, pulling him through the door by the hand. "I'll fix you something in the kitchen."

"How can you eat at a time like this?" he asked, being drawn along the corridor.

"I don't know," she answered. "I need to eat."

***

The rain slowed to a drizzle as the troop led the refugees from the warehouse along the streets of Newholt. The walk was long and consistently uphill as they neared the centre where the palace towered above all.

Eventually, the crowd reached the palace courtyard, where a few guards milled about. One approached Thornton with his hand on the hilt of his sheathed sword.

"What business have you here?" the soldier asked.

Thornton had his arm under Ursula's shoulders, helping her to move along.

"Get back to your post, soldier," the captain growled, "before I kick your arse all over the city."

"Captain Thornton?" The guard saluted. "We weren't expecting you."

"I don't think you lot were expecting much at all from what I see," he replied, moving his gaze up and down the full dress uniform on the soldiers standing about. "Where are your battle fatigues?"

"We were commanded to remain here," the soldier answered as Thornton continued to lead the refugees towards the barracks.

"Who told you to wear that shit?"

"Commander Brondt instructed us to—"

"Commander Brondt said for you to wear that?"

"Well… no… but…" the other stammered.

"Get Commander Brondt," Thornton grunted. "I think I want to make a formal complaint."

"George," Ursula sighed. "Leave him be, please."

Thornton hugged her tighter.

"You're lucky she's here," the captain remarked. "Or I'd have you right now, boy. Get back to your post."

"Yessir." The soldier moved away in haste.

∗∗∗

Alice tore chunks of bread from a loaf sitting on the kitchen bench and stuffed them into her mouth. She chewed quickly and swallowed hard and fast so she could get the next piece past her lips.

Emily stared wide-eyed at the girl as Arthur placed a hot cup of tea on the bench beside her.

"Thank you," Alice mumbled through the mouthful of bread. She lifted the cup and drank it dry in four gulps. "Good. I needed that."

"By the gods," Emily gasped. "Slow down."

Alice was already chewing another wad of bread.

"There are no gods," she mumbled.

"I just boiled the kettle." Arthur shook his head, lifting the empty cup from the bench. "How in blazes did you drink this?"

Alice nodded, pointing to the cup.

"Kayl'sro Alice wants more," Nola'ee interpreted.

"I assumed so," the boy replied, moving to the other end of the bench where he kept a tin of tea.

"Alice!" Emily grabbed the girl's hands, preventing her daughter from inhaling more of the loaf. "Something is wrong. No one behaves like this. What is going on with you?"

"I don't know," she replied. "I'm really hungry."

Her stomach growled loudly.

"That can't be good." Arthur turned to her.

The door near him, leading to the cavern behind the hut, opened. David stepped into the kitchen and wiped his eyes.

"Good morning," he said, walking to the bench. "Oh good. You made tea."

"It's for Alice," the boy replied. "And I think she's about to eat all of our stores."

David turned to see the girl pushing more bread into her mouth.

"Is she pregnant?"

All attention suddenly turned to him.

***

Ursula scooped up spoon after spoon of a stew that was on offer in the mess hall. She was sitting on her fifth bowl and didn't appear to be slowing down.

"This is really good," she said to Thornton, sitting next to her at one of the long tables.

He sniffed his bowl of slop, which had gone cold. It smelt and looked similar to waste from a privy.

"You haven't touched yours," she said, pushing her empty plate aside and dragging his before her.

The sound of a bubbled churning suddenly emanated from her gut.

"Excuse me." She smiled sheepishly. Others sitting at the table watched on in awe as she instantly dug back into the bowl of cold casserole.

***

Brondt stood in the middle of the palace kitchen floor. The staff stood behind him with fear in their faces, watching as the queen ate the flesh from a baked chicken that was sitting on a table near the centre of the room.

She bent over the carcass, tearing strips of meat off with her mouth, using her hands to hold the bird down like some animal. Wet sucking sounds hissed in and out of her mouth as she breathed and chewed. Drool slid down her chin and over the chicken.

"I guess that's all yours, then." The commander gestured.

She looked at him.

"Sorry." She spat small, chewed chunks of meat out as she spoke. "I'm just so hungry and this is so good." She looked at the kitchen staff. "You did such a good job with this."

"All right." Brondt shook his head. He stepped over to her and took the plate away.

"No." She reached out after him. "Give it back. I'm the queen."

"Amicia," he yelled, handing the plate of partially devoured chicken to a male staff member. "You may be the queen, but you are not acting like one. What are you doing?"

Her stomach rumbled as she started to cry.

"I don't know." She moved her hands to her abdomen. "I know I'm acting strangely. But I don't know…"

Suddenly, a flow of dark liquid escaped her mouth.

She fell to her knees as she continued to throw up.

Brondt was at a loss as to what to do.

The expelled liquid grew darker and darker, thicker and thicker, spreading across the floor like rich tar.

"Amicia," he called, stepping through the growing puddle to move to her side.

"It's the darkness," she told him before another barrage of dark bile surged from her.

***

Ursula had made it out the doors of the barracks before she fell to her knees and ejected the contents of her belly. Thornton and Kateryn were by her side within moments.

The darkness spread over the gravel slowly, oozing across the ground.

"Get it all out," Thornton told her, trying to seem as level-headed as possible.

She took a deep breath and hurled another load onto the ground. Tears were streaming from her eyes and mucus dribbled from her nose.

He felt helpless, unable to ease her illness. Unable to comfort her except to hold her hair back and rub her spine.

***

She stared at the black puddle on the grass by the porch. Her fingers gripped the edge of the timber boards as she kneeled not too far from the cabin door.

Arthur was there, beside her.

"How do you feel?"

"I think that was the last of it," she replied. She repositioned herself to sit. "I feel better."

She got up.

"Not too fast," he said, lifting himself with her, holding her by the arm.

"I'm fine," she said, turning to face him. Her eyes were brighter.

"What is this?" he gasped, letting her go and stepping away from her.

She turned to see the others gathered by the door. They, too, stared at her with a shroud of fear over their faces.

"Your eyes," Emily pointed.

"What about them?" Alice asked, some concern resounding in her voice.

"They're blue," her mother said.

"Like stars," Nola'ee murmured.

Arthur moved closer to her.

"I'm sorry," he told her, gently touching her on the arm. "I shouldn't have reacted like that."

"What do they look like?" She sobbed. "Is it horrible?"

"No." He laid a hand on her cheek. "They're beautiful. It's as if they glow."

"They glow?" She frowned.

"Not quite." He ran his fingers through her hair. "Your hair is changing."

Alice looked at her mother.

Emily gestured, tears streaming down her cheeks. "You have snow streaks."

Alice grabbed a handful of her hair from the side of her head and brought it into view. Sure enough, strands had changed colour.

"What just happened?" David asked. "You ate all that food, then that black shit came out of your mouth and now you've got blue eyes and your hair... Can someone tell me what this means?"

Alice looked over at him, letting her hair fall over her shoulders.

"I've been cleaned," she told him. "All darkness has been purged from me."

"And what does that mean?" he pressed.

"There are others like me," she told him. "Purged and prepared."

"Prepared for what, Alice?" Emily asked.

"War."

Thirty-Three

"Oh my," Maud gasped, peering at the pale streaks on Ursula's head, extending down the sides of her face. "You look so different."

Thornton guided her through the confused crowd and to a bench beside one table in the mess hall.

"Would you like something to eat or drink?" Brook offered.

"No," she said. "I'm fine."

"Are you?" the captain asked, running her fingers through her white strands of hair. "Your eyes are different."

"It's all right," she reassured. "It's a good thing that has happened to me."

"What has happened to you?" Rose asked, staring into the young woman's piercing blue eyes. "They're so blue."

"They have always been blue," Ursula chuckled.

"Not like this, they haven't," the other replied.

Ursula looked at Thornton.

"She's right," he told her. "They were darker before. Now, they are so bright."

"I must look hideous," she muttered, looking around to all the gawking faces.

"No," the old soldier said. "Not at all. I've never seen anyone so beautiful."

She leant into him and kissed his forehead.

"Now what?" Vawdrey called. "We've had monsters attack us. A girl throwing up and changing her appearance. What happens now?"

"We go to the queen," Ursula told him. "We have much to do."

The rain had stopped falling. The clouds had moved away to the southwest. A white glow spread upon the eastern horizon, signalling the imminent rising of the sun.

Thornton, with Ursula on his arm, led his men into the palace foyer. An older guard wearing full regalia approached him. His brass buttons were polished and his navy-blue coat and trousers fashioned neatly with straight creases along the length of the sleeves.

"Hard night's fighting," Thornton growled sarcastically as he regarded the man.

"Sir?"

"George," Ursula chided softly.

The captain smirked.

"We're here to see the queen," Ursula told the guard.

"And who, may I say, is here to see her?"

"Let them through," a voice called from a large doorway to their left.

All turned to see the commander approaching.

Suddenly, all the men around Ursula stood at attention and saluted.

"At ease, soldiers," he commanded, before turning his attention to the woman standing before him. He peered at her eyes and hair, scrutinizing Ursula's appearance. "Extraordinary. What's your name, my lady?"

"Ursula," she replied nervously, trying her best to curtsey. "Ursula Wadham, sir. It's an honour."

"You don't need to call me sir," he said, extending his hand to her. "My name is Jonathon Brondt, and the honour is all mine."

The commander turned his attention to Thornton.

"I gather the expedition to the northern settlements didn't go as planned," he said.

"No sir," he replied. "We discovered a concentrated force of those creatures at White Keep. They appeared to have taken up residence in the old ruins by the Great Horn."

"Follow me," Brondt instructed the troop. "The queen is expecting the young lady. I think what they need to discuss may interest us all."

The commander led them deeper into the palace, passing through large rooms and wide corridors adorned with fine furniture and exquisite paintings of people and places. Some of these, Thornton recognised.

It was the first time he had ventured so far into the palace. He had never dreamed of it being so awe-inspiring. His imagination simply saw walls, doors, and windows. Now, his mind was blown away by what surrounded him.

With each turn of a corner, there was something new and wonderful to see; chandeliers and tapestries, high ceilings and decorative skirting along the walls. All was whitewashed and brightly lit with candle stands positioned on hall tables throughout the rooms.

Eventually, they came to the dining room, where Amicia sat at the end of a long table, drinking tea from a small cup. When she saw the others approaching, she got up.

"Please sit," she said, gesturing to the table before the men had a chance to bow. "You must have had a very long night."

"Your Majesty." Thornton lowered his head. "I thank you for this opportunity to allow us to have an audience with—"

"No formalities, please Captain," she told him.

He looked up to her and noticed she had experienced the same changes as Ursula.

Her hair, tied back, had pale streaks extending from the temples. Her eyes were a piercing blue, almost glowing.

"Young lady!" The queen touched the back of a chair beside hers. "Sit by me."

Brondt moved to his regular seat by his wife's side. "Her name is—"

"Ursula," Amicia said. "I know." She sat in her chair and summoned a kitchen maid over with a flick of her hand. A young woman crossed the floor to the queen's side.

"My lady?"

"Tea for our guests," she ordered.

"Yes, my lady." The kitchen girl bowed slightly and moved through a door at the side of the room.

With everyone seated, Amicia moved her gaze to Ursula and grinned.

"It seems we have experienced something special," she said. "Do you know what it is?"

"My lady, I…"

The queen held her hand up. "Amicia, please. You and I are now sisters. A greater power has united us. I wonder if you know for what purpose this has occurred?"

"Amicia," Ursula said. It felt strange calling the ruler by her given name. "I know that all darkness has been removed. I know we need to unite with another. I know there is a battle coming."

"Not a battle," the other corrected, moving her eyes to Thornton. "A war. Those creatures you fought last night are drawn to dark magic. They are slaves to it. Their master summons them and prepares to use them to wage war on all that oppose his will."

"His will?" Thornton grumbled. "So, it is a man that controls these things?"

"He is far more than a man," Amicia replied. "He is the Maji. It's an ancient word that translates as *Light of All*. It is also a deception of terminology. He was a prophesied warlock. *The heir of darkness. The ruler of all.* The son of the White Mistress."

The men exchanged looks around the table.

"My lady, we came from White Keep," Brook started. "These things were everywhere."

"I know," she said. "The White Keep was a beacon for dark power for many, many years. It only makes sense that these creatures be drawn to it. The only reason that they didn't attack the settlement there earlier was because of two things. First, the Maji hadn't reached his full power yet and, second, Ursula kept them at bay.

"I lost many of my abilities over the years. I wasn't able to see any of this until now. With the Mirikin disbanded, my link to any power diminished. But something has awakened during the night.

"A great darkness has been born," she continued. "Greater than the world has ever known. But the light won't be swept away so easily."

"We three must unite," Ursula said.

"Indeed." Amicia reached over and touched the young woman on the hand.

"Three?" Vawdrey looked around the table.

Thornton shot the man a stern look.

"Yes," Ursula said. "There is another."

"A girl," Amicia affirmed. "Our prime."

"Your prime?" Brondt asked. "I thought you would—"

"She is far more powerful than I," the queen admitted. "Than both of us."

"More powerful than this, Maji?" Thornton queried.

"I don't know," she replied. "The Maji has the Seven of Woodmyst and two on his side."

"The Seven?" Thornton growled. "I thought they were friendly to us."

"They were," Amicia told him. "But their will has weakened. He's manipulated them since he was young.

"The damage caused by the Sovereign and her men gave strength to the darkness within them. He set his influence over them, subtly, for many years.

"He lived amongst them; was welcomed into their homes as a child. After his mother's death, he struggled within. The light and the darkness wrestled over his heart. But his love for his mother gave strength to the darkness. Eventually, he gave in to it and embraced it.

"His influence spread through the community, like vines quietly growing over walls and through the cracks in the streets until every it took root in every heart. Woodmyst was his long before he came to power.

"And now," she continued, "he is there. Far from the sea where our ships can reach him. He will see our army approaching. He will use those he has influenced to defend him. Innocents. Women. Children.

"The dark creatures and his forces will move upon the rest of us. They will sweep across the land and destroy all who oppose him."

"Forces?" Thornton queried. "He has others to fight for him? Not only these creatures?"

"He has the commander of Woodmyst," Amicia replied. "The ships and soldiers at Dweagan are his to command."

"His forces outnumber ours," Bacon sighed.

Silence fell upon the troop as they stared downheartedly at the table.

"What can we do?" Jendryng reasoned.

"Escort us to our prime," Ursula told him.

"What?" Brondt shot a glance to the young woman, and then to his wife. "No. You aren't leaving the city."

"I must," Amicia told him. "You need to order the defences of Newholt to prepare. Then you will instruct the stable hands to ready the horses."

She looked around the table to each of the others seated about her as three of the kitchen staff entered the room with pots of tea and cups on silver trays.

"I am sorry, gentlemen," she told them. "But I need your immediate service. We must follow the trail of the creatures."

"Follow the creatures?" Sparrow raised his brow. "That sounds like a great tactical plan."

"Their trail will lead us to our prime," she informed them.

Thornton looked down at Ursula's hand and processed everything that had been discussed.

"I don't like this, Amicia," Brondt complained. "It makes little sense to leave the city at this time. We just survived an attack. Our people need us."

"We could use at least one night's rest in our own beds," Vawdrey added.

The older soldier laced his fingers with Ursula's before locking eyes with her and smiling.

"Vawdrey's right," Bacon put in. "We've been up all night fighting those things. We deserve one night to recover."

"You deserve nothing," Thornton growled, pushing his chair back and standing to his feet. "You are men of the guard. You will do your duty to your last breath if necessary. The queen has given a command. You will obey it. Do you understand?"

"Yessir," they chorused, rising to their feet, standing to attention.

"Get your supplies in order and assemble in the mess hall. You have thirty minutes."

They saluted and waited for the next prompt.

Thornton raised his hand to his brow. "Dismissed."

With that, the men under his command filed from the room.

"I apologise, Your Majesty," he said softly, "Commander. I guess our tea party will need to wait until another time."

"Thirty minutes, Captain?" Brondt rose to his feet.

"Sir?"

"That doesn't give me much time to speak to the generals about our defences." The commander looked to the other man.

"My apologies, sir," Thornton frowned. "I simply didn't want Her Majesty to listen to any more of my men griping."

"Griping is what soldiers do," Brondt replied. "In fact, I heard such tripe coming from my own lips before they started."

"I didn't mean to overstep my authority, sir."

"I'm thankful to you, Captain." The commander moved around the table to Thornton. "I needed to be put in my place."

"Quite frequently," Amicia quipped.

Brondt grimaced.

"The ladies will be fine here without us," the commander said, putting his arm around Thornton's shoulders and moving towards the corridor. "Walk with me."

"Yes sir," the other replied, looking over at Ursula, who was smiling back at him.

"I noticed you are missing two men from your detachment," Brondt said as they moved along the passage.

"Yessir," Thornton replied. "I lost private Arnald Smyth on the road, and Lieutenant Ralf London during the battle last night."

"Good men?"

"They're all good men, sir."

"You should select replacements before we embark on this mission," the commander suggested.

"I'd prefer not to, sir," Thornton replied. "My preference is to continue on with the men I have."

"You could have your pick of the litter, Captain," the commander offered. "Perhaps replace any you feel aren't up to it."

"No thank you, sir," the other replied. "I would fight with and die for any of these men under my command. They are some of the best I have ever had the opportunity to stand with. If my task is to protect the queen on this expedition, then I can think of no one better to achieve that with."

Brondt nodded.

"Fair enough," he said. "I'll yield to your judgement. I will accompany you with my own regiment. Your men are yours to command, Captain. They respect you. I do not wish to interfere with how you keep your band together. Total autonomy, so to speak."

"I understand, sir," Thornton replied.

"Thirty minutes," Brondt said as they neared the foyer.

"Thirty minutes," the captain agreed.

"I'll do my best to meet you in the mess hall."

Thornton saluted and was answered in like by the commander.

With that, the captain crossed the courtyard and made his way to the barracks.

Thirty-Four

Twenty-six horses moved into the foothills at a walking pace. Thornton rode at the head of the group, following the obvious signs left by the dark creatures from the night before.

The multitude of beasts had torn the ground up with their claws, leaving patches of freshly tilled soil, overturned stones, and crushed vegetation. Tracking wasn't difficult.

"I could let the horse steer itself," he grumbled to Brook, riding close behind him.

"They've practically created a new road," the lieutenant said, observing the surrounding damage.

Commander Brondt was next in line, wearing clothing that appeared more casual, covered with his leather armour. Ursula and the queen, both in riding trousers and breastplates immediately followed him. The commander had demanded that the women dress for comfort and protection. They both complied, discarding their dresses for outfits similar to what the men were wearing.

Eighteen more men, including Thornton's detachment, made up the rest of the troop. Four of them trailed pack horses behind their own.

"Keep your eyes peeled for any stragglers," the captain instructed. "I'm sure there must be one or two who were injured in the battle."

"Just one or two?" Brook grinned.

Thornton scanned the mountains ahead.

They were still a good distance from the high peaks, but he knew there was no way to cross them without having to endure some hard travelling.

"Rough terrain ahead, Your Majesty," he called. "Could get a mite chilly too."

"I'll be fine, Captain," she called back. "Just lead the way. I'll be sure to keep up."

"My lady," he replied as he neared the summit of a low ridge.

From his position, he could see the creatures had descended down the side of the hill to a thin gully. From there, they had climbed a steady slope to the left before vanishing beneath the treeline.

This was the eastern edge of the Forest of Khun.

The entire land between where the troop were now moving to the border of Woodmyst was covered with woodland, except for the highest mountain peaks in the region.

Thornton urged his steed down the embankment, continuing along the trail left from the night before.

"It's not too late to turn back," Brondt said to his wife as he peered into the mountains.

"We must do this," she told him. "I understand your concerns. But if we don't unite with our prime, the Maji will definitely take these lands as his own."

"So," Brondt said, looking at her, "you *will* defeat him."

"We have a far better chance together," Ursula informed him. "But there is no guarantee."

"So this could be a waste of time," Brook suggested.

"Could be," Thornton agreed. "But what would you prefer? Go out for a ride or sit in Newholt waiting to fucking die?"

Ursula smiled.

Brondt glared to the back of the officer's head angrily.

"Sorry, my ladies," the captain growled.

"Quite all right, Captain," Amicia giggled.

"Unacceptable," Brondt hissed quietly so that only she heard him.

"The man is battle-hardened, my love," she said. "He has seen far worse than you. A little leniency for him and his men wouldn't hurt. Trust me."

Brondt conceded. "All right."

***

"Seven wagons are being loaded with lumber and tools over by the timber yard," Master Bookkeeper Lewis Drayton said, walking beside the Maji as they crossed the centre bridge of Woodmyst, reading from a parchment in his hand.

People passing by bowed slightly, bidding good morning with a friendly, "My lord," before moving on.

"Food supplies?" Takmel asked, pulling his newly gained, dark damson cloak with gold trimming tightly over his shoulders. It draped over the hilt of his sword, resting on his right hip, and almost reached the ground.

He turned his head momentarily to see four guards walking tall a short distance behind him. They scanned the people moving about on the bridge, looking for potential threats, guarding their master diligently.

"Twelve wagons laden with wheat, oats, sacks of flour from the mill, corn, potatoes, pumpkins, seed stock, dried fish, some live poultry…"

"All right." The other stopped and peered at the river flowing below. Several tiny boats anchored on the surface near the middle of the wide canal, so their passengers could drop a line into the deeper water. "Livestock?"

"Four wagons are being loaded with straw," Drayton replied, checking the list. "We are sending a further nine cows, one bull, ten sheep, twenty horses and the chickens as I mentioned before."

"And you and the other bookkeepers are certain that will be enough to last them through the winter?"

"We based it on the calculations made before we heard from the spies about the additional numbers in their encampment," the old man answered. "But yes, given that we calculated a surplus, it should be enough."

Takmel peered to the sky above, where thick clouds continued to drift about.

The rain had stopped.

The storm was over.

But Woodmyst was still shrouded in a veil of gloom.

He could see patches of light where the morning sun attempted to breakthrough.

"Bad weather, my lord," Drayton said. "Perhaps we should hold off transporting these goods until the clouds have cleared."

"It won't rain," he replied. "We will deliver the supplies as promised."

"As you wish, my lord." The bookkeeper bowed slightly.

Takmel summoned a guard over.

One of the four men following him rushed to his side.

"My lord?"

"Go to the stables," Takmel commanded. "Tell the hands to prepare the best horses for my wives and I. We will pay our family a visit today."

The guard gave a small bow and raced away.

"You're going outside the wall, my lord?" Drayton appeared concerned. "Do you think this wise?"

"You question my ability to reason?" the Maji glared at the bookkeeper. Darkness swirled in the young man's eyes. The clouds above appeared to grow darker.

Fear swept over the old man's face as he peered up to the sky briefly before seeming to shrink, bowing his head.

"My apologies, my lord," he replied. "I merely have your safety in mind."

Takmel relaxed.

His eyes cleared, and the sky brightened slightly.

"My mother-in-law deserves to hear the good news." He grinned. "After all, she is also my sister-in-law now."

***

Alice sat on the ground at her mother's feet. Emily was on the porch of the cabin, running a brush through the girl's hair.

"It's spreading," the woman said calmly, noticing the change in pigmentation in other areas.

"I know," Alice replied, watching the rukyul bounding towards her over the grass.

"Braids or out?"

"Just tied back, please," she answered as the beast slowed its approach, cocking its head as it noticed the difference in her appearance. "Hello, Shadow."

It edged towards her and sniffed her face.

"Ghastly creature," Emily said, eyeing the animal cautiously.

Shadow sat near them and looked over the glade. People were up and about their business. Some tended to livestock, while others continued with the construction of the huts.

Alice would have been amongst them, but Arthur had insisted that she take a day to relax after the events of the night before. She had argued, but her own mother sided with her husband and demanded that she stay home.

Emily tied a blue ribbon into her daughter's hair, creating a ponytail that fell between the girl's shoulder blades.

"There," the auburn woman said. "All done."

"Thank you, Mama." Alice hopped to her feet and kissed Emily on the cheek. She then started down the slope, heading towards the pasture.

"Where are you off to?" her mother called. "You promised your husband you would stay here."

"I need to check on Liana," she replied, the rukyul on her heels.

Emily watched her daughter walk away towards the large cavern.

"How is she?" a voice called softly from beside her.

Emily almost jumped in fright at the sound.

She turned to see her sister-in-law, Linet, approaching with her son Alan in tow.

"She's fine," Emily answered. "Different. But fine."

"Different?" Linet peered after the girl moving across the grass. "She's always been different. You mean her appearance?"

"Yes," the other replied, looking at Alice's snow-coloured ponytail swinging over her back as she walked. "And no. There's a change in her personality. A little more refined."

"More lady-like?"

"I wouldn't go that far."

Linet sat beside Emily, her eyes moving from the girl walking away to her son, who plonked himself beside her.

"You don't think what is happening to her might be a ploy from your sister?"

The question surprised Emily. She furrowed her brow and peered at the woman beside her.

"No," she answered. "No, I don't."

"How can you be certain?" Linet questioned. "I mean, none of us believed the Seven to be involved in any malicious acts. And yet, there they were plotting their way into power the whole time."

"I'm certain," Emily assured her. "A veil was lifted last night, Linet. A great darkness has come into power. But a light has also been ignited. I don't know if it is the work of nature balancing the way of things, or if it is the gods intervening. All I know is that my daughter has been touched. She has been cleansed of all darkness and filled with light."

"So she is perfect now." Linet watched the girl step from the grass-land and into the cavern.

"I wouldn't say *perfect*," Emily said. "She's Alice. She takes after your brother and he was anything but perfect."

Linet grinned as she thought about Tomas. She remembered him as an inquisitive and mischievous boy in his youth. Her memory flashed with images of him climbing trees, chasing livestock and jumping from the roofs of houses on the pasturelands into piles of straw. His daughter was no different, always exploring the woodlands and disappearing from sight as soon as one's back was turned.

"She's exactly like him," Linet said. "Except for the hair."

The two women giggled.

***

The cave was pitch black.

The gloomy clouds outside didn't help with her ability to see into the deep darkness, making her wish she had brought a torch along with her.

She moved on inside, feeling her way along the rock wall with her hands.

"Liana," she called softly, barely more than a whisper.

A gentle rumble emitted from far inside the cave, reverberating through the cavern.

"Come on, girl," she urged the creature.

The sound of something large and coarse scraping against the rock and dust filled her ears. The dragon was moving towards her.

It chirped quietly as it crawled closer.

Alice turned and started for the cavern's mouth.

"Let's go outside," she urged, slapping her thigh as she would summon a dog.

It pursued her a little farther, but would not follow her onto the grass.

She turned to see the beast sitting just inside the cavern, peering at her and the rukyul by her side.

It chirped again.

"What is it, Liana?"

The dragon chirped again.

It was afraid.

Alice peered into the dragon's orbs, moving closer to the beast.

It lowered its head, pressing its muzzle gently against her chest. With soft strokes, Alice moved her hands over the dragon's leathery skin around its nose.

"What's the matter?" she asked concernedly, looking at the beast.

It flickered a glance to the sky and back to her.

Suddenly, it made sense.

The storm from the night before. The way the clouds moved over the glade. These were acts of unnatural forces. Dark forces.

"So," Alice said. "You're sensitive to the things of magic."

Alice moved her gaze to the sky.

The clouds were still moving to the south and the golden ring of the sun was barely visible through the thick, grey covering in the air.

"You're going to have to get used to sorcery, girl," she told the dragon. "After all, I can do a few tricks, myself."

Still petting Liana's nose, she lifted a hand to the sky and waved it as if swatting a bug away.

"Disperse," she commanded.

The clouds instantly rolled away. Beams of bright yellow light broke through and spilled upon the glade.

As the light spread across the grassland, the dragon poked her head out of the cavern, staring at the sky. More and more blue appeared, causing the creature to chirp excitedly, urging her to venture onto the grass.

"Happy now?" Alice asked her with a grin.

Thirty-Five

"What's that?" Brondt called from behind Thornton.

The captain peered through the thick undergrowth to see the outline of a small shelter. Its thatched straw roof was discernible against the greenery surrounding it, yellow and angled to allow precipitation to slide over. Someone had constructed a hut, or covering, in the middle of the woods.

Thornton edged his steed forwards, following the trail left by the dark creatures. It led him around a small thicket and then directly towards the building.

It was a tiny hamlet of five structures, all made with crudely fashioned timber. A large fenced-in yard, assembled with portions of long oak branches nailed to posts, sat neatly to the side of the largest building. It was a stable of sorts with its doors wide open.

The sound of buzzing flies grew louder as the troop passed by.

Amicia put her hand to her face. "What in blazes is that stench?"

Thornton saw it first.

Inside the barn.

A pile of flesh, torn and shredded, rested in the centre of the stable's floor.

He pulled his steed to a halt and peered at the mess inside.

Faces of goats, pigs, horses and men stared back at him.

Hooves, trotters, arms and legs stuck out in places.

"By the gods," Vawdrey gasped.

"Arm yourselves," Thornton barked, pulling his sword free.

The men behind him did likewise.

"Surround the queen," Brondt commanded his men.

"Come by my side, girl," Amicia instructed Ursula.

The two women sat on their horses as the commander's guards manoeuvred their mounts into a circle around them, facing out and away from the ladies.

"On me," Thornton called to his troop, riding slowly into the centre of the settlement where a hearth surrounded by large stones sat, still smoking.

Pots of stew laid overturned on the ground.

Some furniture sat askew and on their sides.

Trails, splashes and puddles of blood stained the doorways, ground and walls.

The doors of the four small timber huts around them were wide open.

"Dismount," Thornton ordered as he dropped to the ground. "Brook."

"Yessir," the lieutenant replied.

"Check those two shelters for survivors with your men." The captain pointed to the buildings on the left. "Cobham, Sadler, check that one. Cheyne, you're with me."

The men split into four groups and moved to their allocated dwelling, holding their weapons at the ready.

Thornton moved in quickly, steadily to the doorway. He pressed himself against the outside wall on the right, with Cheyne on the left.

Both peered into the darkroom beyond, trying to see into the shadows for anyone, anything.

"Anyone there?" the captain called. But no answer came. He looked over at the soldier with him. "You ready?"

The other nodded, preparing to go inside.

"Oh, shit!" they heard someone call from the building next to theirs.

Both turned to see Cobham on his back, jabbing towards the door with his sword.

Sadler stood just inside the building, shaking and shimmering strangely.

It took Thornton a moment to realise that the man's feet were not touching the ground.

"Oh, shit!" Cobham cried again as Sadler's body fell to the ground, twitching.

The man's head was in the jaws of a lanky, dark creature, slowly emerging from the hut on all fours.

Dropping Sadler's head, it focused its attention onto Cobham, who was on his back, pushing wildly with his legs in order to escape. His sword swung and poked towards the beast.

Thornton, running as fast as he could towards the creature, noticed it was dragging its left hind leg behind it. An odd bend in the upper portion informed him that the beast had broken the limb and had been left behind by the others of its kind.

Swinging his sword over his head and downwards, he plunged his blade deep into the creature's back, penetrating through the chest and into the ground beneath it.

It screamed a deafening call until it could scream no more.

"Are you all right, soldier?" asked Thornton, turning to Cobham.

"Ye—" He picked himself up from the ground. "Yes, sir."

Thornton looked around to his men, who were all watching fearfully.

"Burn everything," he growled.

"Captain," Brondt called angrily, riding over. "That's not a command that I think you're in a place to give. We should check the other buildings."

"Four huts," Thornton replied. "The dead are piled up to my shoulders in that stable there. No one survived this." He gestured at the signs of blood and carnage. "Look around you, sir."

Moving his eyes about, Brondt carefully absorbed the scene.

"No offence, sir." Thornton moved towards the hearth. "But if one of those things is still alive inside one of these huts, I'd rather it come out with its flesh aflame than give it a chance to kill another one of my men."

"We burn it, Jonathon," Amicia ordered. "We take no chances."

"All right," the commander conceded. "Burn it."

"Yessir." Thornton kicked at the smoking embers, causing them to glow red. He turned to his lieutenant. "Find some dry branches. Something. Anything to set flame to so we can light this place up."

"Yes sir," Brook replied.

Within moments, the small village was ablaze, and the troop was continuing on, following the trail through the woods.

"Captain," Brondt called as he rode up to the older man's side.

"Yes sir," Thornton replied.

"I want to apologise for my outburst," the commander offered.

"No need to apologise, sir. I should have checked with you before issuing the order to burn that village."

"No," Brondt said, shaking his head. "You've spent most of your life as a soldier without direct supervision. Either on the road or posted elsewhere. Correct?"

"Yes sir," Thornton answered. "My time in Newholt is usually limited to three or four-month intervals before I move to one of the southern outposts. This previous mission was the first time I've been north since the time of the Mirikin."

"Bad memories up that way?"

"Even more now after recent encounters," the captain replied. He glanced back to Ursula riding beside the queen. "And a couple of good ones to even things out."

Brondt looked over his shoulder at the two women. They were in deep conversation, no doubt discussing the events leading up to, and including, their transformation.

"She loves you dearly," the commander told him. "You can see it in her eyes. She looks to you constantly."

"I know," the other murmured.

"And you love her."

Thornton frowned, peering to the path ahead.

"I've not felt this way about another person in a very long time, sir."

Brondt nodded thoughtfully.

"I think that's part of their power," he shared. "Not so much *love*. But *emotion*. I remember the Mirikin well. Their power came from what they shared with the Sovereign at first, and then was followed by the time of the White Witch. In both situations, it was hatred and a yearning to control.

"When Amicia and I fell in love," he continued. "And I mean, truly in love, she changed. Something broke the bond she had with the others of her coven.

"She gradually lost the abilities that she once possessed. I thought my wife was becoming, by all standards..."

"Normal?" Thornton suggested.

"Well..." Brondt shrugged. "Is any woman normal?"

"That may be a matter of perspective," the captain replied. "From their perspective, are we normal?"

"Who can tell?" Brondt looked back to Amicia. They were still talking. "This thing that happened. This empowerment that my wife and Ursula experienced. I wonder if it was brought on by what you and she share?"

"Because I slept with her?"

"Perhaps," the commander continued. "But maybe it's because of love."

Thornton thought about that for a moment.

"So," he said, frowning. "This one we seek. This *prime*. She must be more powerful? Like the Sovereign or the White Witch?"

"I am hoping she is nothing like them," Brondt replied. "But, yes. The prime is traditionally more powerful according to what I know about them."

"And if *love* is a factor into the source of their power," Thornton continued, "and with this new threat moving across the land, it should be safe to assume that the one she loves is a far better soldier than either of us."

"We can only hope." Brondt conceded, considering the captain's words. "We can only hope."

***

"I distinctly remember telling you to stay home today." Arthur paced back and forth in the small sitting room, his hands balled up and the veins in his neck tensed.

Alice, sitting in one of the cushioned chairs, had never seen him so upset before.

"After what you went through last night, I needed you to give yourself time to recover."

"I'm fine," she assured, holding her hands out to him. "Arthur, I feel fine."

He took her hands in his and knelt before her.

"I don't want to see you hurt," he told her. "I saw that filth coming out of you. How do we know if this thing won't return?"

"It's gone," she replied. "I've been purged of any darkness. It's even vanished from the ground outside."

"You should rest," said Arthur. "Please, promise me you will."

She breathed a deep sigh and assented.

"All right," she replied. "But I'll need to check on Liana and feed Shadow and the stallion later."

"I can do that for you," he offered.

"Liana won't follow you," she reminded him. "She has... what's that word you use for when ducklings follow their mother?"

"Imprint?"

"That's the one. She has imprinted on me."

"All right," he relented. "You take care of the dragon. I'll look after your horse and rukyul. Agreed?"

"Agreed." She pulled him closer to her so she could plant a kiss on his lips.

"And no more of this..." He waved his hand towards the sky, mimicking her display from earlier in the day.

"Not today," she promised.

"Not today," he repeated with a wry grin, lifting himself from the floor. "I need to get back to work."

She rose from the chair.

"No." He pointed to the chair. "Rest."

She relaxed and let out another long sigh as he disappeared through the door.

***

The heavily loaded wagons filed through the woods, leading the procession of supplies from Woodmyst to the glade. Behind them were men on horseback, herding a variety of livestock.

Takmel, clothed in his damson cloak and seated upon his steed, followed some distance behind. It was a slow ride, but he was in no rush.

He peered into the sky, focusing on the formation of the clouds above. A thick gloomy soup still stirred above, blotting out the sun's rays upon all the land.

All except one patch ahead of them.

It was as if an invisible wall prevented the clouds from crossing that region, causing them to swim around on either side.

"She's resisting you," Catherine said from his side.

"It's no matter," he replied, peering around at the other eight women riding behind him. "She is but one. We are many."

Two squads of well-armed cavalry troops plodded in formation behind the women with Andris, the Commander of the Guard, in their lead.

"Do you think this show of force will benefit you?" Catherine asked.

"They need to see I am in control now," he said. "It's the only way I can ensure that they comply with my demands."

She frowned slightly.

"Don't be concerned," he told her, reaching his hand out to touch her gently on the thigh. "No harm will come to them. The soldiers are merely a deterrent. The sight of them will be enough to persuade them to obey. We'll continue to supply them with their needs and allow them autonomy from the city. They are family, after all."

"Just..." She winced slightly, not really wanting to say the words. "Don't hurt them."

"I don't feel I will need to," he replied. "If they submit to me, that is."

She peered to him pleadingly.

"Catherine." He took her hand. "Your sister is not a stupid girl. She won't risk the lives of those living near the caverns. All will be fine. I promise."

Thirty-Six

Alice, exhausted from boredom, stretched out over her bed trying to sleep. She so wanted to be outside doing something, anything, rather than stay cooped up inside all day.

But she had promised her husband that she would take time to rest. So, being the dutiful wife that she was, she complied.

She spent an hour trying to read one of Arthur's books. The words swam after a while, forcing her to close its cover and place it on a table by the chair she sat in.

She then attempted to make a loaf of bread. Halfway through mixing flour and water together, her mother walked in and ordered her out of her own kitchen and back into the sitting room.

It was then that she took a nap.

But her body wanted to be outside and in the fresh air.

She wanted to smell the scent of pines and touch the grass with her fingers.

But she had made a promise.

Lying there in her room, staring at the ceiling, she felt herself drifting in and out of consciousness as her will simply gave in.

She felt herself flowing away, like a leaf floating on a gentle stream, as a soft sensation of sleep enveloped her.

It was dark here.

And the darkness grew thicker and thicker.

White, dagger-like teeth glared at her through the black, grinning malignantly from the distance.

The smiling jaws drew nearer and nearer, causing her to feel a deep sense of dread.

More teeth appeared, countless forms grinning in the dark.

The sound of strange clicking built gradually, growing more and more intense as the figures closed in around her.

Her eyes flickered open, and she jumped to her feet.

She pulled on her trousers and tucked in her shirt before reaching for her leather breastplate and swords. Fully dressed with her blades sheathed on her back, she exited her room and strode to the front door.

"Where are you going?" Emily asked as she placed a tray of freshly mixed dough into the oven.

"Get your sword," Alice told her. "Something is coming."

The girl stepped onto the porch and peered across the glade.

Shadow was already on his feet, standing a few yards away from the hut. His attention was fixed on the treeline across the way.

Alice looked to Liana, lying on her side not too far from the rukyul. A great hiss emitted from her throat as she moved her gaze to where the other creature was staring.

"What's wrong with her?" Akasati asked from her seat by the hearth.

"Get everyone back to the camp," Alice ordered her. "We have company."

The Erilian didn't hesitate, picking her sheath and sword up from the ground beside her and racing as fast as she could to the treeline. Once there, she gave a great whistle by sticking two fingers in her mouth.

"What is it?" David's voice called from somewhere in the woods.

"Company," Akasati replied. "Alice wants us all back in camp."

"You heard," the big man hollered. "Everyone move it."

Alice moved away from the hut and into the clearing, stopping a few yards away from the camp to face the pasture to the east. The dragon moved up to cower behind her as Shadow moved to her side.

Liana hissed again, staring towards the forest in the north.

The girl cocked an ear and listened.

She could feel something approaching. Something that made her feel enclosed, as if constricting. Suffocating.

"I see them," Yuri's voice bellowed. "Dark ones."

"Get the younglings," Alice called to him. "Get everybody."

She peered into the trees and listened, focusing her ears.

Clicking.

Strange and barely audible, but it was there.

And it was growing.

"Quickly," she shouted.

Emily dashed to her side, sword in hand.

"What's coming for us?"

"Darkness," Alice answered.

Behind her, David and Arthur pulled the chestnut stallion, tethered to a wagon, back into the glade.

The Agrodien females and younglings followed them.

"Where's everyone else?" the girl called.

"They're coming, Alice," Arthur told her. "They're moving as fast as they can."

Liana hissed again.

The clicking grew louder and louder.

Then Alice saw them.

On the far side of the glade, past the livestock, several dark forms moved just beyond the trees.

Her attention fell upon the few who were tending to the animals. They had heard Akasati's signal and were already on their way, climbing the steady embankment to the encampment.

"Hurry," she told them. "Behind me."

"These things are all around us," Emily said, pointing to an area slightly behind their position to the north. "Yuri is over that way, and he just said he saw one of them."

"I know," Alice acknowledged, pulling one of her swords free and aiming its blade to the east. "But the darkness comes from that direction."

She turned to see almost everyone huddled behind her.

"If you have a weapon," she ordered, "form a perimeter around the others."

David stepped to Emily's side, brandishing his long sword. Arthur moved to his wife's side, holding a wood axe in his hands.

"Where did you get that?" she asked him.

"I was chopping wood," he answered. "My sword is still inside."

With the circle formed around the women and children, they waited.

The clicking increased as more and more dark figures moved just inside the treeline.

Louder and louder, the sound grew, intensifying as their numbers increased.

The creatures leered at them from beneath the trees, offering menacing smiles filled with long, jagged teeth.

Liana hissed.

Shadow flared his teeth.

Alice peered around at the edge of the clearing.

She saw threatening grins on all sides.

They were everywhere.

"What's with that infernal sound?" Baldwyn yelled.

The rowdy clicking was almost unbearable, drowning out all other noises.

Louder.

Louder.

Louder.

Silence.

The world seemed to stand still.

The small community tensed.

Young children sobbed.

Mothers rocked their children.

"What is this?" Arthur whispered, moving his eyes over the forest.

Alice shifted her gaze to the far end of the glade, past the animals that had all herded together in fear, to the trees on the eastern edge.

Several of the creatures moved away silently, creating an opening.

The darkness was here.

She stared in disbelief as wagon after wagon moved into the clearing.

"Supplies from Woodmyst?" Karlena enquired.

Alice watched in silence as the wagons filed into the glade and pulled to a halt in the pastureland.

More livestock was herded into the glade and guided to the other animals.

"I don't understand." Emily shook her head. "Don't they see the creatures surrounding us?"

The girl glared at the gap the creatures had made.

One by one, riders appeared through the trees.

Ten, cloaked in varying coloured garments, led by one in a dark material hemmed with gold, steadily made their way towards the encampment. Uniformed men followed them on horseback.

Their identities were obvious as they drew nearer.

Alice pulled her other sword free. Her scrutiny fell upon her aunt, then Lucy, before resting on her sister.

Shadow set his hackles on edge and growled menacingly.

"Your hair!" Catherine laughed.

Alice ignored her and moved her attention back to Joanne and Lucy.

"Where is your son, Antony?" she asked the woman in black. "Named after your father. And where's your daughter, Holly?" Alice moved her eyes to Tricia, clothed in scarlet. "Where's your son, Thedric? And your husband, Simon?"

"You know very well where they are," Takmel interjected.

"What does that mean?" David queried, looking to Alice. "Where's Simon? What happened to Simon?"

"They've all been murdered," Alice informed him. "They have killed their children and husbands."

"I'm their husband now." Takmel pointed to himself. "Me. I'm their husband and they are all my wives."

"Why?" Emily glared at her sister with tears in her eyes. "Your own baby."

Joanne stared back, seemingly emotionless.

"It was the will of the Maji," she answered.

"Complete devotion," Alice sneered.

"Exactly." Takmel grinned.

"You're a fucking monster," Glaun blurted.

"Careful," Lor warned him. "He could set those creatures upon us."

"You have nothing to fear from these creatures." Takmel laughed as he gestured to the dark forms beneath the trees. "As long as you remain in the area surrounding the glade. Don't cross the mountains to the north, the east or the west. Remain here and you'll be safe."

"So, we are prisoners?" Emily asked.

"You are my family," he replied, and a look of concern swept over his face.

"Then why do this?" Alice queried. "Why bring these creatures? Where did they come from?"

"The creatures?" Takmel looked around at the slender, black figures as he thought of the words to say. "They served my mother. In the time it took her to cross the frozen lands from Blackrock Haven to Wintermarsh, she discovered many wonderments and inhabitants of the mountains and plains covered in ice.

"These creatures were drawn to the power she carried within her. My power.

"When she was at her weakest, they brought her food and kept her nourished. But they were never loyal to her."

"But they are loyal to you," Alice finished.

"Correct. My mother told me about them, but I didn't really understand, until recently.

"My mother's vision for this world needs to be fulfilled. Her work needs to be completed. A land under one rule without opposition. So, I summoned these creatures to destroy the men scattered throughout the land, starting with the settlements in the north."

"Your mother was insane, boy," David blurted. "And so are you."

"My mother was a goddess." Takmel glared at the large man angrily.

"She killed thousands of innocent people," the other growled. "She killed
my friend Tomas, and before that, she killed your father."

"She loved my father." The boy shook his head defensively. "She loved him."

"She forced herself onto him. Raped him so she could have you," David taunted.

Takmel looked annoyed, continuing to shake his head in repudiation. "You only say this because she is not here to defend herself against your words."

"I'm done talking." David tightened his grip on his sword. The black creatures tensed, ready for an attack. "If you are going to destroy all men, begin with me."

"I don't want to destroy you." Takmel held up a hand, silently ordering the beasts to stand down. "You were a good friend to my father. You are all my family. Why would I seek to hurt any of you?"

"I loved your father as I would a brother." The giant frowned. "You are but a stain on Ivo's name and mean nothing to me. You never did." He peered over to Alice, who had pulled both of her blades from the sheaths on her back. "All this time, I blamed the girl for the deaths of my wives and daughter. But it was you. You took my family from me. Didn't you?"

Takmel smiled, touching Catherine on her thigh. "A team of horses destroyed that bridge."

"I should run you through right now," the big man hollered, tears slowly moving over his cheeks.

"After all I've done for you!" The Maji glared back. "Bringing supplies to get you through the winter. Offering my hand as your friend. As your family."

"Family?" the other barked. "I don't think there is one among you who understands what that word means."

"Look..." Takmel waved his hand dismissively. "We can banter all day about how you would like to end my life. But, the truth is, you wouldn't take one step without either these creatures taking you down or my wives tearing you apart with their power."

David peered around.

The Maji was right.

There was no way to survive this.

If the multitude of creatures didn't reach him in time, the Seven would surely see to his doom before he could reach the boy.

David lowered his sword and dropped it to the ground.

"What are you doing?" Alice asked.

"There's too many of them," he replied.

"Not for me," she informed him.

"Alice," Emily called softly. "You might defeat them on your own. But they will surely take more than a few of us with them first."

The girl looked over her shoulder at her mother and husband. All she wanted to do was defend them.

"The dragon and that rukyul should be destroyed," Catherine stated.

"If you touch either of them," Alice said as she held her sister's stare, "I will take your head and feed your flesh to the dogs."

Takmel smiled.

"I had high hopes for you, Alice," he said, moving his attention to Arthur. "I wanted to take you for one of my wives, but you fell for this weakling instead."

Alice prepared herself to strike.

"He's more man than you will ever be, Takmel."

"Don't worry..." the Maji held up his hands in mock surrender. "I recognise your love for him. No harm will come to him by me. I promise.

"Live out your lives here. Grow crops. Raise livestock. Have children. Just, do not try to leave."

"I will warn the world of you, Maji," she hollered.

"I believe you would." He smirked. "Threatening the lives of these people would prove pointless. Saying that I intend to tear your husband's limbs from his body wouldn't even be enough to stop you. So, go ahead. Warn them all that I am coming. A better world awaits us all after I take control. True peace. True harmony. All under my rule. No wars or struggles. No more need for bloodshed. They'll welcome me with open arms."

"And if they don't?" David asked, glaring at the young man.

Takmel turned his steed away, ignoring the question.

"I have my own pets," Takmel said to Catherine, nodding towards the dark creatures surrounding the glade. "She can keep hers."

"But the dragon…" the other complained.

"No," he snapped. "Let them be."

The young sisters' eyes met again momentarily, exchanging a deep detestation. Alice lowered her swords to her sides as Catherine turned her horse to leave.

Joanne glanced up to Emily sheepishly, quickly averting her gaze when she saw her older sibling glaring at her.

"Woodmyst will continue to care for her people," the Maji called back to them as he rode away slowly. "The wagons are laden with supplies to get you through the winter. A resupply will arrive after the snow has melted and I will expect that you will reopen the quarry at that time.

"Needless for me to say that none of you will be welcome in Woodmyst from this day hence. You are all banished. If we sight any from the glade from the walls, we will shoot you with arrows and return you to your loved ones in pieces."

Liana hissed again as the riders moved away.

The community stood its ground well after the horsemen had gone from sight.

They stared into the woods and waited as each of the grinning creatures raced away through the forest, vanishing from sight.

Alice sheathed her swords and placed a hand on Shadow's shoulder. He grumbled softly as she rubbed his thick fur.

"What do we do now?" Oliver Weston asked.

They all turned to Alice, who was starting down the embankment towards the wagons parked on the pastureland.

"Alice?" Emily called after her, tears streaming over her cheeks.

"I need to check the supplies," she replied coldly as the rukyul trotted to her side.

The people of the glade stared on in disbelief as the girl simply walked away, seemingly willing to carry on as if nothing had happened.

But Alice fought to maintain her composure.

Tears welled as she marched towards the awaiting wagons.

It took almost every ounce of her being to focus on the task at hand.

Inside, she felt like throwing herself on the pastureland to cry.

She balled her shaking hands into fists and swallowed the lump in her throat away.

Epilogue

As the day's end arrived and the first stars winked to life in the expanse above, Alice sat on her porch and closed her eyes.

Shadow, the rukyul, rested his enormous head upon her lap as she scratched him gently behind his ear.

The sound of weeping filled her ears as she listened to those who had once lived in Woodmyst mourn over the loss of friends and young ones they had watched grow.

Her thoughts were on her half-brother and half-sister, lost to the will of the Maji. Anger had built in her heart, overpowering her sorrow to the point of rage and a desire to tear Takmel, and his queens, limb from limb.

But that would lead to darkness.

So, she redirected her thoughts and found a reason to be encouraged.

As others lamented, she focused her attention to the north.

"Kayl'sro," the reptilian said softly, not wanting to disturb her, but knowing he had to.

"Yes, Yuri?" She opened her eyes.

"I sorry for you." He bowed his head.

"So am I." She wiped a building tear from her eye.

"We have packed supplies into dragon cave for the night," he informed her.

She peered over to the large cavern to see several Agrodien and northern refugees moving back towards their dwellings.

"Good." She nodded. "Thank you."

He sat beside her, stretching his tail across the porch.

He looked to the sky, where he noticed the clouds dispersing.

"No tears from sky tonight," he said. "We have enough here."

She felt one streak over her cheek.

She saw the faces of Antony and Holly in her mind.

"They were so sweet, and gentle, and innocent," she sobbed. "And now they're gone." Yuri listened as he placed his hand on her back. "They weren't old enough to understand anything. How afraid they must have been."

The reptilian pulled her to him and wrapped his thick arm around her.

Shadow moved his head and whined, sympathising with the girl.

"How dare they!" she cried. "How dare they take the lives of little ones."

Yuri held her tightly as she wept.

"What we do now, Kayl'sro?" he asked.

"We wait," she replied

"Wait for what?" He gave her a puzzled look.

She pulled away from him and mopped her face upon her sleeve. Taking a deep breath to compose herself, she turned her gaze to the north.

"We wait for my new sisters to come."

About the Author

Robert E Kreig was born in Newcastle, Australia and grew up in its outer suburbs.

He has always had a love for books, particularly well-told stories involving action, adventure and fear.

Some of Robert's favourite authors as a young reader included J. R. R. Tolkien, Stephen King, Orson Scott Card, Ray Bradbury and Frank Herbert. As he grew into adulthood, the list continued to lengthen, adding more influential writers such as George R. R. Martin, Matthew Reilly, Nathan M. Farrugia, Dan Brown, James Patterson, Michael Connelly and Lee Child just to name a few.

Inspired by movies like Star Wars, King Kong, Jaws, Jason and the Argonauts and other great adventure pieces, Robert listened to the voices in his head and entertained the strange visions dancing through his mind to assist him with writing his fantasy series The Woodmyst Chronicles.

Robert has penned ten books for the series which follow the lives of many characters, particularly focussing upon a family who must face many trials before the epic conclusion. Clashing swords, strange creatures, flying dragons and sorcery inhabit the world surrounding Woodmyst.

Robert has also written a standalone book, Long Valley.

Robert currently lives in Canberra, Australia where he hopes to one day become a full-time writer.

Other Books By This Author

THE WOODMYST CHRONICLES

From a faraway land...
...comes a new adventure.
The Woodmyst Chronicles is the story of a small community that faces the hardest of trials in a world filled with darkness, violence and magic.

Books In This Series...
THE WALLS OF WOODMYST
THE SONS OF WOODMYST
THE HEIR OF WOODMYST
THE WARLORDS OF WOODMYST
THE HUNTRESS OF WOODMYST
THE SHADOW OF WOODMYST
THE BRIDES OF WOODMYST
THE GODS OF WOODMYST
THE WEAPONS OF WOODMYST
A FAREWELL TO WOODMYST

LONG VALLEY

In the small community of Long Valley, nestled comfortably beneath snow-capped mountains, people quietly go about their business. Everybody knows everybody and there are no worries to give mind to.

But something has awakened.

A tragic accident near the valley's army base sparks a number of terrifying events, placing the local civilians in mortal danger.

A contagion is subsequently released into Long Valley, infecting pets, livestock, wildlife and people.

It's up to the local law enforcement and a small band of citizens to try to keep the town safe.

In the end, it becomes a struggle for survival as the people of Long Valley are overcome by the urge to feed.

THE CALM VOICE

No one in the remote town of Edwards Hill could have known that she was capable of such carnage.

Least of all her parents, the first to die.

Driven by the gentle words of The Calm Voice, she inflicts a barrage of carnage and death, leaving a trail of blood in her wake.

Her goal is to bring death to all who have hurt her.

All she needs to do is listen to The Calm Voice.

All she needs to do is just focus...

Just focus...

Focus...

The Calm Voice by Robert E. Kreig is a dark psychological novel surrounding the actions of one girl on a fateful morning in April 2017. Kristin Matthews is fed up with her life, her oppressive parents, and her bullying schoolmates. A soothing voice thrumming in her head compels her to seek revenge on those who have wronged her. At the top of her list is a trio of girls who have taunted her to breaking point. After careful planning, she embarks on a deadly rampage through Edwards Hill State High School, bent on destroying all her pain one last time. What follows is a haunting description of the day's events, culminating in an ending no one will expect.

www.robertekreig.com

www.whitekeepbooks.com

www.ingramcontent.com/pod-product-compliance
Lightning Source LLC
Chambersburg PA
CBHW031947130726
47904CB00012B/328